Follow Your Heart

EMILY HUSSEY

Book 3 in the Red Centre Series

WINSOME *Books*

Emily Hussey

Note that Australian English is used in this book. Spellings will be different to standard spelling used in the United States. Some of the terminology may be unfamiliar to readers outside of Australia.

Copyright © 2018 Emily Hussey
ISBN 978-0-6482972-22

Editor: Lauren Clarke
Cover Design: Emcat Designs
Cover Images: Depositphotos

Published by Winsome Books 2019
Second Edition 2022

A division of Winsome Enterprises Pty Ltd
Adelaide, South Australia

Also by Emily Hussey

The Red Centre Series
Journey to the Heart (*Prequel*)
The Red Heart
Trust Your Heart
Follow Your Heart

Stand-alone Stories
Ambition and Passion
Maison Angelique

Tales from Harrow Series
Wild Spirit (*Prequel*)
Wild Destiny
Wild Tempest
Wild Fire

Sandy Bay Series
Secrets in Sandy Bay
Escape to Sandy Bay
Return to Sandy Bay

Emily Hussey

CONTENTS

CHAPTER 1

THE LIGHT BREEZE did nothing to dispel the heat sitting heavily on the landscape. A lone crow voiced its displeasure, a cry of discordant complaint.

Melissa Gilbert froze, her eyes fixed on the rocky outcrop. A rivulet of sweat trickled between her breasts but she let it go, certain as soon as she took her hand off the shutter, the moment would be lost. She directed a hot breath up towards her fringe in an effort to blow a strand of hair from her eyes. Secured by her hat, and plastered with sweat, the hair stayed in place. The horse stayed obediently still.

A movement caught her eye. She thought she'd seen it earlier, but they were cunning. They had an aggressive reputation but this one showed all the signs of being patient and crafty. It must have heard her approach and was waiting to see what she was going to do. What *she* was going to do was sit and wait. Which of them would outlast the other?

There it was again. The sandy flank was similar in colour to the surrounding landscape and the animal blended well. A white muzzle and blaze on its chest gave away its location when it rose to its feet and took a cautious step forward, sniffing the air.

Hardly daring to breathe lest she startle the animal, yet hoping it would look in her direction, Melissa squinted into the viewfinder and brought it into focus. Perfect. The dingo stood as though posing. *What a natural,* she thought. *You should be on the catwalk. Or perhaps the dog walk.*

Appearing satisfied there were no immediate threats, the wild dog lowered its head and picked its way around the spinifex clumps. Its progress was purposeful, as though it had places to go or places to be. She followed it through the lens, delighted at the opportunities presented to her.

It was the reaction of the dog that alerted her. It froze for a nanosecond and then bolted. So intent had she been on her stake-out that the noise took a second to register. A small helicopter swung around the adjacent hilltop and swept just above the horse and rider. It came out of nowhere and thundered overhead like something out of *Apocalypse Now,* startling them both. The horse reared in fright. Intent on clutching her precious equipment, Melissa lost her balance and was unceremoniously dumped from the saddle. The horse bolted and fled. The thudding of hooves in the distance indicated that it had no intention of stopping anytime soon.

The ground, strewn with boulders embedded in the hard clay, did not provide a cushioned fall. Stunned, Melissa lay where she had landed, doing a survey of limbs and body. Her camera was still clutched to her chest. The lens was new and had cost a small fortune. If that was damaged, she would be royally pissed.

She could move her arms and legs. There was a stone pressing into her back, making it imperative she change position and do something about getting herself up. A shaft of pain hit as she straightened her legs.

"Bastard." She hissed the word through barely controlled pain. Slowly, she rolled onto her side and pushed herself into a sitting position. A tentative exploration revealed she was only winded. She could still move her leg, so it wasn't broken. Bruised perhaps. She rolled onto her knees and grunted softly as small stones embedded themselves into her flesh, then raised herself into a wobbly standing position. The sound of the chopper diminished and then ceased. She retrieved her broad-brimmed hat and jammed it back on her head.

Grit studded the palm of her hands and she wiped them on the side of her jeans to dislodge it. She took a tentative step and gasped. She bit her lip before looking around to see if the horse had stopped. It was nowhere to be seen. Rather, her father's horse was nowhere to be seen. She had saddled up *his* stallion when she left the homestead. Hopefully Caesar had headed for home and hadn't come to any harm. There would be hell to pay if he had.

The loose surface broadcast the tread of approaching footsteps She refused to look around. She knew who it would be.

"Are you okay?"

"As if you care. Piss off." She started walking in the direction of the homestead, trying not to limp. It would be a long walk.

"Melissa, stop. I didn't mean to frighten you, okay? I wasn't expecting anyone to be here."

She kept walking.

"Melissa, for chrissake—it's too far to walk. Hop in and I'll drop you back at the homestead."

She swung around. The glare would have killed at twenty paces. He was fortunate they were at a distance of about twenty-one.

"Chris Harris, if you think I'm going anywhere near that aerial jellybean you've another think coming. I've seen enough of your flying for one day. I'm safer on the ground. Piss off." She resumed walking, resolutely walking.

"Look, I've said I'm sorry. I won't—"

"No, you didn't."

"Didn't what?"

"Didn't say you were sorry."

"Alright, I'm sorry." He yelled at her back, following several paces behind her. "If you want to dehydrate out here and let the dingos eat you and the crows pick at what's left, that's fine by me but your dad will probably have my guts for garters. Get in and I'll fly you home."

She slowed her pace and turned, hands on hips. "Fat chance he'd care," she muttered, but Chris was right. It was a long way back and the afternoon was heating up. Someone would probably come looking when the horse turned up without her. If she got home first, perhaps no one would ever know that she had taken the horse, or that she'd been thrown.

She turned and walked back to where he'd left the chopper. It was a small machine used locally for mustering. She could feel Chris watching her as she stalked past him and clambered into the cabin. She strapped herself in, and looked straight ahead. Just because she was allowing him to fly her home didn't mean she'd forgiven him.

With a sigh that bordered on a huff, Chris followed and belted up. Giving an all-stations report on the radio, he set the rotors in motion. A high-pitched whine progressively deepened and the machine rose, tilted slightly and moved off in the direction of the Plenty River homestead.

❧

Chris landed close to the station buildings. He shut down the engine and the rotors slowed to a residual spin. Melissa unclipped her seatbelt. Her father stood outside the homestead and had watched their approach and landing. He stood with hands on his hips, and his stance said he was not happy.

"Damn! Rotten timing," Melissa said.

Chris looked bewildered at the comment but shrugged his shoulders with a gesture that said 'Not my business'.

"Now I'm here, I'll give your dad the rundown on progress today. He kinda looks as though he'd like some explanation. I'll update him before getting back to the muster crew."

"Please yourself. Whatever you do, it'll be the wrong thing." She took a deep breath and exhaled slowly. "Thanks for bringing me back, by the way."

He risked a quick smile in her direction, but Melissa ignored him in favour of her father.

Dan Gilbert strode towards them as they clambered from the cabin. "Melissa! Who said you could take Caesar? He came back five minutes ago all of a lather. What did you do to him?"

"Yes, I'm okay, Father, thank you for asking."

The sarcasm was wasted. His demeanour didn't change.

"You weren't around to ask before I left but I can't see it was ever a problem. Caesar needed the exercise anyway. Cleo is close to foaling so I couldn't take her."

"Hmph." The grunt sounded anything but concerned. "What happened?"

"My fault, Dan." Chris joined the conversation. "I was flying tight and low and came across them unexpectedly. The horse was spooked and headed for home. I thought I'd better drop Melissa back here." He looked apologetically towards Melissa before turning back to her father. "Phil Baker will report to you later, but we've got most of the mob. There are still some stragglers I need to locate and round up."

"Well, you'd better get back out there. There'll be another mob out at Black Well tomorrow. I want this lot finished today and ready for trucking on Friday."

Dan Gilbert was not known for exchanging pleasantries. He was a hard task master and gave no quarter. Melissa wasn't sure what made her speak up. Perhaps it was annoyance at her father's blunt approach. Perhaps it was contrariness. The words were out of her mouth before she'd stopped to think.

"Actually Dad, I've invited Chris to dinner tonight, so you can talk to him about future work then, though it would be nice to have some other discussion for a change. Say six thirty, Chris? Will that be okay with you?"

If Chris was surprised, he handled it well. Invitations to the big house were not common. Station hands and contractors had their own quarters and were expected to not intrude. Melissa's father always maintained a distance between himself and the hired help. She directed her attention to him, daring him to contradict her.

"Sure. I'll be cleaned up by then. I'd better be off. The others will be wondering where am. See you tonight." Turning abruptly, he strode back to the Robinson and took off again.

Melissa decided it to make herself scarce, before her father voiced an opinion about the plans for the evening. She went to check on Caesar, finding someone had already removed his saddle and released him in the home paddock. It was probably Pete, the station hand who was usually about the place somewhere. She took an apple from the sack in the saddle shed and whistled to the stallion. His ears pricked but he held his distance for a while before cantering up to the fence and claiming the treat.

"I understand you getting a fright but why did you desert me, you wicked boy? You should have known it would get me into trouble."

The horse was more intent on the apple but put up with a neck rub. "Don't land me in the shit like that again, okay?"

Melissa sighed as she turned and made her way back to the homestead. She did her best to walk normally but her leg gave her some grief. Probably just strained, she told herself. No real harm done. She didn't want to give her father more ammunition to use against her. He must have seen the camera so would have realised what she'd been doing.

Now she needed to navigate the evening as well. She'd better tell Jenny about their guest. It had been a crazy idea to ask Chris to come for dinner. It was just a spur-of-the-moment thing. In part she knew it would annoy her father and sometimes that was an irresistible urge. It also meant that her father was less likely to be so critical if there was a witness at the table. Why shouldn't she invite someone to dinner if she felt like it? Sometimes she yearned for company her own age.

Melissa found the housekeeper rearranging cupboards in the kitchen. This was her domain and she had total control over what came in and what went out of that kitchen. Had done for years now, ever since Melissa's mother died.

"Umm, Jenny—we have an extra person for dinner tonight. I hope that doesn't inconvenience you?"

"Not at all. I can always accommodate one more. I didn't realise we had visitors."

"We don't. Not really. Chris Harris is coming—the mustering pilot."

"Isn't he the one who was ill recently?"

"Yes, but he's back at work so I assume he's fit for duty."

"This is a change. Your father doesn't usually invite the contractors to dinner."

"He didn't. I did. Is that a problem?"

"Melissa, you know you can invite whoever you choose. In fact, I'm delighted. You don't socialise enough in my opinion. You're too isolated out here. I'll put on a roast. That's easy enough and it will keep your father happy. Plenty of roast vegies as well."

"Thanks, Jenny. I'll be in the dark room if you want me."

Stripping the film from the camera, Melissa processed it in the chemical baths which were already set up. This was her domain. The amount of time she spent on photography annoyed her father, but he'd allowed her to establish the dark room when she had developed an interest in her mid-teens. She kept out of his way where possible and kept her life private as well. The fact she wasn't fulfilling his expectations only served to annoy him further. She looked at a print from the beginning of the roll, where she'd captured her father as he strode towards the station ute at first light. She would never show him. She put it aside and turned her attention to the rest.

Chris made sure he was exactly on time. What had prompted Melissa to lie about inviting him? It was an awkward setup. He was curious and not exactly apprehensive, but aware he would be under scrutiny. When dealing with Dan Gilbert, it was best to be on your toes. He rushed through his ablutions, and his hair was slightly damp when he climbed the veranda steps and knocked on the front door.

Jenny answered his knock. He liked Jenny; she was a breath of normality at Plenty River. She beamed a welcome.

"Chris—come in. Dan's in the dining room. Go on down."

He paused uncertainly. He'd not been in this part of the house before. Never used the front door in fact. A wide hall stretched before him, cool and dark after the bright heat of the day. He glanced back at Jenny.

She took the hint. "Second on the left. I'll let Melissa know you've arrived. She's still in her room."

He found Dan sitting in a leather armchair at the far end of the room, book in one hand and glass of whiskey in the other. He was a sturdy well-built man, with a weathered skin that made his eyes seem a brighter shade of blue. His hair, now

9

thinning and faded, was once a sandy ginger. Usually, it was concealed under a broad-brimmed hat but tonight it was freshly washed and neatly combed. He stood and proffered his hand.

"I like a man who's on time. Pity my daughter can't do the same. It's not as though she has far to come. Can I offer you a drink?"

"Same as you're having will be fine, but just a small one thanks Dan. I've been given the all-clear but I'm taking it easy."

The older man poured a nip of scotch into a glass and added a splash of soda. He indicated to Chris that he should take the only other armchair and both men sat down.

Dan raised his glass in silent toast. "Good idea. Don't see much of it but that Q-Fever can be nasty. I remember some of the old blokes getting it years ago but otherwise you're the first person I've come across recently who's gone down with it."

"And I sincerely hope I'm the last." Chris inhaled the smoky aroma from the liquid and took an appreciative sip. It was a good single malt. He mentally searched for common ground. "We got the Yaldara mob today. I had to head out towards Mulga Downs to get the last of them, but we brought in all the stragglers. Phil Baker gave me a few clues on where to look. You'll be pleasantly surprised at the final head count."

There was a grunt from Dan, hopefully appreciative. Chris glanced around. *Where's Melissa? I'm not sure how far I can push this conversation.* He sipped his whisky, savouring the hit to his palate before pushing on. "So, you want to start on Black Well tomorrow?"

The two men were deep in discussions about the muster and cattle numbers when the creak of the door alerted them to Melissa's arrival. She had swept her long auburn hair into an elegant roll, and pulled on slim-legged black trousers, topped with a tunic of soft violet silk. Strappy sandals and lashings of mascara finished the look.

"Sorry if I've kept you waiting but it sounds as though you've had a few things to talk about. If you move to the table now, I'll let Jenny know we're ready."

Chris stood and surveyed the table uncomfortably. *Sheesh—I should have worn the tux.* The beautiful polished piece of furniture could comfortably seat a very large dinner party. It was set as though for a formal dinner. Dam moved to the head of the table.

Melissa returned ahead of Jenny and the three of them took their places with Chris and Melissa either side of Dan. Discussion was stilted while Jenny served their meal, placed a bottle of red wine within Dan's reach, and retreated, shutting the dining room door behind her. She evidently wasn't joining them.

The roast was a hit. Both men made short work of the generous serves which had been placed before them. A silence stretched. Chris cast around for topics of conversation.

"So, Melissa—no lasting damage from today?"

Dan Gilbert looked up from his meal. "Why should there be any damage? What happened?"

"Caesar threw me when Chris flew over us. I landed heavily. I was winded, that's all." Melissa made light of it although Chris had noticed her quietly massaging her leg under the table through most of the meal.

11

"So that's why you're limping."

"It's nothing, Dad. Just bruised I think—that, and the ego."

"What were you doing out there anyway?"

"I was trying out my new lens. I only picked it up last week and I wanted to see what it could do. Before Chris came, I was following a dingo. I hoped she might have a pup or at least might lead me to one. Chris put paid to that."

"Sorry—if I'd known you were there I would have kept right away." *How was I to know?*

"Don't be silly." Dan Gilbert was dismissive. "You had a job to do and Melissa was only indulging her hobby. She's the one who should have used some common sense and kept out of your way."

"Dad, it's not just a hobby. The fact you don't appreciate my work doesn't mean others feel the same way."

"Yeah, but are they people who really matter, Melissa? Only your city cronies and what would they know?"

"Actually, they know quite a lot. I wouldn't get the contracts I do if my work wasn't taken seriously."

"Taking photos of a lot of skinny, over-painted people dressing up in strange clothing doesn't seem to me to be serious work. There's enough real work that you can do here at Plenty River. Learn more about the business for instance."

"I already do your bookkeeping. What more do you want? I'm entitled to my own life!"

This was getting uncomfortable. Chris looked from one to the other. *What have I stirred up here?* He sat through a frosty moment before turning to Melissa. "Now you've got me intrigued. I didn't get around to asking what you were doing out by Tero Creek today. You have an interest in photography?"

"No, I don't have an *interest*. I *am* a photographer, and no matter what my father might think or say, I'm well respected in my field. I'm a fashion photographer and work on contract for various fashion houses." She moved her chair, angling her body towards Chris and away from her father. "Today was for my personal project. When I'm on location, I could be working anywhere—Sydney, Rome, Bali—you name it. Then my work concentrates on people and the clothes and accessories. When I'm home, it's different."

"Different is the understatement of the year. You must lead a very glamorous lifestyle in the big smoke. What's the focus of your work out here?"

Dan Gilbert audibly snorted at this comment but busied himself with the bottle of wine.

"Oh, you know—station life, flora and fauna and things like that. I like to record my world and what I can see through the lens."

She sounded defensive. Lifting her chin slightly, she glanced at her father anticipating a derogatory comment. Dan pointedly examined the label on the bottle. She turned back to Chris.

"For what it's worth, there is nothing glamorous about the fashion work. The days can start before dawn and finish with sundown. There's a lot of standing around waiting for the shoot director to make decisions or for the models to be ready or for the rain to stop or keeping out of the way of the local militia or whatever."

She reached for the bottle of wine and topped up their glasses. "When I get back to Plenty River, I'm glad to be home and away from all the drama. I'm not denying it—the job has taken me to some fabulous places."

"Some would kill for opportunities like that. You've never been tempted to change to the other side of the camera? You've got the poise and the figure."

"What, me? A model? No thanks. Standing around in skimpy swimwear in the middle of winter and trying to look as though I'm on a sunny beach in the middle of summer is not my idea of fun. I'll stick with my camera and creative control—with enough clothes on to keep me warm."

"Oh, the girl's got some sense after all."

Dan didn't hide his derision. Chris deliberately ignored the comment as he addressed Melissa. "I'd be interested in seeing some of your work. I assume some is in the public arena."

"If you're angling for an invitation to 'come and see my etchings' don't hold your breath. I don't make a display of my work."

Whoa! That wasn't what I meant at all. Chris's threw an assessing glance at Dan. Dan merely rolled his eyes at his daughter's words.

"Melissa, give the man a break."

"I wasn't meaning to be intrusive," Chris said "I was just intrigued. I had no idea you owned a camera, let alone that you were a professional photographer. Not that there's any reason why I should have known," he added.

Melissa considered him through an awkward silence. "If it weren't for you and your low-flying antics, I'd have shot
14

more film of that dingo. I haven't printed anything yet so I'm not sure how they'll turn out." Her tone became accusing. "I've waited a long time to capture that dog."

"Bloody vermin," Dan interjected. "I would have shot it all right, but not with a camera."

Melissa didn't bite and refused to look at him. Her pursed lips left no doubt about her feelings on the matter.

"I hope there are no lasting effects from your spill today," Chris said. As a change of topic, it was a fairly obvious tactic.

"If there are, I'll follow it up with the physio in town." She stacked up the dinner plates. "Can I offer you some coffee?"

"While you two continue your nattering, I'm going to catch the late news and weather forecast. It's good to remind ourselves sometimes that there's a world beyond the horizon."

With not so much as a glance in their direction, Dan levered himself out of his chair and strode out the door. The room felt depleted when he had gone. He didn't have the sprightliness of a younger man, but he still emanated a sense of strength and solidity. Not a person to mess with and not many would try.

"So—coffee?" Melissa asked.

"Yes, that would be good. Thanks."

Jenny had put a coffee pot on the sideboard earlier. Chris sat back in his chair watching, as Melissa poured them each a cup.

"Milk? Sugar?"

She placed the milk jug and sugar in front of him, along with a platter of cheese Jenny had left. Chris helped himself and settled back in his chair.

15

"Where did you do your training?"

"In Sydney. I boarded there during my school years and studied photography during my final year." She carried her own cup of coffee back to the table and sat down before continuing. "I enrolled in a technical course after graduating. I didn't have the support of my father as you've probably noticed and so I struck a bargain with him. I did a bookkeeping course so I could look after the station books and in return he agreed to me studying photography." She gave a tight triumphant smile. "I persuaded him to let me set up a studio in the old school room. He never imagined that my passing obsession—as he called it—would come to anything, so for him it was a small concession."

"From what I can see, it's still an obsession. How come no one in Alice knows what you do?

Her laugh was without mirth. "I doubt anyone there would care. I was cast years ago as the ice-maiden and nobody has ever bothered to really get to know me."

Chris raised his eyebrows but didn't say anything. Melissa took a deep breath and exhaled slowly before continuing.

"When I was younger, I had a governess and did School of the Air. When I was old enough, I went to boarding school, out of my father's way. I never had the chance to mix much with the locals. When I returned at the end of term, I found the kids my own age had their own networks and I was always the outsider. They were not happy times."

"Sounds tough." He spoke matter-of-factly, but with sympathy.

"Yes and no. I had my friends in the city and I stayed with them during the school holidays. I made some useful contacts
16

during those times and they helped me once I qualified and started looking for work. You need all the help you can get in this game."

"I think that's the case in any industry." Chris looked around the room, his gaze resting on a print on the end wall. It was mounted on a board but not framed, so the focus was on the picture. He stood up, and took a couple of paces towards the picture, peering at the detail.

Dan Gilbert was the subject and his head was turned looking directly into the camera as though it had just caught his eye. The look was assured, and the stance firmly asserted his right to be in the frame, but captured also was a hint of sadness reflected in his eyes. It was like looking into a man's soul and beyond the facade. Behind him, the sun was veiled by a swirl of dust kicked up by cattle. A kelpie was mid-dance at their feet. It captured a moment in the life of a man who lived by, with and on the land.

"Did you take this? Is this an example of your work?"

"Yes. My father is not an easy subject. I have to make the most of the moment when the situation presents itself. If I want anything other than a candid shot, forget it. He just shuts down and won't cooperate. If I stick a cow in the frame and tell him the animal is the focus it's easier, but not much."

"Probably not many of us like posing for photos, so he has my sympathies. Quite a contrast though between this photo and capturing images of young women standing under studio lights in the latest fashions."

"Not just women, but men too. Models come in all ages and in any gender. There are the technical aspects no matter where you are—looking at the lighting, the composition, the right lens, etc.

"I'm starting to understand. My apologies again for disturbing you today."

She shrugged. "You weren't to know, and if I'd really done my homework, I would have realised you were in the vicinity. There'll be other opportunities and anyway, when I see what I captured it might be just what I was after."

Placing his cup on the table and looking with regret at another piece of cheese, Chris stood up.

"I've enjoyed the dinner and the company but I've an early start in the morning. I'd better make tracks. Do you have any more photographic excursions planned for tomorrow? Just so you know, we'll be working in the direction of Black Well."

"Tomorrow will be a dark room day and I've a few other things to do around here. I expect to be off on a contract soon, so need to make the most of this time while it's available. Don't worry; I'll keep out of your way. I'll show you out."

At the main entrance, he stood, hesitating.

"Thanks for the invitation. It was unexpected, but I enjoyed the evening. If you look me up when you're in town or passing through, I'm more than happy to introduce you to a few people. You could expand your local field of acquaintances."

"That won't be necessary. I think I know all the people who are worth knowing in Alice and it's too late for anything else. Good night."

Both her words and manner were abrupt. As she moved to shut the door, a dingo howled in the distance.

Chris looked in the direction of the howl. "Don't tell me your problems, mate. I don't have any answers."

❧

Melissa allowed herself a small smile as she cleared up the last of the plates from the dining room and took them down to the kitchen. There she found her father making himself a cup of tea.

"So, young lady; what was that all about?"

"What was what about?" She stacked the dishes on the sink and avoided looking at her father.

"Don't play the innocent with me. Why did you drag him to the dinner table tonight?"

"Drag him! Hardly. I extended an invitation and he accepted. It was no more complicated than that."

Dan was silent for a moment, observing her with an inscrutable expression before speaking again. "Chris Harris is good at his job and a reasonable sort of bloke, but don't go leading him on, Melissa. There's no future for you there; or for him, either."

CHAPTER 2

THE DEVELOPED PRINTS were everything she'd hoped. She'd been able to zoom in to reveal whisker clarity. Even with the disturbance, Melissa was pleased with what she'd captured. The lens had been worth every cent.

She didn't bother showing them to her father. It would have been a wasted exercise, but Jenny was suitably impressed. Melissa knew she would be. The woman always encouraged her work. The lady in question was in an area of an enclosed veranda that they called the morning room, because it caught the morning sun.

As she expected, given the hour, Melissa found Jenny with mug of tea by her side and a novel in her hand.

"Hey Missy; do you want a cuppa?"

"I'll help myself in a minute. I thought you might like to see my latest efforts. I've been trying out the new lens and these prints are the result."

The older woman jammed a piece of paper between the pages of her book and studied the first of the prints. She examined them all in turn, making small appreciative comments as she did.

"Wow. I can see your patience paid off. You've really captured the attitude—the essence if you like, of the animal. In this one, you're virtually looking into his eyes. Melissa love, you've done a fabulous job. It's not just the equipment, you know. The lens is only a tool but it's the skill of the person using that tool which counts."

Melissa flushed with pleasure. Jenny was the only person she'd had to turn to for guidance and reassurance while growing up. She was no technical expert, but Melissa valued her opinion.

"I am pleased with them. Think what else I could have done if Captain Whirly Bird hadn't come thundering over the horizon.

"Chris Harris? Just doing his job, Missy. You can't really blame him."

"I know. His timing was atrocious, that's all. I could have throttled him. I was on a roll when he turned up."

She wondered what Chris might think of them. He had expressed an interest in seeing her work after all. Perhaps when he returned to his quarters at the end of the day, she would seek him out and show him.

She was still debating whether she wanted to do that when she discovered from Pete that the mustering contract had finished, and Chris had flown back to Alice late afternoon. It had been a silly idea anyway. Why would he have any real interest in her work? He'd only been polite over dinner.

It was good to be back in town again. That was the good part of his job. He spent time in the air, and out bush for several days or even a week or more, but then he came back to town and civilisation. Like a beer down the pub or catching up with mates.

The bank was his first port of call. His job came with benefits. Sustaining them required money. On the way out, he bumped into one of his favourite people. Sarah. That was another thing about being in town. You kept running into people you knew.

"Hey Curly. You're a sight for sore eyes. What's new?"

"I've told you before, don't call me that." She stuck a hand on her hip in mock indignation. "Just because you've been away for a few days, doesn't mean you can get away with it. She tilted her head to one side. "Where were you anyway?"

"Mustering at Plenty River. Dan Gilbert wanted to bring a mob into market."

Sarah pulled a sceptical face. "That must have been fun for you. It's not exactly a barrel of laughs out there."

"It wasn't that bad. It just takes a little while to get to know some people. Anyway, I was there to do a job, and that's what I did." There was no logical reason, but he didn't want to tell her about his invitation to the big house.

"Well, you're back now, and that's all that matters. Coming down the pub this Friday? Everyone will be there."

Yeah, Joel Pemberton among them no doubt. "Probably." He rubbed the side of his nose and screwed up his face as though thinking deeply. "I'll have to check my diary."

"You do that," she said and winked at him. "It will probably be the best offer you get all week." She shifted her bag to the other shoulder. "I need to keep moving. I only slipped out to do the office banking. See you Friday."

He followed her with his eyes as she walked down the Mall towards the StationAir office. He was over her—well not really because there had never been anything to get over. More wishful thinking than anything. Joel was a lucky man. He let go of the breath he'd been holding with a slight shake of his head. *Move on mate*. He pushed open the door of the bank.

It was a pain—literally and figuratively. The ache in her leg meant she still had a slight limp and it affected her sleep. Of course, it had to be her bad leg. She couldn't get comfortable and when she did drop off, a dull ache woke her a couple of hours later. She had already planned a trip to town so scheduled a trip to the local physiotherapist at the same time. Hopefully, he could pull a rabbit out of the hat and effect some miraculous pain relief.

The day was one of those clear summer days that accentuated the strong colours of the Australian landscape, with a hint of the intense summer to follow. In acknowledgement of the rising mercury, Melissa pulled her hair back into a loose pony tail, held by a tortoiseshell clasp.

Coming out of the travel agents, where she had booked her flights for the coming week, she decided to grab a cup of coffee. She had plenty of time before her physio appointment. She meandered down Todd Mall, window shopping and side-stepping clusters of tourists.

23

She spotted him before he saw her. Chris had come out of the Bank and was walking in her direction. His aviator sunglasses perched on top of his head instead of his nose, pushing his fair hair into spikes behind them. He sauntered with an easy pace indicating here was a man with some direction in life but no immediate drama.

She paused uncertainly. Did she want to meet up with him? Inviting Chris to dinner had been a whim she didn't fully understand herself. It had been to deflect her father's attention as much as anything. It didn't mean she wanted to see him again.

She dithered too long. Chris spotted her and raised a hand in greeting with an easy grin. She waited as he neared, wondering how to handle the encounter.

He hailed her on approach. "Fancy seeing you here! How's the leg? I see you're still walking."

"No thanks to you, it has to be said. I'm in town to see the physio, and to book some flights for next week."

"Physio... I hope that helps... I'm so sorry..."

"So you said before. Look, don't worry about it. You couldn't have known I was there. I was just cross because I'd been stalking that dog for so long." Melissa didn't mean to sound so curt but feeling anxious did that to her.

"Let me make it up to you. I'll buy you a cup of coffee." His appeal bordered on the plaintive.

Her sunglasses slid down her nose, and she pushed them up with one finger, her mouth simultaneously making a moue of distaste.

"Okay—I'll buy you a cake too."

"Cake? Do I look as though I need cake?"

"Why do I get the feeling here that I'm on a hiding to nothing? Anyone would think I was about to bust the other leg."

"Chocolate."

"What?" His tone mirrored his puzzled expression.

"I would like some chocolate cake."

He shook his head as though not comprehending what he'd heard. "Well, I like a woman who knows her mind. Chocolate cake it is. Step this way. Melissa, you have a habit of surprising me."

She smiled at that and felt the belly-knot of tension start to ease. Holding people at arm's length was a difficult habit to break. At least Chris was inoffensive. What you saw was what you got. There would be no harm in a cup of coffee.

"I expect good coffee," she warned. "None of the dishwater rubbish that gets doled out to the tourists up here."

"No, ma'am. Do I look like a person who drinks dishwater? If you step this way, I know just the place. One of the benefits of spending time in town is that I get to check out all the local cafés."

They were well-matched in height, and Melissa kept up with him stride for stride. She stole a sideways glance. If he ate out a lot, it didn't show. He didn't have a body-builder physique, but he was still trim, taut and terrific—as much as she could discern anyway.

As they walked, Chris nodded or exchanged greetings with other locals, and it was evident he was well-known. She noted some curious glances in her direction and some polite nods, but nobody spoke directly to her. She was not a familiar sight in town, and those who did know her were never sure how to approach her. Melissa knew this and accepted it as the way things were. Life was simpler that way. That was what made this event seem so strange. Impromptu coffee meetings with men she only casually knew were not her style at all.

They turned down an arcade leading off Todd Mall. It had a central unroofed section that let in the sky—and the heat and the rain. Vines had been planted and trained to grow up over a central trellis, creating a leafy canopy to the tables that were located outside. These tables were now occupied by a mixture of tourists, complete with wide-brimmed hats and cameras, and high school students who should have been but were not wearing any. Hats were not cool.

Chris held open the door of Marnie's café, allowing Melissa to pass before him. Being mid-morning, trade bustled. Marnie still managed to greet all who came through her door with a smile and a cheery "Good Morning".

Besides conventional chairs and tables inside, there were some low-slung armchairs positioned near coffee tables on which newspapers and magazines sat in a messy heap. A poster on the wall indicated that the Centralian Writers' Group met there on the first Thursday of the month. All enquiries were welcome.

"We're in luck. There's a table over by the wall. We'll stake our claim and then we can place our order," Chris said.

They barely had time to reach their seats before a voice rang out.

"Melissa darling! What a wonderful surprise."

She knew who it would be before looking around. There was only one person with a voice like that. It was as loud as its owner.

"Russell! I should have known you'd pop up somewhere today."

The man in question was incredibly tall and incredibly skinny. His wrists protruded from his jacket sleeves, reminding Melissa of a stick insect. His white-blond hair hung below shoulder level, the colour a contrast against his ruddy complexion. He wore a multi-coloured patchwork jacket over skinny jeans and calf-length olive green tooled cowboy boots. In this environment, he stood out as an exotic species. He looked not of this world and certainly not of the Alice Springs' world but there was no Tardis in sight.

Seizing her by the shoulders, Russell deposited two air kisses on either side of her face.

"I would have seen you tonight anyway. You are coming, aren't you? Seeing you now is just a bonus."

Melissa extricated herself from his embrace, holding him at arm's length. 'You're looking spectacular, as always.'

Russell beamed at the compliment. "Now who is your friend? Sweetie, have you been hiding something from me? I don't blame you with all the hunky men around here."

He flashed an 18-carat smile at Chris, who looked alternately confused and bemused. Taking his cue, he stuck out his hand.

"I'm Chris. Not so sure about the hunky though."

"Russell. Delighted to meet you. It's okay— I never poach someone else's man. Is Melissa bringing you tonight?"

"Umm…" He raised his eyebrows at Melissa, who by this stage could feel a flush rising on her cheeks. Several locals watched the exchange with interest. A bit of gossip and drama went a long way in a small town.

27

"You never change, Russell," Melissa responded drily. "Chris is an acquaintance and I'm sure he doesn't bat for your team so leave him alone. In answer to your question, yes of course I'm coming tonight. It's one of the reasons I'm in town and no, Chris isn't coming."

"Why ever not?"

"Because I haven't asked him, and I doubt he'd be interested. I only ran into him a few minutes ago."

"And just what is it I'm not going to and wouldn't even be interested in?" Chris looked mildly miffed at the conversation happening around him.

Melissa flicked Chris a glance. "Russell is staging an exhibition of his work at the Araluen Cultural Centre, and tonight is opening night. I'm going along to wave the flag and offer support."

"And to make the most of the opportunity to see some award-winning paintings," interjected Russell. "So, Chris— are you coming?"

"I'm not doing anything else this evening, so I don't see why not. I've not been to the opening of an art exhibition before."

"Then you absolutely must come. I insist. I'll expect both of you at 6:00. Must rush. I need to check the final installations. So pleased I ran into you. See you tonight."

With a wave he was gone, a few stares following his departure. Melissa turned her attention back to Chris. "Russell can be bombastic. Don't feel you have to go tonight."

"I'd like to go actually. I'm just in the mood for something different. I'll grab the coffees and then you can tell me more about it."

Melissa watched as he fronted the counter. *It will be a change to not go to something on my own, but I hope he's not too uncomfortable there. It will be far removed from the locals he usually mixes with. I might regret this.*

Conversation resumed around them, and when Chris came back with carefully balanced coffee and cake, no one was paying attention to them anymore.

"So—who's Russell? Should I have heard of him? Tell me about his exhibition."

"Russell is an old friend. We met at technical college together in Sydney, only I was in the photographic stream and he was studying art. In the time I've known him, he's experimented with a variety of styles and I think he's currently in his earthy landscape phase."

Picking up her fork, Melissa prised off a piece of the cake. It looked wickedly decadent. "The theme of the current exhibition relates to desert environments, and that's why the opening's being staged in Alice Springs."

"That sounds, well... interesting."

Melissa allowed herself a small smile as Chris's bemused demeanour belied his words.

He continued. "I'm sure a little culture in my mundane life won't go astray. Why don't I pick you up and we can go together? I hate walking into these sorts of things on my own."

"These sorts of things? I thought you said you hadn't been to an opening before."

"Only the opening of a keg and I don't think that counts. It's the different social setting that has me a little self-conscious."

29

She burst out laughing. "I never pegged you as being hesitant or shy, Chris. Sure, I'll hold your hand. Figuratively speaking that is."

"Are you staying at the town house? I' can pick you up, say at five forty-five?"

"I don't think so. You probably drive a rust-bucket. I'm not going to be seen arriving in that. My credibility would be shredded."

"You think? It might be enhanced. Don't you find that Rollers are just so passé?"

"Since you ask, no I don't. I'm rather partial to them myself."

"Mine's in dock at the moment, but I promise I'll wipe the seats first in the truck. Is that okay?"

Melissa fixed him with a steely glare, but a slight twitch to her lips gave her away. The man was amusing to an extent, and certainly persistent. With a small sigh, she acquiesced, hoping this was not something she would later regret.

CHAPTER 3

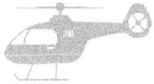

EARLY EVENING, CHRIS knocked at the door of the town house that the Gilberts used when they were in Alice. She peered past him to the street, looking for the battered Toyota Hilux in which she expected to be travelling.

A gleaming Mercedes sat at the kerb, with not a speck of red dust marking the panels. She looked from the car back to Chris and saw he watched for her reaction. He was clearly enjoying the surprise. When he opened the passenger door for her, she the smell of polished leather greeted her. This was a car that was well loved and well looked after.

"I hadn't picked you as a luxury car man," she remarked as they buckled themselves in.

"Nor had I really—rather I had but didn't think that it was feasible on a lowly pilot salary. This car used to be my grandfather's. He stopped driving after a recent illness and knowing I'd always loved the car, gave it to me. I had to promise to take him for a drive from time to time. This car was his pride and joy."

"He must have thought a lot of you."

"I hope so. He was in the air force years ago and was pleased when I chose aviation as a career. It followed in his footsteps, you know?"

"That would have made him very proud."

"I reckon it did. He lives in the city, but whenever I go back home, I try to take him up for a spin. He took me for my first flight when I was a kid and it's great to be able to return the favour."

"I envy you. That's a really special relationship."

Melissa looked out the side window to avoid any further conversation on the topic. Secretly, the mode of transport pleased her. It had a sense of style, and style was something she appreciated.

She didn't often dress up in Alice Springs, but then she didn't often attend Gallery openings there either. Her slip of a dress was supported by shoestring straps and the silky fabric featured a range of blue-greens that were shot through with a fiery red. It was reminiscent of a deep coloured opal and it was this factor which had drawn her to the dress on her last city shopping expedition. A gold belt and gold spikey sandals completed the outfit. She'd pulled her hair back on one side with a clip, leaving the rest to frame her face in a curtain of russet. It suited her tall, willowy figure. The whole appearance was a change to the big city drop-dead black that she might otherwise have worn.

By contrast, Chris was the one who was wearing black, and that also surprised her. It was a change to the jeans or khaki he usually sported. She liked it, and not just because it was a foil to her. She hadn't expected it, but they made a good couple.

They heard the music before making their entrance. A flautist, a violinist and a local didgeridoo player sat in the forecourt to the gallery, with their music serenading, teasing and cajoling as the guests wandered past. The unusual combination of instruments suited the occasion. Melissa knew the didge player and gave him a brief nod as she passed. His eyes followed her but playing was an all-encompassing activity which didn't allow for external interaction.

A few people already mingled in the gallery. They circulated, drinks in hand and heads inclined first on one side and then the other as they evaluated the paintings. Some moved in for a closer inspection of the technique or of particular details, meaning others had to dodge around them to get an unobscured view. Some stepped back a pace or two to take in the bigger perspective. Russell moved between his guests, greeting them with exuberant affection.

"Melissa, Chris—glad you could make it." He kissed Melissa on both cheeks, and Chris took a backward step before the puckered lips could be proffered in his direction. He didn't avoid a back-slapping hug.

"Have a look at the work and let me know what you think, Chris." He gazed deeply into Chris' eyes. "I really value your opinion. Being a virgin to the world of art, your perspective will be untarnished by current trends."

"As long as you don't expect anything in artist-speak," Chris said. "I know what I like, but don't always know why I like it."

Russell laughed and clapped him on the shoulder. "Grab yourselves a drink and take a wander. I'll catch up with you later."

33

He moved towards other guests, but not before giving Chris a little pat on the bottom.

"Such a pity. Don't let this one go to waste, Pet."

This last comment was directed to Melissa, who had watched the whole exchange with amusement. She considered Chris with new eyes. Perhaps Russell was onto something. She would ponder that but first, the artworks.

Drinks in hand, they wandered in a clockwise direction, studying each picture in turn. Some of the colours were vibrant, but elsewhere reflected the subtle and delicate hues of the desert and her moods. Chris could relate to some of the exhibits, but found other paintings were confusing. Spotting the scarlet desert peas, jumping off the canvas with their dramatic and confronting colour pleased him.

"Now that's something that I recognise and can understand." There was a touch of relief to this comment.

"Is it necessary do you think that the subject material is familiar to you?"

"I suppose not, but it helps to have some context. For instance, here I can relate to the colours. This is what I see every day, particularly from the air. Not sure what the painting means but I know that it features this environment. It's like indigenous artwork in a way—a symbolic interpretation of where we live. Not a chocolate box view in sight."

"I doubt you'll ever get chocolate box from Russell! In this one, you get such a sense of open space. For a city slicker, he's captured it well."

As they moved from painting to painting, Melissa nodded to various people she knew. A photographer was taking publicity shots and they exchanged a few pleasantries. It was
34

difficult in a small town not to know those who were in the same industry or shared interests. At one point, Chris paused and looked around at the crowd instead of at the walls.

"Do you know, besides yourself and now Russell, I don't think I know a single person here. For Alice Springs, that's amazing. There's a whole new community in this room, one quite different to the people I mix with in aviation."

He didn't ponder it too long. A waiter passing with a tray of champagne claimed his attention. Melissa stood back, letting Chris form his own opinions but when he was ready, they discussed the works and what the paintings portrayed. They selected their favourites and analysed their merits and Russell's use of technique.

"I want to look once more at the dessert flowers. That appeals to me the most."

The painting was displayed under directional spotlights. As Chris led Melissa towards the back of the gallery so they could view it again, she felt his hand in the small of her back. It was the lightest of touches, casual almost, but the impact she felt was anything but. A frisson of charged heat ignited her skin and it had nothing to do with the temperature outside. She felt a surge of warmth, others couldn't notice her reaction.

She flicked a quick glance at Chris and realised that he had just spoken.

"Sorry, what did you say?"

"Have I been talking to myself? I just said I really like the way he's captured the light without making the colours look harsh or confronting."

She laughed. "We'll make an art critic of you yet. I think we've seen everything at least twice. Grab another drink before the speeches start. By my reckoning, that should be any minute."

At Russell's insistence, they joined him and a small group including the gallery curator for supper after the exhibition closed. Chris responded immediately. Melissa hesitated. *I'm not sure these are really Chris's type of people. He might be incredibly bored by the experience.*

She spoke to Chris as an aside before heading out the door. "Look, just because you brought me here doesn't mean that you have to stay for this. That wasn't part of the deal."

"Melissa, if I didn't want to go, I would say so. It would be rude, wouldn't it, not to support your friend in his hour of glory? I'm not flying again until tomorrow afternoon so that's not a problem."

"Okay—just don't say I didn't warn you. The conversation will probably be all city art and hot air."

"There's always a lot of hot air around this place so we should be fine. I'm enjoying the opportunity of leaving my comfort zone. It's about time."

The restaurant was a chic bistro, specialising in indigenous and Australian cuisine. It was one of the cool places to be seen—this week anyway. The walls were decorated with a mixture of indigenous art and photographic prints of the Centralian area. They were blown up, mural size, and the menu featured some of the prints. The venue was appropriate for Russell's celebration. It was almost full, but at Russell's insistence, the staff pushed a couple of tables together and accommodated them. He was not in a mood to be thwarted and probably in anticipation of a sizeable account at the end of the night, they were happy to oblige.

Melissa noticed some bemused glances in their direction and nodded an inobtrusive greeting with the head waiter. She disliked attracting attention but with Russell leading the party, that wasn't an option. At least, she could remain on the periphery.

Chris pulled out Melissa's chair before claiming the adjoining seat. "Did I tell you how stunning you look tonight? Drop-dead gorgeous in fact." His eyes slid over her in frank appreciation as he spoke.

"You're not so bad yourself. I don't think that I've ever seen you in anything other than denim, khaki shirts and RM Williams boots."

"That's because you've never seen me at in art gallery before. You've no idea what a style icon I am."

Melissa openly chuckled and felt herself relaxing with it. The idea, given what she knew of the man so far, was quite preposterous but suddenly she wondered what it would be like to have him in front of her camera lens instead of a wild dog. Would she stalk him in the bush, or position him in the studio, lights on exposed and gleaming skin and with a sultry gaze that seduced the camera? It was an engaging thought.

She found herself taking a back seat to the conversation, responding when spoken to and sometimes contributing but not really initiating a new thread. Having taken some pain killers after her visit to the physio earlier in the day, she was mindful of minimising her intake of alcohol and that gave her a platform from which to observe her companions. She never felt comfortable centre-stage anyway.

Russell was still on an exuberant high and his bonhomie was spread over the gathering. There were a satisfying number of red dots on paintings, all the right people had attended, and he'd given a couple of media interviews that should publicise the exhibition further. Even under normal circumstances, he tended to dominate a gathering. His height and extrovert manner saw to that. Now he was especially loud, enveloping them all in his elation. Today, Alice Springs, tomorrow, the world. No surprises there. It was vintage Russell, sweeping everyone along in his wake.

"What a fantastic night," he enthused. "I should have done this years ago."

"It might not have been a success then," Melissa suggested. "You could have been working in a different style in earlier times and that might not have appealed to this market."

"That's true. What about you? When are you going to exhibit in your home town? That should be a no-brainer for you."

"I don't think so", Melissa demurred. "My fashion work gets published around the world already and nobody is really interested in my private work."

The woman to her right raised her eyebrows.

"I might be. Why don't we talk about it some time?"

Belinda, the curator at the Cultural Centre, was an old friend and she and Melissa caught up briefly on mutual news and associates.

"Why don't we catch up next time you're in town," Belinda said. "We can have a proper talk then."

Melissa pursed her lips, considering the suggestion. Belinda was in the right position for knowing what was happening where and to whom. "Sure," she said. "That sounds like a plan. I'll call you and make a time."

Conversations swirled around the table, covering the art world, people they knew and of course a re-hash of the exhibition highlights. The surprise of the evening was Chris. She had known him for a couple of years, though not intimately. Her father used his services when the need arose for mustering contracts and of course there was the odd social occasion, such as the Harts Range Races and the ball that followed the three days of racing festivities. They didn't exactly move in the same social circles. Life was simpler when you didn't get entangled in other people's lives. If there was one thing that flourished in the region, it was gossip. Sneeze, and everyone knew. Sneeze twice and you probably had bird flu. Sneeze three times and you must be at death's door. She preferred to keep to herself.

"You're quiet tonight, Melissa."

Looking up from her reverie, she realised Chris was watching her. "Aren't I always?"

"I don't know, but I suspect not. It's just a case of getting you in the right company where you feel comfortable."

She fiddled with the stem of her glass, avoiding his gaze. Chris was trying to read her and she wasn't ready to open up to him or anyone. She'd learnt some lessons in life the hard way. If you don't allow yourself to be vulnerable, you are not likely to be hurt. She wouldn't make that mistake again.

Melissa noted the confidence Chris exuded in a different environment. When she saw him working, he was usually focussed on the job. He was reserved when talking with her father, but that was normal for most people. Dan Gilbert was not a man who encouraged intimacy. Chris now engaged in a lively discourse with Russell, explaining the finer points of aerial mustering. The artist placed his long creative fingers on Chris's arm, gazing soulfully into his eyes.

"Fascinating. You must have such fine motor control. What I wouldn't do to find a man with hands like that!" He gave an exaggerated sigh. "You're so lucky, Pet."

As earlier, the comment was meant for Melissa though his gaze remained firmly fixed on Chris. Melissa glanced at Chris to judge his reaction. She was familiar with Russell's dramatics but wasn't sure how often camp overtures were made to Chris.

If he was embarrassed, he didn't show it. He caught her glance with a quick smile and an even quicker wink, so quick that she wasn't sure she'd seen it. Perhaps he might even be enjoying himself.

By the time the dinner group made leaving noises, the restaurant staff were resetting tables for the next day. Russell conveniently excused himself to go to the bathroom coinciding with the arrival of the bill. Melissa pursed her lips in exasperation. Typical. Russell was full of noise but a past master at appearing to be benevolent to others without spending a cent. Nothing had changed. The others at the table had split the bill between them and organised the tip by the time Russell returned. Any unpleasantness for him such as actually putting his hand in a pocket was avoided.

"Melissa, it's been so wonderful catching up with you, especially seeing you in your environment instead of the city.

It's a fascinating town," he declared. "I had no idea there was such a cultural oasis hiding out in this desert. You're lucky to have grown up here; it's so inspirational."

She burst out laughing. It was good to see Russell again and she was happy for him and his well-deserved success, but honestly—he had no idea what he was talking about. He patted her hand in a gesture of affability. "Next time you're both in Sydney, you must come and see me, and we'll do dinner again."

"Oh, but we're not…" Melissa started.

"Thanks—we'd love to. We don't have any immediate plans to travel, but we'll discuss our options," Chris said, extending his hand. Russell seized the proffered arm and pulled Chris to him in close embrace, planting a kiss on each cheek. This time a slow flush spread over Chris' face and lit up his ears.

"You asked for that," Melissa remarked later as they walked out to the car park.

"I wasn't aware I had, but I'm on a steep learning curve." He rubbed his cheek reflectively as though afraid that there was a residual mark on his face that said, 'A multi-coloured stick insect kissed me here.' "He's quite a character, isn't he? He asked if I could take him flying but I'm not sure about being in close proximity at a height of five thousand feet with no way to escape."

"Sounds like you're learning fast. Russell is harmless really—mostly bluff and bluster. He's got his reputation to protect. He's worked so hard at developing his persona. If you really want to give him a surprise, kiss him back."

"I'll take your word for that. I'm in no hurry to put it to the test."

The restaurant was on the edge of town and away from the main road. A light breeze whipped their shoulders, a welcome relief from the earlier heat of the day.

The shadow of the MacDonnell Ranges loomed over the carpark. It seemed that they were not in a built-up area but in a more bush-like setting. The occasional call of a night bird helped to reinforce this impression.

Theirs was almost the last car remaining in the car park. Chris opened the passenger door for Melissa, aware of a faint scent as she slid inside. How come he hadn't noticed that earlier? It contrasted with the earthy smell of the leather seats. She gave him an enigmatic look as he eased himself into the driver's seat. It puzzled him. What was she thinking to give him a look like that? She knew how to confuse a bloke.

He pulled onto the road, the beam from the headlights swinging around to light up a corridor of eucalypts. "I couldn't help noticing," he said, "on the back of the menu there were credits to Melissa Gilbert for photographic works. Were all of those murals on the walls the results of your work?"

"Yes, that was a local commission. The owner of the restaurant and I went to boarding school together. When she was doing the restaurant fit-out, she approached me about providing the prints. It was a welcome change to showcase some regional landscapes instead of beautiful people wearing beautiful clothes."

"Why didn't you say something when we arrived? There were some stunning prints on the wall. I was impressed."

"This was Russell's night. It was all about his work, not mine."

"It didn't get you a cheaper meal."

"This is business. I charged a fair price for my work and Justine charges a fair price for her meals. I wouldn't expect anything less. I can be just as pragmatic as my father."

Chris scratched his chin. "I can see there are similarities, but I need more time to really comment." What he really meant was, I don't know you well enough—yet.

Melissa flicked a sideways glance at him but didn't respond. The rest of the journey was conducted in silence, but it wasn't far. He pulled up in front of her town house, and switched off the motor. The silence was loud. It was a long time since he'd been in this situation and now there was no time to think. He needed to say something. Would she expect him to kiss her?

Chris turned in his seat to look at her. "Earlier today, you mentioned you were booking some flights. Are you going somewhere?"

"I picked up an assignment back in New South Wales. I fly to Sydney next week."

"Will you be away long?"

"I don't know. The job should only last a week, but there's some prep work to do and then some studio work at the end of it. I should also do the rounds of some of the agencies. Out of sight is out of mind. I have to be careful when I come back to Alice that the industry doesn't forget I exist."

"I'd be surprised if they did that, if your fashion work is as good as the images I saw tonight. Will you see Russell while you're there?"

"I haven't any specific plans, but it's always a possibility."

"It's eons since I've been in Sydney," he mused. "I'd probably get totally lost now—quite the country boy in the big smoke."

"It wouldn't take long to find your way again. Anyway, thanks for the lift tonight—and the company." She reached for the door handle. "Perhaps I'll see you out home on your next mustering contract."

"Well, hopefully before that. I've enjoyed tonight. It was out of my comfort zone, but I needed to be pushed. I think I've needed it for a while."

"I'm glad you enjoyed the experience. It's been… interesting."

He leaned forward and softly kissed her cheek. "If it doesn't push *you* too far out of your comfort zone, I might give you a call some time? Perhaps you could show me more of your work."

"Perhaps." She gave him a sideways look. "I have some prints of a dingo that might interest you." Not waiting for his response, she slipped out of the car, shutting the door behind her.

He turned the ignition key but waited a moment, watching her open the front gate and walk up the path before pulling away. *Yes, I would like to see the prints of that dingo. That and a whole lot more besides.*

44

***

From the security of her doorway, Melissa watched the tail lights of the Mercedes disappear. She was relieved Chris hadn't invited himself in for a coffee or to look at her etchings. She needed some time to process the day and how it had unfolded. There was a lot to think about. For instance, how and when she might see him again, and why the thought gave her a degree of pleasure.

CHAPTER 4

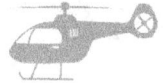

AS THE PLANE banked over Botany Bay and lined up on heading for the runway, Melissa peered out the window. It never ceased to amaze her that there were so many people crammed into the metropolis. Back home, when she saw a roof from the light aircraft in which she commonly travelled, she knew exactly whose roof it was. Here, there was a sea of anonymous red roofs, all packed closely together. The city skyline and the outline of the bridge presented a visual relief on the horizon.

Anticipation always hit prior to landing. It was that heightened sense of awareness, the appreciation of form and colour and a magnification of the noises around her. It was a virtual smorgasbord that assaulted the senses. She looked forward to catching up with friends and experiencing again the smells and the tumult of the city—for a while anyway. She knew by the time she left, she would be hanging out again for the space and quiet of home.

The taxi drew up at the terrace house at the same time as Angela reached the gate, laden with grocery bags in each hand.

"Melissa!" she squealed. "You're looking good, girl. You're a vision of sunshine and health compared to my city pallor. There must be something beneficial in that country air."

"I think it's the *absence* of anything in the air that counts," Melissa responded dryly, taking some of the bags. "No diesel fumes, no hydrocarbons, no general grime and pollution. I'm sure that stuff isn't good for your skin, let alone your lungs."

"You're telling me nothing! I'll put the kettle on, and you can fill me in on all your news. Where's your next contract?"

Angela was a location scout, and she and Melissa met a couple of years earlier while on a job. The two women hit it off and on return trips to Sydney, Melissa rented a spare room in Angela's Annandale terrace. It suited them both. Angela had some income and company for those periods but as it was only for a while, she didn't feel her privacy was being compromised. Melissa had somewhere to stay that was comfortable, friendly and dependable. She could indulge in the cosmopolitan lifestyle for a while.

They both enjoyed catching up on the news and gossip. Melissa outlined the job she had lined up down the coast and the people with whom she expected to be working. Angela talked about the new season's fashion collections and the trouble she was having in finding a unique location for the videos and photographic shoots.

"You should see the gowns—they're dramatic and inspiring. I've only seen the sketches of course, as the collection is a work in progress but I'm looking forward to seeing the final product. The colours are so vibrant."

"I'm sure you'll find the perfect location. You always do. I can keep an eye out on this job, if you like. The south coast is dramatic and rugged in places, plus it's not too far for you to go."

"I know, but I think it's time for something different. If only they would give me a bigger budget. I'd scout out a Pacific island or somewhere like that." She frowned pensively. "Are there any semi-active volcanoes around? Think what spectacular photos that would create with some of fire and brimstone in the background."

"Um, I don't think so. You'd never get insurance for a start, and where would you find models who were prepared to run the risk of being swallowed by molten lava, to say nothing of the photographers? This particular photographer says *no way.*"

"Melissa, you've no sense of adventure! Put your stuff away. I can't be bothered cooking tonight. I suggest Vietnamese takeaway to celebrate your return and we can catch up on all the goss. Have you met anyone interesting since you were last here?"

Melissa thought fleetingly of Chris, the image of his black-clad figure admiring the paintings quickly replaced by the pilot in the bush, caked in sweat and focussed on the job.

"Not really, you know how it is."

"No, I don't. Why don't you tell me?"

Melissa laughed but refused to look at Angela. "There's nothing to tell. A remote station property is not exactly teaming with likely candidates."

She knew Angela was looking at her quizzically but declined to engage any further. It wasn't as if there was

48

anything between her and Chris. They hardly knew each other. One evening in each other's company didn't really count, and besides--their lives were very different. There was nothing to tell.

The pace of city life swept Melissa along in its wake. There were people to meet, details to verify and preparations to make for the next contract. She had to be sure of having the right equipment and being able to show the models and the background in the best possible light--and of course the clothing. It was all about the clothing this time. No wildlife here.

A couple of days later, she jammed some practical clothes in a hold-all before heading out of town in her rented car. The job was all sand, wind and salt, part enjoyable and part challenge.

Eduardo, shoot director could be a prima donna. It wouldn't be Eduardo if there weren't a few histrionics. When Melissa first met him, he had been Edward, often shortened to Eddie. As he developed his experience and reputation within the industry, plain Eddie was consigned to history and Eduardo arose chrysalis-like instead.

Eduardo was a more colourful character than Eddie. Even his own mother barely recognised him, or so he said in rare moments of honest self-appraisal. Depending on the company, his accent was likely to revert to broad Australian at those times.

Despite the façade, he was a professional. Melissa knew his vision on the job usually translated to a result which delighted the client and of course resulted in repeat work for them all. He was the only person she tolerated calling her Mellie.

The first evening, Eduardo plopped down beside Melissa in the lounge area of the motel dining room.

"Great job, Mellie. I had a quick look through today's shoot. I can always rely on you to capture the mood and emotion. You really understand what I'm trying to communicate. I'd suggest you should be in front of the camera yourself except I don't want to lose you behind it."

"Not likely. I wear clothes for pleasure not for work and from what I've seen, those models work hard. I also prefer to eat and drink what I like without worrying what it does to my prospects."

"Your prospects look fine from this angle," Eduardo said eying off her figure with a suggestive leer. "There must be something in that bush air. Perhaps you could bottle and sell it."

"Mm. Angela was making similar comments. You'll have to come out some time and see for yourself. She was talking about looking for a location for your next shoot. Plenty River would be a logistic nightmare, but it would be different from anything you'd done so far. Plus of course, I wouldn't have to travel—a win for me at least."

"You know, that's not such a crazy idea. Leave it with me and I'll see what I can do. It all depends on the budget and the timing and I'd have to talk to the client, but it just might work. Uluru, here I come."

"Steady Eddie", she teased. "It's a long way from Uluru but the scenery can be just as dramatic. I can help with some of the organising from my end. Keep me posted on your plans."

❧

Eduardo spoke to the client, and Angela investigated the logistics and practicalities of Plenty River. Some hard discussions took place behind closed doors, but it all came together quicker than anticipated.

Incredible as it seemed, the crew was on its way to the station. Melissa flew back a week earlier to make the final arrangements. Dan Gilbert didn't hide his thoughts on the prospect of a bunch of city slickers running amok over his property. Why would they want to come all that way to pose against the spinifex, or with cattle or rocky outcrops in the background? He didn't oppose it however, in one of his rare moments of generosity towards Melissa.

"Just make sure they don't get in my way and if they get bitten by a snake, that's their problem. I don't want to know. If they get themselves lost out here, I've got better things to do than to look for them. And make sure they can drive on these roads!"

This last comment was flung over his shoulder as he headed out for the day. He would not be part of any welcoming party when they arrived. That was fine by Melissa. The more he kept out of their way, the better. Jenny was more excited. It was a welcome break from station routine.

"Do you think they'll mind if I watch? It will be interesting to see what goes on behind the scenes. I can get a better understanding of your work as well. I'd love that."

"Of course, you can come." Melissa gave her a quick hug. "No one will mind, and they should be grateful for the opportunity we're giving them. You can drive out to the work site with me. I've been doing some thinking and have a range of locations I'll suggest to Angela. All we need now is for the weather to hold up—not too hot and not too cold. Just right."

"I'll put my order in," Jenny said. "How many people are coming? I should think about some baking."

"No Jenny, you don't need to bake a thing. They'll have budgeted for all their catering. Ultimately, the client will pay for it."

"I'm sure they'll have morning or afternoon tea here at least one day. I'll be prepared just in case and what isn't used can go in the freezer."

Melissa knew Jenny would do some baking regardless of what she said. The freezer option was a good one. That just left one call to make.

She pictured the man at the other end of the phone. That black had looked surprisingly good on him.

"Hi Chris? I haven't caught you at a bad time, have I?"

"Melissa! Of course not. Are you in town?"

"No, I'm out at Plenty River, but I wondered if you and perhaps your mate Mark might be available for a contract later in the week."

"You're talking about a flying job? Where to, for how long, and doing what? If you give me some details I can chat to Mark and consult our bookings. I thought your father had finished the mustering."

"He has. This is for something totally different. I've organised a fashion shoot at Plenty River and some of the locations I've scouted are not so easily accessible with conventional vehicles. They won't have a lot of time for long-distance travel either. I thought we could drop people into location by chopper. Would that be feasible?"

"You mean we would have to fly a bevy of beautiful women around the country? What do you think? I can hear Mark salivating already."

"Settle down, tiger. These women are totally focussed on themselves and anyway, he might be carrying the male models; or members of the production crew."

"Does that include you?"

"I'll be the photographer on this shoot although I'll travel in the station 4-wheel drive. There'll be a videographer as well covering that aspect of filming. The shoot director might want to use the chopper for filming. Should be a breeze for someone with your experience."

"I'll check with Mark and get back to you, but I don't think there's anything we can't rearrange. Changing the subject, when are you in town next? Perhaps we could catch up for a meal?"

"Oh… yes… well… we could do that."

Melissa thought rapidly. There was no valid reason why not. Even as her thoughts questioned what she was doing, she could hear her voice confirming her program.

"I'll be in town next week to finalise some details and to pick up Angela from the airport. She's the location scout and is arriving ahead of the rest of the crew. I could see you the evening before if I came in a day early."

This was so out of character for her. By the time she put the phone down, arrangements were made, and it was too late to back out.

It was just dinner. She could do that. It didn't mean anything.

Chris disconnected the call. A grin split his face as he imagined Mark's response. It would be a welcome change. There was nothing preventing them from taking the job. He reached for a booking sheet. This would be entertaining. Melissa was full of surprises. He'd like to see her in action. With the job entered in the system, he pulled the phone towards him. He'd better make a reservation for the dinner. After that, he'd call Mark. He couldn't wait to hear the reaction.

It was planned that Angela would fly out from Sydney a couple of days earlier than the rest of the crew. Melissa would meet her at the airport and take her out to the station, giving her colleague a tour of the locations she had provisionally selected. She was excited about Angela visiting her for a change. She'd never had the opportunity to invite friends home when she was younger and school friends never came to stay during the holidays. She knew her father wouldn't have welcomed the intrusion. Now she was independent enough to extend her own invitations.

The drive into town took nearly three hours, but it Melissa had made the trip many times. She passed the gate to Mulga Downs on the way, home to neighbours Alex and Kathy Woodleigh. She and Alex had spent a lot of time together as kids, being the only young people for miles around. Alex's mother Rose had also taken a motherly interest in Melissa's welfare and had made sure Melissa knew she was always welcome.

There was a time when Melissa had assumed, as had her father, that she and Alex would end up together permanently. Kathy's arrival on the scene had put paid to that idea. She now maintained only polite contact with her neighbours and even then, only when necessary. She didn't look at the entrance to Mulga as she passed.

She pulled up at the town house with enough time to shower and change before dinner. Chris hadn't said where they were going although there weren't many options in town. She opened a few windows and turned on the fan to blow out the stale air. That was one of the problems with the house being shut up for periods of time. It could get stuffy. By the time Chris arrived, in the Mercedes of course, the house was fresh and so was she. She listened as his footsteps came up the path.

"You're looking good."

He leaned forward and dropped a light kiss on her cheek. She regarded him from under her eyelashes—a Diana look.

"Sorry," he said. "I'm still learning how to be sophisticated." Grasping her by the shoulders, he planted a kiss on each cheek. "How am I doing?"

Her lips twitched. "I think you're doing fine. A fast learner." She picked up her bag and house keys which had been waiting by the door. "Where are we going? Obviously somewhere that's the height of sophistication in downtown Alice?"

"There are a couple of options," he said, opening the passenger door. "I hear the new Spicy Chicken diner that took over the old petrol station at the end of town is pretty good."

Melissa was unsure what to say. Surely, he was kidding? Sitting at a booth in a fast food joint was not her idea of a night out. If that was what he thought, he could stop the car right now.

The grin was a give-away. "The look on your face is priceless. Of course, we're not going to the Spicy Chicken, though I have heard favourable reports. I thought we'd try the dining room at the Desert Sands Resort. They serve up a credible meal."

Melissa relaxed. She should have known Chris wouldn't pull a stunt like that, but then she didn't know him well. She found him intriguing, but something told her that she would get to know him much better. The greater surprise was the little voice which kept piping up saying that she wanted to know him better. Where had that thought come from?

The dinner provided the first opportunity for them to sit down and really talk. The waiter took their order and brought a pre-dinner drink before Chris raised the topic of the fashion shoot.

"So, tell me more about this job you've roped me into. Mark can't believe his luck. He's been dining out on it all week, regaling all and sundry about the fabulous models he's going to be flying around the country. They get more famous and more stunning with each telling."

"It's pretty much as I outlined on the phone. I'm picking up my friend Angela at the airport tomorrow but most of the others will be arriving in a couple of days. Angela is the location scout. I've got an air-conditioned minibus ready to drive them out to the station. A van is en-route with the clothing and essential equipment and props. Hopefully those guys haven't got lost. I've given them a map directing them to the station once they hit Alice."

"Where are they all staying?"

"I've commandeered the staff quarters which are largely empty at the moment, and some will be accommodated in the house. With Angela arriving first, she's got first dibs on a room. It's not Ritz accommodation, but then they're not staying at the Ritz. It will be an experience that they won't get elsewhere."

"Sounds as though you've got it all under control. Are you always so organised?"

"Think so. Probably got it from my father; his tolerance for disorganisation is minimal." She gave him a wry look. "You may have noticed. Anyway, I learnt quite young that if I wanted anything to happen, it was up to me to organise it. Strategic thinking is a university course these days. I picked it via the University of the Bush."

"So, it's just you and your father who live…?"

57

"Yes." *Don't pry, Chris. I'm not ready.* "What brought you to Alice? How long have you been here?" Time to ask him questions.

Chris's eyebrows lifted slightly but he took the change in conversation without further comment.

"It was the job. The location interested me, and I knew there was a reasonable chance this was where I might end up working. It's a great opportunity from which to build up experience that opens doors later. Mustering involves precision flying. Either you're good, or you're not. Permanently not. I've been here nearly three years now and I've learnt a lot."

"So I've seen. Low-level flying for a start."

"Yeah, well... that's an important part of the job. You're not going to give me a hard time about that, are you?"

He turned a beseeching look on her. Melissa wasn't sure whether it really reflected his feelings or if he was just turning on the melodrama. "No. Not anymore. Well, not unless I think it's necessary anyway."

She smiled at him. She tended to be reserved with people she didn't know well and knew her natural demeanour could come across as aloof. Indifferent at best and withering at worst. She was under no illusions about her reputation. The smile evolved, in spite of herself.

Chris grinned in response, re-filled her wine glass and picked up his in salute.

"Melissa, don't change. I like you. You're a woman of surprises."

Her eyes widened, but she didn't say anything. Just sipped her wine and glowed in response. She didn't want to let on how delighted but disconcerted she was feeling.

When Chris drove her back to the town house, he not only opened the passenger car door but walked her up the front path. There, he grasped her by the shoulders and turned her to face him.

"Thank you for your company this evening. I've enjoyed getting to know you. It's just the beginning, but I'm in no rush. You're an intriguing woman."

The kiss was sweet, explorative. It promised more. Earlier in the evening, she'd tentatively wondered how she would react if he kissed her, and then how she'd react if he didn't. The question was too hard and so she ignored it and instead focussed on her wonderful chocolate mousse dessert. It was a rare luxury and she was going to make the most of it.

If she'd thought this was as good as the evening was going to get, she was mistaken. The kiss was a whole lot better. It stirred feelings that she didn't realise she had, to the point where she felt both bereft and terrified when he broke away, looked at her with that half-smile that was his trademark, lightly kissed her again and then left her, with a promise to see her soon.

CHAPTER 5

THE CAVALCADE MADE itself known with a cloud of dust before becoming visible on the long driveway from the cattle grid at the turn-off, past the graves and onto the cluster of buildings comprising the operations centre of the station. There was the main house of course, where Dan, Melissa and Jenny lived. Close by were the staff quarters, occupied at times by jackaroos, jillaroos, the station manager and contractors. Otherwise there were a collection of sheds and outhouses, which provided cover for various station vehicles and equipment, and the workshop in which repairs and mechanical interventions took place.

The station dogs were the first to greet the visitors, their barking more effective than any early warning system.

"Buster... Digger... Heel!" Melissa roared the commands as she opened the side gate and dragged the dogs inside. Some of the models and crew might not be accustomed to exuberant working dogs. She shut the gate and strode towards the vehicles wearing an uncharacteristic smile.

"You made it. Welcome!"

Her cordial welcome hid the feelings of excitement tinged with anxiety that she felt. They were on her home turf. She wanted them to appreciate it. She and Angela exchanged amused glances as they saw the crew unwinding themselves from the vehicles and stretching cramped legs. There were a few stunned looks.

"My god Melissa—do you make that journey all the time? It's so far! Where do you go for a freakin' coffee?"

"And you said there are dingos out here. Do they eat adults too?"

"One can but hope," muttered one of the drivers.

"Do you have flush toilets?" asked a leggy blonde who had a slightly pained expression on her face. Melissa took the hint and ushered her into Angela's care and the indoor facilities. Eduardo embraced her in a warm hug with a look of wonderment on his face.

"I was sort of expecting to see you as a version of Queen of the Desert. It's not exactly desert is it, but there's certainly a hint of drama here."

"I think the dramatics are about to unfold over the next couple of days," she responded sweetly. "Welcome to my life."

She turned to address the cluster of bodies.

"Okay everybody. Pleased to see you got here in one piece. This is Plenty River Station, not quite the edge of the universe, but almost. The dingoes will give you a wide berth, *but*… there'll be plenty of other critters to give you a nasty bite. Keep your shoes on and long trousers are a good idea. If you'd like to follow me, I'll show you to your rooms and you

61

can dump your bags and freshen up. Then, if you make your way into the dining room, we'll have afternoon tea waiting for you."

Jenny had insisted on organising this, and on reflection, Melissa agreed that after their journey, her colleagues would appreciate some station hospitality. Plenty of time later for the catering van to feed and water the hungry hoards.

Despite their protestations and wise cracks, the crew were used to less-than-five-star locations and of course when it involved one of their own, were prepared to rise to the challenge of adventure without too much complaint. With afternoon tea out of the way, Eduardo ran through the sequence of events and what he was hoping to achieve in the next couple of days. Angela described the locations Melissa had shown her and how in her view, the collection to be featured might best be displayed.

Melissa described what she would like to achieve in each of those locations, with reference to time of day and lighting. She also told them two helicopters were arriving the following morning to help in getting to some of the more remote locations. That caused a degree of excitement.

"Do we get to see Uluru from the air?"

"Not a chance. It's hundreds of kilometres from here."

"Damn. That would've been so cool."

"Oh, I've always wanted to fly in a chopper. Will I go up, Eduardo? Pretty Please?"

"No promises for anyone. If anyone goes up, it's going to be me." Eduardo was wickedly resolute.

Observing the interchange, Melissa wondered how Chris was going to cope with this lot and the ribbing that was part of the job. If he could muster bush cattle, it shouldn't be too bad. Or so she hoped.

D-day would be tomorrow and already she had butterflies thinking about it. She turned back to her guests, and the arrangements for the following day and the early start. This was what she needed to focus on.

Breakfast was served before dawn. It was a light affair, as they needed to be on site and ready for the first light of day. The catering van would have a more substantial meal available in a couple of hours. Melissa led the cavalcade of vehicles towards the first location. The rocky outcrop faced east, and the early morning light would provide wonderful illumination to the selection of clothes against the reds, browns and ochres of the dramatic background. The morning birds heralded them, carolling notice of the intrusion across the landscape. Small marsupials scurried from their path. Melissa managed to capture a shot of a red kangaroo which paused for a while, ears twitching as he watched the activity happening in his backyard, before bounding off. A couple of smaller female roos followed behind.

They set up camp in the half light, getting ready for the first magical morning rays. Melissa didn't need long to get organised, and nor did the rest of the crew. They were professionals and followed patterns established on previous work. They moved into position and got on with it.

"The air here is so clear," one of the models remarked. "It's not until you come to an environment like this that you appreciate just what you must be breathing in the city. It even has a different taste. Chilly though; I wasn't expecting that."

"It is at this time of day," Melissa agreed, "but it will warm up with the sun. Can you just look over to the left? Chin up… I'll be as quick as I can and then you can put your wrap back on."

"Darl, you're channelling too much earth mother there. Think desert nymph… alluring…tantalising… in control of your environment. Give me a look of power and control."

Eduardo bellowed his usual challenging directions as Melissa and the models worked together, making the most of the beautiful light which bathed the scene in golden hues, hinting at the day that unfolded. By the time they paused for a break and refreshments, they all felt they had done some solid work. The catering van, powered by a generator, had accompanied them and now the delicious aromas of coffee, eggs, bacon and croissants intruded on the morning. Nobody needed a second invitation. Everything smelt overwhelmingly tantalising. Even the fastidious weight watchers were tempted.

"Mellie, you've brought us to a fantastic backdrop. The client should be really pleased with the results. It's not an environment the city boy in me really understands but you've done well." Praise from Eduardo was praise indeed. He didn't bestow it often.

"Thanks Eddie. It's nice to be appreciated." She didn't mean to sound glib. She really was happy to hear it.

"We work so well together," he continued pausing for a mouthful of coffee. "I may have a contract coming up in Europe. If you like, I can put your name forward as the shoot photographer. No promises, but together, we make a good team. You always understand what I'm trying to achieve and then go one better. Plus, you never question what I'm trying to do. I like that."

Melissa didn't argue, that was true. She had long since learned to take on board what he was saying and then to follow her own professional instincts anyway but in such a way that Eduardo thought it was his idea. Wiping a dribble of butter from her chin, she turned one of her rare smiles on her friend.

"Eddie, that would be a fantastic opportunity. I'd like to get more international work. I've established myself in Australia, well in some circles anyway, but I'd love to work with some of the big names and fashion houses overseas. Who knows where it might lead?"

"It's an opportunity for you and me both. Stick with me Mellie, and together we'll travel the world to fame and fortune."

He headed back to the food supply for seconds. A thin man who survived on nervous energy, he had no need to monitor his intake. Faintly, above the noise of the chat, a mechanical vibration could be heard, becoming gradually louder. Melissa swept her hair back from her face as she peered at the horizon. Was that Chris or was it Mark?

It was both, flying in tandem. They emerged from the sun and circled low over the camp before sinking to the ground in a clearing a short distance away, the eddies of dust whirling around them.

"Great, here come the fly boys," called Eduardo. "Now we're really in business."

The focus on food paused while everyone scrutinised the two figures just discernible in the cabins. They shut down the engines and the rotors continued to whine while slowing to a stop. As the pilots emerged, Melissa moved forward to greet them, aware of an unfamiliar feeling of anticipation. It was a long time since a man had aroused these sensations in her. Not since Alex Woodleigh really and now she doubted those feelings had been real. Had she just been living up to expectations?

"Morning. You're just in time for cuppa, or a second breakfast if you're hungry," she said, hands on hips.

"You know me. I'm always hungry," said Mark. "We were up quite early—this'll feel like lunch."

With his trademark half-smile, Chris moved forward as though to embrace Melissa. She had a moment of panic. Not here. Not in front of everyone. Flashing him a quick smile she broke off eye contact and gestured towards the catering van. "Help yourselves while it's still hot, but I'll introduce you to Eduardo first. He's the director for the shoot."

She led the way to where the crew were standing a respectful but curious distance away, bickering amongst themselves as to who would get to go up. Chris paused, looking around as though getting his bearings.

"C'mon, mate. What are you waiting for? I can smell it from here." Mark clapped him on the shoulder and followed Melissa. He didn't need inviting twice when there was food around.

"I thought you said there were no men around here?" Angela asked, one eyebrow raised in interrogation. "You didn't mention they just drop in from the sky. What else have you forgotten to tell me?"

"Men? Chris and Mark are local contractors. My father engages them for the aerial work when he's doing a muster. They come and do the job and then they go. I never have much involvement with the hired help."

She didn't know why she said that. It was an instinctive response. She couldn't look Angela in the eye, but noticed Jenny giving her a strange look.

"Hmm. Looks like a missed opportunity to me." Angela's tone was as appraising as the looks she cast towards the two men. She followed them to the catering van. She was not one to pass up on an opportunity, even if Melissa was.

With the crew watered and fed, it was back to business. There was a quick discussion about the next location and who needed to be on site, and what they needed with them. Melissa was taking the four-wheel drive.

She addressed the crew. "The choppers will be quicker, so I'll make a start now for the next location. I can take four of you with me, and some of the equipment as well. Eduardo, you sort out who's going with who. Jenny will be following me in her vehicle, so others can go with her."

The hair and make-up people came with her. For them, it was all part of the adventure. Eduardo, the videographer, and the four models travelled in the choppers. She arrived a little after the machines had touched down in the next location. Two pop-up tents were quickly erected to serve as change rooms and the make-up specialist set up a table in the shade, after inspecting the ground carefully for ants, scorpions, spiders, snakes and anything else she could think of.

Chris and Mark stood to one side, watching with interest the scene unfolding in front of them.

67

"Beats chasing cattle, mate," commented Mark. "This is much easier work."

Chris grunted a reply. He watched Melissa as she set up her equipment, took test shots and fiddled with her settings. She didn't pay him any attention but focussed one hundred percent on what she needed to do.

Melissa was aware of Chris watching her and was disconcerted. The two pilots, not having anything to do at this stage, were free to observe proceedings. Outsiders weren't usually hanging around on a shoot. She did get intense about her work

The easiest way to deal with her audience was just to ignore them and pretend they weren't there. Mark tried his best one-liners with one of the models, who smiled sweetly but swiftly made him aware that right now it was all about work, not socialising. In case there was any doubt, Eduardo soon put that thought to bed as he bawled instructions to the assembled crew.

"Do I need to remind you all that this is a work trip, not a holiday?" he bellowed at the company in general. "Where are the models? C'mon, c'mon – get up on those rocks and don't dare snag the merchandise. Melissa—are you ready? If we don't hurry up, the sun will burn us all and monster ants will probably eat us alive."

Given his propensity for exaggeration, nobody was particularly perturbed at this possibility, but they were all keen to get the job done.

If you think this is hot Eddie, you're in for a surprise later today. Melissa rolled her eyes at his antics and continued at her own pace. The models were given the tick of approval for their hair and make-up and moved into position. The stylist checked the outfits and how they were displayed. The session began.

The heat built up through the day, and the crew felt it. While the models changed into the next outfits, everyone else dived into the nearest shade. Melissa took off her hat and mopped at the perspiration collecting beneath the brim. Her jeans, practical for working in this environment, felt heavy and stuck to her legs. She drank thirstily from her water bottle.

"So, which do you prefer—fashion or dingoes?"

She looked around. She'd been so absorbed in her work she'd momentarily forgotten Chris was there.

"Whatever I'm shooting at that moment, I guess. That becomes my focus and I don't think about other options."

"Perhaps, but what I've seen here I would describe as dedication to the task. What I've observed before has been passion."

"An interesting perspective. I'll need to think about that. Have you two had a cold drink? Can't have our pilots getting dehydrated."

Mark winked as he raised his water bottle at her, indicating he was fine. Chris gave her a thumbs-up. "Don't worry about us. Plenty of water, thanks."

For the first time that day, she made eye contact. She wasn't even sure why she had been avoiding it. He smiled his crooked half-smile at her and instantly her memory was flooded with the sensations of that door-stop kiss. The heat infusing her was both mortifying and tantalisingly sweet.

"I need to check my lenses," she muttered and fled back to the Land Cruiser. She knew she was running away, but she needed breathing space. It wasn't just the memories of that kiss. His comments about her dedication versus passion struck a chord. It made her think.

The prospect of the overseas work excited her. Anyone in her position would kill for an opportunity like that, but there was huge satisfaction from her private work. She didn't promote it but any recognition that she received was hugely rewarding. Perhaps she could use the reputation that she gained through her fashion photography to springboard a side career in other areas. For now, it was fashion that paid the bills.

Equipment in hand, she returned to the waiting crew.

"Okay everybody, break's over, time to go." Eduardo was in hyperactive director mode again. He clicked his fingers. "Hey, fly boy. Crank up that machine of yours. I want to get some aerial footage."

Melissa froze. He shouldn't speak to the pilots like that. What did Eduardo think he was doing? Chris and Mark were not members of the crew.

The two men did not respond, but Melissa could tell from their slightly stiffened posture that they'd heard. Eduardo clicked his fingers again. Twice more in fact.

"Are you deaf? We need to lift off. Get your arses into gear."

Melissa groaned inwardly. This could mean trouble. She tried to catch Eduardo's eye. He could be so difficult when he was in one of his moods. If she could diffuse the situation and then pull him aside …

"Eduardo…" she began, just as he clicked his fingers yet again.

At this, Chris turned around with a deadly and deliberate stare. "Do. Not. Click. Your. Fingers. At. Me. I am not a performing monkey. You can flap your arms and fly if you want to lift off and walk back for all I care. When you speak to me, you mind your manners and use please and thank you."

There was a silence in the camp. Eduardo glared at Chris. He was not used to being challenged, nor being told how to behave.

Collectively, everyone held their breath.

As effectively as Jekyll and Hyde, Eduardo disappeared, and Eddie stood in his place. "Look mate, I didn't mean to be offensive. We're running to a tight schedule here and I got caught up in the stress of the moment. I'm sorry I clicked my fingers, okay?"

The two men stared at each other. Chris didn't respond, and Mark moved to stand at his shoulder. It was a movement of solidarity.

"If I say pretty please, will that make a difference?"

"Not really. Just standard *please* and *thank you* goes a long way." Chris stalked back to his chopper. At the door to the cabin, he looked back over his shoulder. "If you're coming, you'd better hurry up before I change my mind."

Eduardo and the videographer scurried to the aircraft and strapped themselves in. Melissa observed from the sidelines, utterly aghast at the turn things had taken. Why didn't she warn Eduardo to modify his behaviour in that environment? Why hadn't she intervened and reprimanded Eduardo herself? A small voice said, *Because you didn't want to get on Eduardo's bad side, that's why. You didn't want to cramp your chances of future work.*

As these thoughts ran through her mind, her eyes caught Chris's through the canopy of the chopper. This time he wasn't smiling. There was no sense of connection at all.

CHAPTER 6

THE CHOPPERS WERE only chartered for the one day. Melissa made a point of thanking Mark and Chris for their assistance before they lifted off for their return to Alice. Chris was clearly still unimpressed by the earlier interactions.

"Are your mates always so rude, or just to the hired help?"

"Chris, it's not usually like that. Eduardo is so intense when he's working; he just gets carried away."

"That's no excuse. You people in the fashion industry might be used to that sort of behaviour but that's no reason why I should put up with it."

"You people? What's that supposed to mean? It's rather a sweeping statement."

"Well, I didn't hear anybody protest about the rudeness of your mate, so I can only assume that everyone accepted it as normal."

"By everyone, I suppose you mean me. Didn't it occur to you we were all taken by surprise? That doesn't mean anyone, myself included, condoned what Eddie did."

"So now it's *Eddie*? You obviously know him quite well. I think I'm glad I don't."

It was a conversation going nowhere and didn't last much beyond that. There were no suggestions of further contact and Melissa was too embarrassed to either encourage or expect it. She watched the machines lift off and disappear into the late afternoon, leaving behind the swirling dust eddies reflecting her own emotions. Beyond giving Eddie a piece of her mind, there wasn't anything else she could have said. A pity. It spoiled what was otherwise a good day's work.

❧

"Fa-a-ark! That didn't turn out as I expected." Mark secured the aircraft and followed Chris into the office attached to the hangar. "I think I need a beer. What about you?"

"I'm not in the mood, mate," Chris replied. "It's been a long day. I'll take a rain check."

"What a piker," Mark jibed. "You can stay for one, surely?"

Chris sighed. One wouldn't hurt. What had hurt was the incident earlier that day. "Okay, but I'm not settling in for the night."

Mark fetched two cans from the office fridge and passed one to Chris before tugging the ring-pull on his, releasing a fine misted spray. "You don't seem your usual cheery self," he remarked. "You didn't let that fuckwit get to you, did you?"

"Of course not."

"What then?"

"It's just… I dunno really. I was pissed off, but it's not just that." He pulled the ring tab on his can and took a swig. The two men sauntered to a pair of battered armchairs near the front window that were positioned with a view of the runway. "It got me thinking, that's all. I enjoy my job and the opportunities I've had in Alice have been fuckin' unbelievable."

"No arguments from me."

"I just don't want to be forever in a situation where some half-wit from the city thinks it's okay to spit in my face; metaphorically speaking."

"Speak whichever way you want. The guy's lucky we didn't drop him at the back of beyond and let him walk.'

"I was tempted," Chris admitted, "but I didn't want to make things bad for Melissa."

"Don't you think she can look after herself?"

"Probably, but she hired us to do a job and I wasn't about to run out on her."

"True." Mark squinted against the late afternoon light streaming in the window. "Fairly quiet, wasn't she. I had no idea she did that sort of work."

"I think there's a lot about Melissa that none of us have known."

Mark looked at him quizzically, but Chris didn't respond. He didn't want to talk about Melissa. He didn't particularly want to talk *to* her either.

"If you're ready for a change mate, there's one option I've been thinking about." Mark spoke tentatively, as though unsure of Chris' reaction.

"You've been thinking. This could be dangerous. Don't leave me in suspense."

"Working for Centralian Aviation Services has been good, but between the two of us we've established a wide network of contacts. Why don't we buy ourselves a couple of choppers and branch out on our own? Our own business—you and me."

"Just buy a couple of choppers! How much money have you got in your back pocket?"

Mark shrugged. "Not much, but we can borrow. I'd tap my old man on the shoulder for starters, and if we front up to the bank with a list of forward bookings, they'd look kindly on us." He made it sound so simple. "We could do it, Chris. Whaddyer reckon?"

Chris glanced out of the window. A Qantas passenger aircraft was coming in and touched down smoothly with a small puff of smoke as the tyres connected with the runway. He never tired of watching those guys.

He tried to marshal his thoughts. He and Mark worked well together, and between them, they could swing a few contracts their way. *This is a huge commitment on so many levels. I need to think about this.*

"A change has been on my mind for a few months now, but this wasn't one of the options I considered. I need to think about it. I mean, there are the ethics as well. We'd be taking business away from CAS." He looked over at Mark. "Where do you see yourself in two, five, ten years' time? Have you thought about that?"

"Yeah, I have and it's building my own business. That's what it's all about. There's no rush. I didn't expect an answer today. Think it over and let me know what you decide.

~

The client was impressed with the results of the shoot: the way the clothes were presented, the setting, the lighting and in fact the whole package. The models were the faces of the collection, but credit belonged to the crew. On the back of that, more contracts were lined up in Sydney. Melissa took the call from Eddie while breakfasting in the morning room.

"We've had a fantastic response, Mellie. The client loved it. I loved it. That was a brilliant suggestion of yours, even though it was in the back of nowhere and plagued with heat and flies and all manner of ferocious marsupials."

'I like the way you tell it, Eddie." she said dryly. "Straight to the point; no bullshit or drama.'

He just laughed. "The point is, we're getting a few bookings off the back of this job. What are you doing sitting up there? You need to get your arse back to Sydney. This where the work is."

Her mind went into overdrive. He was right. She needed to base herself in Sydney if she was going to develop her career and reputation, and from what Eddie was saying, probably sooner rather than later. There was nothing to keep her in Plenty River. The ice hadn't thawed between her and Chris and there was no point in hanging around.

"Mellie? Are you still there?"

"Yes… yes, I'm here. I was turning over what you said. You're right of course. I do need to be in Sydney. Splitting myself between there and here isn't going to work if what you

77

say is true. Leave it with me. I need to make some arrangements."

She disconnected the call and sat for a while. She would miss Jenny, but her father would hardly notice she was gone. As for Chris, she'd made one attempt to contact him since the photo shoot, but he'd been out of range on a job. She didn't bother again, and he hadn't contacted her either. There was nothing to stop her going. She went to find Jenny.

The harbour was beautiful. Sydney could be grimy in places, appearing dishevelled and slovenly—like a blowsy woman who has had too much of the good life and not enough sleep. The harbour made up for it. The city had a dependent relationship on the water and its surrounds and for that gift, in the eyes of the beholder all was forgiven.

Eduardo even secured her a gig at an A-lister birthday bash, mingling with the guests and taking photos of women who were wearing some of the outfits either purchased or on loan from the fashion house client. It was still all about the clothes but was easier than remote location work. Angela came along as her assistant, which made some of the logistics easier, and the two women enjoyed the schmoozing and celebrity spotting.

"Melissa Gilbert—what are you doing here? I haven't seen you in ages."

She couldn't immediately place the voice. Turning back to a woman she had just passed, Melissa recognised her as a girl she had known from boarding school in Sydney.

"Joanna! I'm here on a work gig, but you obviously move in salubrious circles. Stand there while I take your photo. Angela will take down your details."

They exchanged news and history updates. Joanna pointed out other people she might know at the function, and Melissa explained the direction her work had taken, and her decision to relocate to Sydney.

"That's a fantastic career move. We'll have to catch up outside of work. Tell you what— the family are sailing on the harbor tomorrow. Why don't you join us?"

An invitation! And on the Harbour. Living in Sydney was about to get a whole lot better.

"If you don't think I'll be intruding on a family event, I'd love to."

She hadn't been close to Joanna at school but was pleased to renew the connection. They exchanged phone numbers and confirmed details about where to meet and what the day entailed. A hat, sunscreen, comfortable clothes and appropriate footwear were all she needed.

She arrived at the Balmain wharf earlier than the agreed time. She couldn't risk being late. The boat was moored on the North Shore, but Joanna insisted it was no problem for her father to pick Melissa up on the way past, so she didn't have far to travel. Balmain was only a few kilometres away from Annandale, and she managed to find an all-day park not too far from the water.

She leaned against a bollard, inhaling the smell of the sea. Balmain was well inside the harbour heads, but seagulls circled overhead and the breeze carried a salty tang. It brought with it the promise of a fabulous day. What struck her most was the change in colour scheme. Not the vibrancy she was used to but more subtle hues of grey, blue and green, with dancing black shadows between the waves.

Squinting against the sun, she watched the boat approach with Joanna waving from where she balanced at the bow. Joanna reached out to take her hand and Melissa leapt onto the deck while the craft was held steady. When he was sure she was safely aboard, Joanna's father increased the throttle and swung the boat around towards the open water, navigating around the various pleasure craft also on the harbour.

Other family members acted as crew, which gave the two women time to reminisce and fill in the intervening years since school. It was a glorious day, with the harbour at its best. Melissa stretched out on the bench in the cockpit, a breeze on her face and a light misting of spray coating her as they slid through the water. The slap of the waves against the sides and the gentle rocking was mesmeric. *This is the life. What kept me away so long?* The champagne and refreshments were the icing on the cake. She willingly agreed to catch up with Joanna again when she was returned to the wharf, late afternoon.

Her new life was a world away from Alice Springs. She enjoyed the contrast—the weather, the food, the social life, the cultural opportunities, and of course the regular work which came her way. Being consistently in the city paid off in establishing and building on her reputation and she appreciated the boost to her professional recognition. She still missed the open spaces of Plenty River, and rang Jenny at regular intervals, providing an update of latest news and events.

"But when are you coming home again?" Jenny was trying not to put a dampener on the news of a prolonged stay when Melissa rang her after the sailing trip.

"It's not forever Jenny—I have to make the most of the opportunities when they turn up. Anyway, you can always visit me here."

"Well, there's always that I suppose. I'll let your father know your news.'

"I'm sure he's hanging out for an update. Has he even noticed I haven't been around for a few weeks?"

"Missy, don't be like that. You know he does. He cares about you very much. He's especially proud of all you've achieved."

"Really? He has a strange way of showing it. He pays more attention to Caesar than he does to me. If I took some photos of that horse, he might give greater credibility to my work.

Jenny sighed but didn't make further comment on the father-daughter relationship. Instead, she changed the topic.

"I saw Chris Harris on my last trip to town. He's doing some work for a mining company that's working out west. He said it was a welcome change."

"To what? The fickle fashion industry?"

"I don't think that was what he meant. I'm sure he was talking about cattle."

"It's probably all one and the same to him."

"You're in a sweet mood today, aren't you? Is that what the big city does?"

"Just telling it like it is, Jenny. If anything, he probably prefers cattle."

81

The rest of the conversation passed in generalities and local news. It was Chris though who occupied her thoughts when the phone call ended.

The work in Sydney arose quickly after her last conversation with him, and it was only a short time later her bags were packed and she was back at the terrace house in Annandale. There hadn't been a chance to say goodbye and she wasn't sure if there was any point. If he'd spoken to Jenny, he would know where she was and what she was doing. Perhaps she could ring him anyway. It wasn't as if she owed him anything, but she was uncomfortable thinking of how that discussion ended.

She took a deep breath and dialled the number. There was a brief silence before the ring tone sounded and kept on ringing. With a stab of disappointment, she decided he must be away on a job. She might as well hang up. Then he picked up at the last moment.

"Melissa! I wasn't expecting to hear from you. The grapevine tells me you've gone back to Sydney."

"A grapevine called Jenny, you mean. I didn't get to speak to you before I left and I just thought that I… well, what I mean is…" She broke off just not quite sure what it was that she was trying to say. "Look I'm sorry how things panned out the day of the shoot. I should have managed the situation better than I did."

"Melissa, forget it. I already have. Life's too short to get hung up on people like your mate Eddie."

There was a moment of strained silence. What on earth had possessed her to make this call? She shifted the phone to the other ear and glanced out the window of her room. There was a small café across the road and groups of people were seated at the outdoor tables with their morning coffees. A couple of dogs lounged at their feet and a baby snoozed in a stroller parked by one of the tables. It was a cosmopolitan tableau a world away from the dust, flies and heat of Central Australia. It was a very ordinary scene in an urban context, and one in which Melissa was happy to immerse herself.

"You're right, I know. It's just been playing on my mind. The same grapevine tells me you're doing some work for a mining company. That makes a change."

"It does, and a change is very much on my mind. I know it sounds clichéd but after that bout of Q Fever last year, I got to thinking. It's not that I'm tired of what I've been doing but being in hospital for a while gave me some head space. I've settled into a comfortable rut and if I don't do something about it, that's where I'll stay."

"But Chris, you've always seemed so upbeat and in control of your life. That's one of the things I like about you."

"Well, that's nice to know—about liking me I mean." The familiar humour was back in his voice and in her mind, she pictured the lop-sided smile that must surely accompany it.

"Don't fish. That's all you're getting."

"I'll take what I can—for now." He paused briefly. "I'm not bored but I'm ready for new directions. I'm just not sure what they are, though I do have some options to consider."

She looked out the window again. The street outside was bathed in dappled afternoon sunshine. She was looking through a framed entrance to another world. "Why don't you come to Sydney?"

Emily Hussey

The words were out of her mouth before she'd known what she was about to say. They prompted a small knot in her stomach. This wasn't like her at all.

"Sydney?"

"You said you wanted a change. Why don't you make it happen? There must be work available here. Put the word out in your networks. Come for a visit and check it out."

There was a silence—a loud silence during which she threw herself into a panic. What if he said yes? What if he didn't?

"Just check out the opportunities for work? It's a long time since I've been to Sydney." A persuasive note crept into his voice. "Perhaps you can show me around? You know; the sights and highlights of the big smoke."

"You're expecting a personalised tour guide now?" Her voice softened. "No promises about the experience but I do have some local knowledge. I can even pick you up at the airport if you send me the arrival details."

"You're a convincing woman. Seize the day and all that. Sydney's as good as anywhere, but I really look forward to catching up with you. Stand by for an update; I've got some packing to do."

Moving to the window at the close of the conversation, Melissa observed the tableau outside. She fiddled with her neck chain as she watched. Some of the patrons had moved on but others had taken their place. The scenario looked similar but wasn't the same. Chris wasn't the only one living through a process of change.

Well, that was a surprising call. I didn't expect to hear from Melissa again. Chris stripped off and stepped under the shower. He let the water course over his head, flushing the dust with it. The pummelling on his shoulders felt good. He turned up the heat. Bliss. His thoughts turned back to the phone call. Sydney had not been one of his options. He wouldn't have considered it before because Melissa was there. The phone call changed that.

Towelling himself dry, he pulled on a clean pair of jeans and a t-shirt. He was joining Mark and a few others for a barbecue at the accommodation block used by the StationAir staff. The sizzling smell of sausages met him when he pulled up. Mark was already there in front of the grill and waving the tongs around in masterful fashion.

"Ma-a-te—'bout time you got here. I was thinking I'd have to eat it all myself. Grab yourself a beer."

Chris sauntered to the fridge that lived on the veranda and extracted a stubbie, checking first that nobody else wanted a refill. Brian was there, chief pilot with StationAir and so was Sarah. They both lived in the apartments. Joel Pemberton was a recent addition, having moved to Alice and shortly after making a move on Sarah. Chris had never taken to Joel, but if he made Sarah happy, that was okay.

"So," Brian said, "how're you feeling these days, Chris?"

"Never better. Fully recovered. I'm thinking of taking a few days off though."

"Don't do anything too rash. Heading back home to see the family?"

"No, I'm thinking of going to Sydney. It's a while since I've been there. A mate from training days lives there, so I can catch up with him."

"You won't last long," Mark said. "It will be so overwhelming you'll be tripping over yourself to get back here again."

"You're probably right," Chris said. He didn't tell them about Melissa's role in his visit or the directions their conversation had taken. For starters, he wasn't ready to talk about Melissa, and he still needed to make up his mind about Mark's business proposition. He shoved all those thoughts aside and joined in with the gossip and chat.

∂

"I thought there was something you hadn't told me," Angela accused. "No way were you going to sit on that station at the back of Bourke and not pay attention to the men who appeared out of nowhere."

Yeah, he did that all right, thought Melissa but she didn't share the story. She wasn't ready to talk about Chris and, as she kept reminding herself, there was nothing to tell.

"Don't let your imagination run riot. There aren't many men suddenly appearing, as you put it. My father's only been using choppers in recent times. Before that the mustering was done on horseback or with motorbikes and still is to some extent. Anyway, my father didn't like me mixing with the staff."

"Staff? Is that how they were regarded? I would have thought attitudes were more relaxed so far from civilisation."

"You don't know my father. He has rigid boundaries, and everyone knows and understands that. None of the men would have dared approach me. The only person who never paid much attention to my father's attitude is Jenny. She does and says what she wants, and he accepts it from her. If she ever left Plenty River, she would be difficult to replace, and he must know that."

"Were things different when your mother was alive?"

"I don't really remember. I was a child when she died. My memories aren't reliable any more, but I think if it weren't for the accident, there would have been a different atmosphere at home."

"Oh, that's so sad. You must miss her."

"I suppose so." Her tone indicated a no-go topic. "I prefer not to talk about it if you don't mind."

"Sorry, I didn't mean to upset you."

"You haven't. It isn't something I'm comfortable discussing." She stood up. "Coffee? I was about to make some."

"Sounds good. Before I forget—that A-lister booking you have for this week. I've checked my diary and I can't do it with you. I might be able to find someone for you if it's going to be a problem."

"No, that's OK. I'll manage. It's easier with the two of us but I'll cope on my own. To be honest it was good not to have to walk in by myself for that first job, but I'll be more confident now, especially as I might know some of the guests. It won't be as terrifying."

"You? Terrified? One would never know it. You are the most self-contained and in-control person I know. Speaking of which—I know you've got first dibs on Chris, but let me know if that friend of his is going to visit with him, okay?"

There was no way Angela would be convinced there wasn't a relationship happening between her and Chris, so Melissa didn't even try. Just friends a long way from home. That was what they were.

This time she was the one who knew where to go for coffee. With an assurance that inferred a greater familiarity with the city than she really had, Melissa met Chris at the airport and took him to a coffee shop in Balmain. It had glimpses of the harbour— promises of views really. Chris took in the scene with obvious satisfaction.

"So, here I am. I can smell that distinctive Sydney aroma. It's unique. I can't believe I've done this. I owe you one."

An almost childish surge of delight swept all the way to her toes. All was obviously forgiven.

"I'm glad of it though," he continued. "It'll be good to have this break."

Chris had the healthy glow of someone who spent a lot of time outdoors and Melissa felt a momentary pang of homesickness. She soon got over that as she basked in the warmth of his smile, as natural and embracing as he was himself. She'd had delicious churnings of anticipation as she waited for his plane to arrive. All the time wondering if she'd done a stupid thing in suggesting he visit. It was too late now for those thoughts.

"If you're looking for new opportunities, this is a good place to start."

"You're right. I did some research before I left Alice but it's not the same as being here and able to speak to people in person. I'll contact the Helicopter Industry Association. They might know of any opportunities coming up." He reached across the table and took her hand. "Enough talk about work. It's good to see you again. You're looking great. City life must agree with you."

He gave her a frankly appraising look. Melissa found that disconcerting. His skin was warm, but the touch was unexpected. Her initial response was to pull hers away, but then she relaxed and left it there. Most people knew enough to keep their distance, but Chris ignored that reserve. With his easy smile and his way of looking directly at her, he leaped over some of her self-imposed barriers.

There was one axiomatic truth that governed Melissa's life. Don't allow yourself to get too close to other people. When you really need them, they won't be there. Better to not develop a connection in the first place.

She withdrew her hand. "It has its moments. Have you finished your coffee? I'll drop you off at your accommodation and you can unpack and get settled. It's not far from here."

Chris was staying with a mate who'd trained for his licence at the same flying school. The two men had kept up an irregular communication, depending on where they were at any given time. Currently Oliver was based in Marrickville, close to Sydney Airport. Melissa delivered Chris to the front of the cottage.

"Coming inside?" he asked. "You can meet Ollie."

"I'm sure he doesn't need a strange woman intruding on his domain, and the two of you probably have some catching up to do. I'll leave you to it." *I don't want to get dragged into making polite small talk with someone I don't know.*

Chris shrugged but didn't push it. "I doubt he would ever think you strange. Up to you though."

He unloaded his suitcase from the back of the car, and Melissa joined him on the footpath. Now he was in Sydney, her feeling of self-preservation suddenly snapped into gear. She didn't need to be drawn too deeply into Chris's life.

He set the suitcase up on its wheels and turned to face her. "Thanks for picking me up. I appreciate it."

Grasping her shoulders, he dropped a light kiss on her cheek. "I'll call you, okay?"

She nodded with more enthusiasm than she felt. "Sure. Enjoy your catch-up with Ollie."

He waved her off as she pulled out from the kerb. She gave a toot of farewell and headed for the sanctuary of Annandale. Suggesting he come to Sydney was one thing. Getting too involved was another entirely. She couldn't even answer for herself why she had proposed the idea in the first place. Sometimes life was complicated. Silly, when she genuinely liked the man.

If Chris was surprised she disappeared so soon, he didn't show it when he called late the following day. "Feel like catching up for a meal? There are lots of interesting Asian eateries around Marrickville—very different to what we have in Alice. I can even come and pick you up. I've hired a car for the week so I can get around easily."

"Why does that not surprise me? Is it a Roller?"

"Not even a Merc. It's a tiny jelly bean of a car. I don't need anything too big in Sydney traffic. Shall I pick you up at seven?"

She shifted the phone to her other ear, a small frown creasing her brow. Relax, she told herself. It's just an invitation to dinner. "Yes, that would be lovely. I'll look forward to it."

Melissa was waiting on the footpath when Chris arrived. Twenty-four hours could make a surprising difference. Today she was more relaxed about the connection, or friendship, or whatever it was.

"Hi." Climbing in the passenger seat, she leant across and greeted him with a kiss.

"You're looking good today, sweetheart," he said, eyes fixed on the rear vision mirror as he pulled back onto the road. "I think I know the way, but you may need to help with directions in case I become a little unsure of the route. Ollie gave me some suggestions for where we might like to go."

"Useful friend, this Ollie."

"He is. I've told him all about you, of course. You'll have to meet him before I go back to Alice."

She just smiled. One step at a time.

91

CHAPTER 7

THEY NEGOTIATED THROUGH the suburbs and located one of the restaurants on the recommended list. The noodle soups were a delicious change to cuisine in Alice Springs. Over the meal, Chris filled her in on his day. He'd followed up a few work-related leads. There were some positive responses; nothing definite. As he said, there was still the rest of the week. It could take a while to make the right connections. In the meantime, it was all good networking and hopefully when a vacancy came up, he'd be in the front line for consideration.

"I like the way you're always so positive," Melissa remarked. "Whereas I'd be thinking no definite offers of employment were an indication I was doomed for failure, you see it as a positive opportunity for the future."

"Sure, but I wouldn't say you're ever doomed to failure. You have a certain dedication to your craft—obsession even—and others seem to hold your work in high esteem. You're receiving ongoing work offers, aren't you?"

"Yes, but..."

"No buts about it. You're talented and in my highly sought-after opinion, you'll go far."

Her lips twitched. "Highly sought-after? And just who is it who seeks your views on important matters such as the merits of my professional career?"

"Well, Jenny for starters. I'm sure there are others. There will be anyway, once they know how valuable my opinions are."

"I have the highest respect for Jenny, but I know she'd admire my work with a Baby Brownie. In this instance that doesn't count. I await the evidence of these 'others' with interest."

"Ah Melissa—you need more faith in yourself. I'm sure you're destined for great things."

She could feel herself relaxing. It was a refreshing contrast to some people in the fashion industry, who thrived on a complex mixture of insecurity and ego. Like Eduardo for instance.

She knew better than to bring up his name. Somehow, she didn't think that Chris would welcome it.

"Melissa?"

She looked up to see an amused smile.

"You've got a dribble of soup on your chin."

Grabbing the paper serviette, she swiped at the offending streak before it could drip onto her top.

"Now that's put a dent in my sophisticated image. Last time I eat here," she joked.

"I was tempted to wipe it off for you." This was said with a tone that indicated he knew Melissa would have absolutely hated him to have done that.

She gave him a look which said it all. It was at that point she had an interesting idea. "Talking of sophisticated images, did you bring any clothing other than flying and casual gear?"

"Why?"

"I have a job tomorrow night and you might like to come along as my roadie. This is different to my usual fashion shoot. It's an A-lister cocktail party and I have to dress to blend with the crowd. That means black tie for men. I'm taking photos of the outfits. It's probably not what you had in mind in coming to Sydney, but it might be interesting all the same; a chance to see how the other half lives."

Chris carefully placed his chopsticks across his bowl and with his elbows on the table, rested his chin on his interlaced fingers as he regarded her. "Did you honestly think I would've packed a penguin suit for this trip? I'll have a chat to Ollie and let you know. He is about the same size as me so perhaps he'll have one I can borrow."

"That's sorted then."

"Not so fast. *Assuming* Ollie has a suit, and *assuming* I'm able to borrow it, and *assuming* it's clean and presentable, just what exactly am I supposed to do at this event where I'll stick out like a sore thumb?"

"From what I've seen of you in previous company, you'll blend in very well, so don't give me that excuse. As for what you can do, you can carry my gear, help me set up the photographic station for the posed rather than candid shots and you can help me to sweet talk and charm the guests. You won't find it difficult."

Her eyes met his and this time it was Melissa who gave the half smile.

"Sounds like you have it all planned," he said. "I'm not sure this is my thing but hey, I'll give anything a try—at least once anyway. Chalk it up to my new Melissa-influenced experiences."

And you're not the only one who's branching out. Inviting Chris along was straying far from her usual behaviour. Aside from Angela, she tended to operate alone. It had always been that way, no matter what she was doing. If you didn't rely on anyone else, you were never going to be disappointed when they didn't meet their obligations or keep their promises.

When Chris dropped Melissa back at the Annandale terrace, he jumped out and joined her on the footpath.

"Thanks for joining me this evening. I'll check with Ollie and let you know about the suit and tomorrow. Even if he hasn't got one, I am sure I could hire an outfit."

"I'm not expecting you to go to any expense. It was just a suggestion. I thought it might be an interesting experience."

"And it's with that thought in mind I don't mind hiring if that's what it takes. I've always wanted to be a snapper's assistant."

With eyes that didn't leave hers, he leant forward and drew her to him. It was the sweetest of kisses, lingering, tantalising, and promising more.

"Did you know you're just the right height?" he whispered into her hair.

It was such a ridiculous statement that she threw back her head and laughed, a full belly chuckle that was most un-Melissa like. It had the desired effect. This time she relaxed into him and the kiss was deep and passionate.

~

He cut an impressive figure. Melissa didn't know where Chris had acquired the suit, but it could have been tailor made.

"Madam," he said, extending his arm. "May I escort you to the car?"

"With you looking like that,' she replied, "we should be going in a Roller. Sadly, we'll have to put up with Angela's Mazda, which she has kindly lent me for the evening. At least it's clean. They may have valet parking at this event. It's so embarrassing to hand over the keys to a grotty car."

"I wouldn't know," Chris replied. "The parties I've typically attended, it's been a case of parking the ute in the adjacent paddock. This is a whole new experience."

"You don't look as though you're heading for a bush bash now. You scrub up very nicely."

Privately, she was relieved. Her professional reputation was also at stake. Presentation and style counted for such a lot in this work.

It was a mild night, and they caught glimpses of lights on the harbour as the road wound around towards Vaucluse. The butterflies increased the closer they got. This always happened before a big job—she was anxious to get everything right and checked and rechecked her equipment several times before leaving home. Once she was on site and organised, the feelings subsided. She knew this and accepted the preliminary jitters as a normal part of professional nerves. It meant she was never slipshod in her preparations.

As Melissa surmised, parking was at a premium. The streets surrounding the address were already taken up with luxury vehicles, even though they had arrived early.

"Where am I going to park? The caterers are taking up the driveway."

"Just pull up behind them and I'll help you unload and carry your gear inside. Then I'll park the car up the street while you get yourself organised. I won't be long."

"I knew it was a good idea to bring you with me."

"We aim to please." That crooked smile was flashed briefly before he seized her bags and bowled up towards the security guard who was already stationed at the doorway.

"Evening, sir. May I see your invitation?" the guard asked.

"It's all right," Melissa called from the rear of the car where she was still gathering a couple of items. "He's with me."

"May I see *your* invitation then?"

"I don't have anything official, but I'm the photographer for Elite Fashions, and this is my able assistant. Don't worry. We'll move the car shortly. I just need to unload first."

Once their credentials had been verified, the security guard directed them to move the car to the underground car park.

"It's not available to everyone, you understand, but I can provide parking to those people who need to have easy access. There's an elevator from there to the house above so when you're ready to pack up again, it will be less hassle."

While Chris sorted out the car, Melissa erected her pull-up background screen featuring the Elite logo, the lighting and the silver reflective umbrella. This was where she would do the posed shots. When Chris joined Melissa upstairs again, he was visibly impressed.

"You should've seen what was parked downstairs. I'd happily just be the car-washer here. I wonder if they have a helipad as well?"

"I doubt it. It would have to be on a floating pontoon if there was. The house fronts onto the water."

"Hmm—I like their style. Speaking of which, I like your style. You are looking stunning tonight. You'll put the guests to shame."

"That's not the intention. The aim is to fit in, not to outshine." Still, the compliment was welcome. It boosted her confidence. She tried not to subscribe to imposter syndrome, but there was always that inner person who said *Who do you think you are, trying to do a job like this?* Seizing a glass of sparkling mineral water from a passing waiter, she drew herself up. *Stand tall*, she told herself. *Let the party begin.*

Guests were arriving, and Melissa asked Chris to direct them towards her set-up. She wanted to get photos while everyone was at their freshest and before champagne-induced red eyes peered from the frame.

"People can get untidy as the evening progresses. We'll hijack them as they walk in the door and after we're reasonably sure most have arrived, we'll circulate for the more candid photos."

"And what would you like me to do? Anything that will stop me looking like a wide-eyed interloper?"

"Just be your charming self. Greet the guests after they have deposited their jackets or wraps and usher them in this direction. We need to get the information on this form—name, contact details, which label they are wearing and get them to sign a release so that we are authorised to publish their photo.

Give them a card and they can contact me later if they wish to order prints. Other than that, smile, tell them they look wonderful and usher them on their way before the next guests step up."

"Perhaps my mustering skills can come into use after all."

"Just don't start snapping at their heels like the dogs. We'll be out of here before we know what's hit us."

He laughed, but schmoozed like a pro. He complemented the women and gave the men a manly handshake, directing them towards Melissa without seeming overly pushy. Not everyone wanted their photos taken, and that was fine. The brief from the client was to capture the glitterati wearing their specific label. The resultant photos would be placed in print where they would be noticed. There was always the chance she could sell some of the photos of people wearing other labels.

There were a couple of people Melissa knew, including Joanna and her latest beau. They exchanged words briefly, with the promise to catch up later in the evening. She made sure the photo of Joanna showed her outfit to the best advantage.

By the time Chris and Melissa left the photo set-up and started mingling, the evening had a more relaxed vibe. There had been plenty of expensive champagne, and waiters moved through the crowd with trays of gourmet offerings. Most people seemed to know each other, and so clusters formed, conversed for a while and then broke up and reformed elsewhere. Melissa focussed on the candid shots, while Chris dutifully filled in the paperwork, detailing the names of the people in the group and any other pertinent information, which either Melissa whispered to him or the guests volunteered.

"Are you from the media?" one of the guests enquired. "I thought someone was going to be here from a television station."

"Sorry, no—we're not allied with a specific media company," Melissa replied. "I'm sure there are people from one or two stations here, but as guests. That's a wonderful gown you're wearing. Is that a Collette Dinnigan? The colour really suits you."

"You're not bad at the smooth talk yourself," Chris muttered in her ear after they'd moved on. "No wonder that dingo stood still for you. I can just hear it now. *What a wonderful coat you have on, Mrs Dingo. It's a beautiful shade of desert sand. May I take your photo for the latest issue of Wildlife Australia?*"

"Behave," she hissed, while smiling at the woman and her partner, but anyone looking closely would have seen a barely suppressed smirk."

Looking around, she saw she'd captured most of the people in their vicinity. "Perhaps we can take a break for a while. We don't have to stay for the entire evening. Once we've covered everyone here who's willing, we're free to go. I'd like to catch up with a couple of people though."

"Okay," Chris replied uncertainly. "I can hang out at the bottom of the garden while you circulate. I don't want to cramp your style."

"Don't be silly." She snatched another passing mineral water. "You won't cramp my style. These are just old friends from school."

She pushed her way through the crowd as Chris followed hesitantly. He was on unfamiliar territory here. When Melissa reached Joanna, the two women embraced.

"Are you enjoying yourself?" Melissa asked. "It's nice now to have time to chat properly."

Her friend laughed. "Running into you is getting to be a habit. Are you covering all the social events now?"

"Only the best ones, Joanna. That's why I keep running into you. It's been a fabulous party. Fabulous frocks as well. My client should be very satisfied with the photos, and so should the guests. All in all, a successful night."

"I see you have a new assistant." The look Joanna gave Chris was frankly appraising and Melissa instinctively moved closer to his side.

"Joanna, this my friend Chris Harris. He's down from Alice for a week while he checks out work prospects in the big smoke.

"Really? What sort of work are you looking for? Are you a photographer as well?

He laughed politely. "Not at all. A photographer's assistant at best. I'll leave the snapping to Melissa." With a flicked smile, he raised his glass in token toast to Melissa before continuing. "I'm a helicopter pilot so I'm looking for work possibly in search and rescue or perhaps with the police or some other government agency. I'm researching the options and that's easier to do in person than from a distance."

"Well good luck with that. I don't have any contacts in the aviation industry so can't help you there." She reached out to grasp the arm of her companion, drawing him closer. "Melissa, I know you saw him through the camera lens, but I didn't actually introduce you. This is my partner, Bruce. He wasn't able to come the day we went sailing."

The two couples exchanged civilities. As the two women chatted, the men gravitated to each other. Bruce was interested to hear of the sort of work that Chris normally did, and Chris obliged with an overview of a typical day.

"That's how I met Melissa," he explained. "In the last couple of years, I've filled a few mustering contracts on Plenty River, her father's property. It's about three hours' drive out of Alice, but we run into each other in town on occasions or at one of the social events in the region."

"I don't think you'll find any work like that in the city."

"It's time for a change. Don't get me wrong, I've enjoyed it but I'm ready for new challenges. Enough about me. What line of work are you in Bruce?"

"I'm in the media. I'm an account director with Channel Nine."

Melissa looked around on overhearing this. So there was someone from television at the party, just not the sort of person the other guest had hoped for.

"Sounds important," Chris said. "What exactly does an account director do?"

"Business development, managing relationships, that sort of thing."

"Sounds fascinating." His tone indicated polite confusion.

"Sure, it's not as clear cut as flying, but it pays and that's the main thing. Well, not only that; I enjoy the challenges of my job."

"That's all right then."

Chris beamed and the two men touched their glasses in the beginnings of a mutual admiration society.

Melissa noticed this with amusement. They'd sniffed around each other like a pair of cattle dogs before deciding that each passed the okay test and settled down to the important topics like the successes of their sporting teams. Life could be so simple for men.

It reminded her she still had a job to finish. "Chris? I should just do the rounds once more and see if there are any more photographic opportunities. After that, I think we're done."

They made their farewells to Joanna and Bruce with promises to 'catch up soon' and completed another circuit of the party. Their last move was to capture a series of photos of the hosts in several different locations in their house and well-manicured garden, before calling it a night and packing up the gear. It had been a good evening, but Melissa was feeling the emotional exhaustion that always hit at the end of a job. It reminded her of how much stress was involved in the build-up to each event. Hopefully it didn't show.

"I enjoyed that," remarked Chris on the winding journey back towards the city. "It was so far removed my reality."

The city lights were intermittently visible on the horizon, signalling the presence of night life and excitement like a multi-coloured beacon. He reviewed the night's experiences. It had been an eye-opener. Who knew people lived like that?

Emily Hussey

Not this hick from the bush. He would file the story away for the next barbecue back in Alice.

"Not sure how I'd go doing it all the time," he continued, "but it's interesting exploring other people's jobs. The location was a bonus. Now you're off-duty, why don't we stop off somewhere for a night cap? Somewhere where the doorman says, "Step this way Sir, Madam" when he sees an incredibly well-dressed couple heading his way."

"I think I could be persuaded. If we head into Darling Harbour, we'll be able to get a car park and find somewhere that meets your obviously high standards. Only one drink for me though given that I'm driving."

"We'll make it a good one then," Chris said. "Something with a touch of class."

When they were seated in the cocktail bar of the Novotel Sydney, the lights on the harbour delivered a magical perspective. The chairs were angled so that they had a clear view of the water. Their drinks were colourful and probably potent. It was a fitting way to wind up their evening. If he made the move to Sydney, this could happen quite often.

"I think we're a good team, don't you?" he queried. "We haven't had a single disagreement all night."

Melissa nearly choked on her drink. "Don't tell me you expected a squabble?"

"Of course not. I was just remarking that we worked well together."

Melissa regarded him over the rim of her glass. "Are you looking for an ongoing role as photographer's assistant? I have to warn you the pay's lousy and opportunities only arise occasionally."

"That wasn't what I had in mind."

He contemplated the woman opposite. She was not a woman who gave much away. He had no idea what she thought of him, but there was something intriguing about Melissa Gilbert. He might be punching above his weight, but what did he have to lose?

The intensity of his look sent a quiver down her spine and Melissa turned her eyes to the water again in an attempt at self-preservation. Her breath caught when he reached over and took her hand. "I've no idea what the future holds. So far, I haven't turned up anything definite in relation to work but this visit has made up my mind. I want to make some changes. When I return to Alice, I'm handing in my notice. I'm going to move to Sydney and continue my search for work. I'd like to see more of you when that happens." He lifted his eyes to hers. "How would you feel about that?"

She watched the boats that were gliding past on the water. On board, she could see groups of people, socialising, chatting, relating to each other. Some of them were clearly in relationships. Was this what she wanted? Could she rely on Chris? Would he stand by her? She wasn't sure what he was proposing.

She turned to look at him, willing herself not to show the panic she was felt. "I've been more relaxed with you than most other people. Not sure why but you're right; we do get on well together. For now, I'd like to take things slowly. No promises."

105

"Slowly is fine. We've all the time in the world." He paused. "Did I tell you I heard from Mark today?"

She welcomed the change in topic. Taking a slow, deep breath, she knew Chris had done that deliberately. It took the pressure out of the situation, even though his words were never far from her mind. Through the rest of their conversation, they hovered at the edge of her consciousness, threatening to detail her thoughts.

The drive to Ollie's cottage was largely conducted in silence. Post-event tiredness had set in, and there was a lot occupying her thoughts. As he kissed her good night before getting out of the car, he whispered gently, "I won't rush you, Melissa Gilbert. I'm going to savour every moment."

The heat in the pit of her belly threatened to explode. The anticipation was delicious. She wasn't totally convinced this man was for real, but the prospect of finding out was one that teased. She found herself tantalised by the possibility.

Chris was due to return to Alice in another three days. It was difficult spending that time together, as Melissa had a job up the coast at Gosford and he was door-knocking throughout the aviation industry. It gave him time alone to sort out his thoughts. Now he was removed from Alice, he could put Mark's offer into some perspective. It was a good offer, a great offer even but the timing was wrong. Right now, it was not for him.

The more he thought about it, the more he was inclined to move on. Not just out of his old job, but out of Alice. If he stayed any longer, he would stagnate, both in his life and in his career.

He would be sad to leave on many levels. He knew Mark always had his back and perhaps if he and Sarah… *Don't go there. She's happy and if anyone deserves a second chance, it's her.*

Time to call Mark. He picked up the phone. He didn't waste time on small talk. "It's a great idea, Mark. I've thought long and hard about this one."

"I can hear a *but* coming. Out with it."

That was the best way. No pussy footing. "Like I said last time we spoke, I need a change. That time in hospital made me confront my own mortality. I think it came a bit close for a while. I always thought a crash would be the greatest danger I faced. I never believed a weird form of cow flu would carry me off."

"You gave us all a fright. I thought I would have to dust off my suit."

"I'm touched to hear it," Chris said. "The thing is, I've been sliding into a rut."

He didn't want to mention his failed approach to Sarah. Mark probably knew anyway. Hell, they'd both been sweet on her… "It got me thinking. There's a whole world out here and I haven't seen enough of it. This trip to Sydney has reinforced that fact. I could go back to Alice one day, but I don't want to load myself with debt and anchor myself to the one place this early in life.

"It's okay, mate. You don't have to explain. I sort of expected this anyway. Does Melissa Gilbert have anything to do with this decision?"

107

"Melissa? Why would you think that?"

"I dunno. I'm just a country boy, but even I've got eyes—and ears. It sounds crazy to me, but make the most of it, mate."

Chris laughed to himself later. Was nothing ever secret when it involved Alice Springs? He and Melissa did have a meal out on his last night in town but skirted around the future beyond his assurances that he would be back soon, and how much he was looking forward to new directions in life, 'thanks to you.'

Melissa was surprised to receive a phone call from him just before his flight was due to leave. They had said their farewells the night before.

"I've done it," he said, "and it's all because of helping you."

"What are you talking about?"

"You remember meeting Joanna and Bruce? Well I didn't say anything before as I wasn't sure anything would come of it, but I've had a couple of meetings since then with Bruce and his senior colleagues. I start as soon as I can organise the move."

"Are you telling me that you've got a job in television?" She was rightly incredulous.

"I am, but not in the way you might expect. I'm flying the Channel Nine chopper. I'll be back here as soon as I've finalised things in Alice."

CHAPTER 8

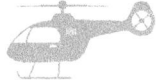

FOR THE SECOND time in in a matter of weeks, Melissa cruised through the pick-up bay at Sydney Airport. It was one of the few times she wished she was back in Alice where meeting incoming passengers was a quick and simple affair. Cars crawled along the congested airport roads, drivers gesturing with annoyance as others cut in front of them or worse still, came to a complete stop.

Chris waved her down, and she ducked into the kerb, allowing him to throw his suitcase in the boot before scrambling into the passenger seat. They exchanged a quick kiss before she flicked on the indicator and pulled back into the melee.

"Phew!" he said. "Welcome to Sydney. It'll take me a while to fully adjust to this level of traffic. I appreciate you picking me up again. It probably warrants a medal for bravery."

She risked a quick glance and smile in his direction before focusing again on the traffic. "I'll take whatever's coming."

"Really? That's enough to get a man excited. I'll put some serious thought into what the reward might be. For now, I'll be happy if you get us clear of this and back to Ollie's in one piece."

He had a few days to settle in before starting his new job. Ollie had agreed to let him move into the spare room in the Marrickville cottage, so accommodation was taken care of. The bulk of his possessions and the Mercedes were arriving from Alice by truck, but there were a few banking and administrative issues to address.

He took Melissa to dinner on his second night in town, after consulting Ollie on a suitable venue.

"Sorry, I can't pick you up in the Merc yet, but at least we can eat somewhere decent. I'll pick you up in a taxi at seven, and we can continue from there."

"Where are we going? Not the Spicy Chicken I assume."

"You'll see when we get there." He was almost gleeful in his secrecy. "It's a thank you for picking me up. You might want a wrap by the way, in case it gets chilly."

She was bemused by the secrecy and thought perhaps he was planning on the revolving restaurant at the top of Centrepoint Tower or something like that. He wasn't. The taxi took them to Circular Quay, and from there they boarded a water taxi.

"This is travelling in style," she gasped as the boat skimmed over the waves, rising then hitting the water again with a rhythmic thwack. "I've not been in a water taxi before."

"Nor have I, but that's what moving to a new location is all about, isn't it? Trying new things."

The driver throttled back, and they cruised towards another wharf. A low-slung building festooned with lights sat to the side, at the water's edge.

"We're going here?" she asked in surprised delight. The signage declared it to be the Catalina Restaurant. Reading that, she realised they were in Rose Bay.

He grinned, clearly pleased with her reaction. "It was the most appropriate place I could think of. It's the location of the first international airport, when flying boats took off from here. It's got all the right ingredients. The harbor, aviation, and good food."

While they watched, the taxi driver sprang ashore and secured the boat with the mooring rope. "It's also my way of thanking you for prompting this change in my life."

He took her hand to steady her as she stepped from the boat onto the boardwalk. Then, he kept hold of it as they made their way towards the restaurant. Melissa couldn't remember when a man had last held her hand. Perhaps never. She liked it. There was something comforting about the contact, and almost a promise of more.

She didn't know what strings he'd pulled, but he'd managed to book a table by the window, overlooking the water. It was altogether a wonderful night, from getting there, to the meal, and the atmosphere. That was before she considered the company.

Sitting opposite Chris, Melissa considered him in a way she had not done before. He was not conventionally handsome, but there was a keen intelligence that shone from his eyes, and his smile and sense of humour were never far from the surface.

Comparing him to some of the models she'd photographed, his looks were more appealing.

"So, do I pass muster?" He'd noticed her appraisal.

"That makes it sound like you're still back in Alice," she parried. "You'll do, Chris Harris—particularly when you manage evenings like this." *Oh god—that sounds so condescending.* For once, she was the one who reached across the table, briefly taking the hand that wasn't holding his aperitif. "Absolutely you pass muster. I'm glad you've come back."

❧

"You will come, won't you Missy? It would mean so much to him."

Jenny adopted the voice she always used when trying to persuade Melissa to do something.

"Well why doesn't he ask me himself?" Melissa ran her fingers through her hair in a habitual gesture of irritation. It was always left for Jenny to make these calls and it wasn't right.

"The Woodleighs are coming over from Mulga Downs, and there'll be others you know. It's not every day your father has a milestone birthday."

"I suppose the preparations are all up to you, Jenny."

"That's not a problem Missy, you know that. There won't be a huge number of people here and it gives us a chance to give the good crockery and cutlery an airing. I've already planned the menu and as much as I can I'll prepare in advance."

"All the good stuff. Wow. I can't remember when we last entertained to that degree. Actually, it's a long time since we've done any entertaining at all. It might have been my twenty first."

"About then," Jenny agreed. "I'll quite enjoy it really. I'll get some help in the kitchen though. Pete's wife Tanya has agreed to come in for the evening. Even getting some help with the washing up will be marvellous."

"Okay, yes I'll come—if only to help you. He doesn't realise how lucky he is to have you running the household."

"I'm sure he does. Your father's not very good at expressing those sentiments." She hesitated. "Is there anyone you'd like to bring, Missy? You always can, you know."

Melissa thought briefly of Chris. It was some weeks since he'd started working in Sydney, but she hadn't mentioned anything about him. Jenny would know via the bush telegraph that Chris had moved and might have reached her own conclusions.

Aside from the fact that getting time off work would be difficult for him, this soon after starting a new job, there was no way she was going to subject him to her father's interrogation or bluntness. She didn't want Chris to know this, but Dan Gilbert would not see a helicopter pilot as a suitable partner for his daughter. She couldn't trust her father not to say something totally inappropriate. The relationship was still in its infancy, and she wasn't ready to invite others into what was still a very personal affair. To tell people would be to threaten the magic.

It was Chris who drove her to the airport instead of letting her catch a taxi.

"You will come back, won't you? It would be ironic if I packed up and moved to Sydney and then you decided to return to Alice."

"Don't be silly. Anyway, I thought you moved here because you wanted a change."

"I could have moved anywhere for a change, but I chose to come to Sydney. Let's just say there were some influencing factors," he said with his smile.

"It's only a short trip. I'll do my duty by my father, help Jenny and probably pack up a few things to bring back with me. I'll return before you know it."

"Your father must have missed you. He'll be pleased to see you again."

"Yeah, right," she muttered, "as if he'd ever show it."

When quite young, she'd learnt not to rely on her father at an emotional level and there was no reason for things to start changing now.

The Land Cruiser, which had been left at the town house in Alice, turned over the second time she tried it. Melissa had no idea how long since it had been driven, but she needed it for the drive out to Plenty River. Pausing only to pick up some last-minute requirements for Jenny, including fresh flowers and the latest editions of some magazines, she headed up the Stuart Highway.

The car rumbled over the grid at the turn-off from the road. She was home. The vibration of the car matched the mixture of trepidation and a sense of home-coming that she felt. The dogs tore out to meet her, tumbling over themselves in their enthusiasm and attempts to be first. She expected Jenny to be attracted by the commotion, but to her surprise it was her father who paused at the front door and then made his way down the path.

"Melissa," he said by way of greeting. "Good of you to come."

"Well, it's not every day my father turns sixty-five. I couldn't let you celebrate without family support."

She got a brief nod of acknowledgement before he grasped the shopping bags and headed inside with them, leaving her to follow with her luggage. That was the most exuberant welcome she was ever going to get from Dan Gilbert.

The dinner was not until the following evening, which meant Melissa was able to help Jenny, as much as she was allowed. That afternoon, they caught up on general news and gossip and Melissa sorted some of her things for taking back to Sydney. She also managed to spend time with Cleo and her new foal, taking a series of photos. The colt was as yet un-named, but Melissa was leaning towards Aristo.

The following day and under direction she acted as general kitchen hand and washed an endless stream of dishes. She took the flowers out of the buckets in which they had been soaking and assembled floral arrangements to be strategically placed around the house. That just left setting the table, choosing some music and preparing the guest bathroom. The two of them had it all under control by the time Tanya arrived to help with plating, serving and of course the cleaning up.

A couple of aircraft flew in from neighbouring stations and another car load made the journey by road from Alice. Most of the guests were overnighting, given the distance from their home base and the fact that alcohol would be served with dinner. They all arrived early enough to freshen up after their journey.

The Woodleighs, Alex and Kathy, and Alex's mother, Rose, were the last to arrive. Mulga Downs was only about a forty-five-minute drive away and Rose had known the Gilberts for decades. She and Melissa's mother had been young brides together and had supported each other in their early years of marriage. Rose had felt the loss of Elizabeth Gilbert keenly.

The guests gathered in the lounge room for pre-dinner drinks. The main reason for the evening might have been Dan Gilbert's birthday, but it also provided a welcome opportunity to catch up in a relaxed atmosphere with friends and neighbours. They discussed cattle prices, domestic and international markets, families, recent travels and general regional gossip. It was a convivial gathering.

Melissa dressed particularly carefully, knowing Alex and Kathy would be there. She'd even bought a new outfit in Sydney, ensuring she was at her most stunning. A little voice told her it was immature, but a bigger voice said that she hoped Alex realised what he had missed out on and that Kathy felt a little over-shadowed.

"Kathy, Alex..." she called in greeting, exchanging a perfunctory air kiss with Kathy and a more affectionate kiss with Alex. "Marriage obviously suits you. You're both looking remarkably well."

She noticed the complicit look they exchanged before making their polite responses. Feeling she had done her hostess duty by them, she moved on with a few passing pleasantries.

She knew all of the guests and was able to make the right enquiries about family members, and the local gossip, all the things that her father wouldn't ask about. She made sure she spoke to everyone before picking up her camera.

"Dad—just stand over by the mantelpiece. I want to take your photo."

"What do you want to do that for?"

"Because you haven't been sixty-five before and it's one of those rare opportunities when you're relaxed and presentable. Just be quiet and do as you're told. I want a photo of you, and Jenny too."

Like father, like daughter. Brusqueness was the order of the evening. She used a little more charm with the guests and recorded them all for posterity. The recent work in Sydney had given her the confidence to use her camera in the social setting. Once, she wouldn't have even thought of it. As she reasoned to herself, why should she take photos of everyone else's parties and not her own? Jenny beamed her approval and gave Melissa a quick hug in passing.

"It's a wonderful idea, Missy. It will be a great record of the evening. You're such a good girl."

At least someone appreciates me. She quietly lined up another candid shot, and then slipped into the kitchen to capture Tanya at work. Pete, her husband was there as well, checking on proceedings and was in the act of slipping a tasty morsel in his mouth.

"Sorry," he spluttered through a mouthful. "I just wanted to see how Tanya was getting on."

"No worries, Pete. I'm sure she'll appreciate the company. Have you tried these? They're really yummy."

117

She held out a tray of blinis with smoked salmon. A grin threatened to split his face as he helped himself to a couple. She liked Pete. He was quiet but had a subtle and very clever sense of humour. It indicated there was not much he didn't notice. He'd grown up on the station as well, his mother being one of the area's original indigenous inhabitants.

"Thanks Melissa. You're a good sort."

"Flattery will get you everywhere. Go and stand by your wife and I'll take your photo."

They were an affectionate couple, and Melissa felt a sudden pang. First Alex and Kathy, now Pete and Tanya. Could she have included Chris in this event? She fantasised briefly on appearing to the dinner party as yet another happy couple, clearly with eyes only for each other. If only life was that simple. She had little faith in happy endings.

The meal, when it was served was a testament to Jenny's organisational and culinary skills. She also joined them at the long dining table. Hers was an indefinable role—much more than that of housekeeper.

Station beef featured in the meal of course, but with advance planning Jenny had been able to incorporate a seafood appetiser and an array of vegetables. Melissa had assisted in making the desserts, and there was a splendid birthday cake, with the recipe and decorative ideas gleaned from the *Australian Women's Weekly* magazine.

Dan took responsibility for serving the drinks and raised a bottle questioningly while looking at Alex. "What's your preference—red or white? I've got a nice full-bodied Shiraz from the Barossa Valley and a crisp white from the Adelaide Hills."

He prided himself on his cellar and had brought out the best of his collection for this occasion. The crystal glasses sparkled and showed off the wine to advantage. He moved around the table, but Kathy covered her glass with her hand, indicating that she wanted neither.

"Not for me. Mineral water's fine, thank you Dan."

"You're not flying tomorrow, are you? You can let your hair down tonight." Dan paused, looking down at the young woman seated in front of him. His tone indicated a measure of indignation that anyone would pass up on such a fine drop.

"I'm on a health kick at the moment. I'd love the mineral water though."

"You're not, are you?" Lily Masters from Daily Springs had picked up on the exchange. At her outburst, other chat around the table ceased and everyone turned to look at Kathy, who immediately coloured and looked to her husband in wordless entreaty. Alex covered her hand with his and it was he who confirmed the news that by now they all suspected.

"Yes, we're pregnant. It's early days so we're not really broadcasting it. We certainly didn't want to detract from your evening Dan."

"Don't be silly, that's marvellous news, Alex. Your father would have been so pleased. This deserves a toast." Dan reached for the champagne.

Pregnant! It was like a knife-twist. Of course they would want a family. That's what people did when they got married. Melissa reached for her glass, raising it in salute. "Congratulations to you both." She turned to Rose. "You must be so pleased—a baby at Mulga Downs."

119

The older woman's eyes sparkled. "You've no idea how hard it's been not spilling the beans. Yes, my dear, I'm over the moon."

It wasn't the only toast of the evening. By the time coffee and liqueurs were served, it was a far more convivial and relaxed group than had assembled at the beginning. Even Dan was full of bonhomie as he topped up glasses with either port or a liqueur of choice. Melissa began to feel the strain. It had been a long day and maintaining the dutiful daughter façade took its toll. On top of that, Alex and Kathy's news had rocked her. She really wanted to ring Chris, just to hear his voice. It would be even later in Sydney though, and perhaps he had an early morning start the next day.

After the last of the guests had retired, she had kicked off her shoes. She and Jenny collected the stray glasses from a variety of hiding places. Dan was sprawled in a lounge chair, reviewing the evening as they tidied around him. His mellow mood began to change as he cast his mind back over the baby news he'd toasted so supportively.

"That should have been you, girl. You should've married Alex Woodleigh and then there would have been a grandson on the way. You even managed to mess that one up. Our families have always been close, but you… you let that woman snare him without putting up a fight. I don't even *see* Alex as much as I used to."

Melissa faced her father. Her voice was controlled but the white-knuckled grip on the glass was a give-away. "One; whoever I marry is none of your business and two; Alex and I had a say in this grand scheme of yours and weren't going to be marshalled into marriage just to suit you."

She wasn't going to admit she'd been devastated and humiliated when Alex had chosen Kathy over her. Her father's accusations re-awakened that hurt.

"Dan, that's in the past," Jenny said firmly. "Alex and Kathy are well suited and obviously very happy. There's no point in bringing this up again.

Melissa put down the glass she was holding and with both hands placed on the table, leant across it, fixing her father with an icy stare. "You've made it as plain as you can. I disappointed you when as first born, I turned out to be a girl, and then I was the child who survived. I disappointed you in not marrying Alex. It's all about you, isn't it? It always has been—you, you, you. Did it ever occur to you that I had lost my mother and little brother, and perhaps I needed my father's support? You could never see beyond your own disappointments."

She straightened up and took a step towards the door before turning back. Her voice reflected the hostility she felt.

"Let me tell you, as a father, you've been a disappointment too. I've got the message. I'll take myself back to the city and you needn't be bothered with me anymore."

She fled from the room. If it were possible, she would have started running and not stopped until she could go no further.

He followed her into the passage. "Melissa! Come back here!"

"You don't order me around, Dad. You don't have that right anymore."

"Let her go Dan—just let her go."

There was nowhere to go except to her room. Once it had been a sanctuary, her place of retreat and safety. Now it seemed foreign, as did her life on the station. There was no longer a place for her here. There was a soft knock on the door. She knew who it would be. She opened the door allowing Jenny to enter.

"Missy, love—don't let him get to you. You know what he's like when he's had a few drinks. He doesn't mean anything by it; you know that."

"I don't know that Jenny. He blames me for their deaths and always has. I was only a little girl. How could I know what was going to happen? He wishes it was me and not William who died that day and then he'd still have his precious son and heir. I always hoped he'd change. I thought he'd learn to love me as a father should. That's never going to happen, is it?"

Tears coursed down her face and she didn't try to stop them. For the first time, she let the tears flow freely. She paced back and forward between her bed and the window, sniffing loudly.

Jenny reached for the box of tissues, pulling out a handful and shoving them at the younger woman. "I think you need these. If you're expecting a magical change, no, that's not going to happen."

"I'll be off first thing in the morning. There's no point in hanging around any longer. I'll take myself out of his life and he and his bitterness can rot for all I care."

"Don't leave with things like this Missy. Family is important. You and he only have each other."

"It's a pity that he hasn't understood that. You're the only family I've ever really had Jenny, once Mum and William were gone. Promise you'll come and visit me in Sydney. I can't bear to think of you stuck out here with him. You should leave too!"

The older woman opened her arms and Melissa fell into them, weeping the release of years of tightly held emotion. Jenny stroked her hair, making soft shushing noises. "It will all blow over Missy, really it will. I know you want to go in the morning but don't forget he's your father and this will always be your home."

"I'm not sure it ever was," Melissa replied bitterly. "I can't think of it that way anymore."

She drove out of the gate soon after first light, pausing briefly at the grave site of her mother and William, located a short distance from the house. There were no tears—she felt as though she had sobbed herself dry—but she had no idea when she could visit them again. She was shutting the door on that part of her life.

❧

Chris met her at the airport. She'd rung him from Alice, letting him know that she'd changed her flight and would be coming back a day early. She'd sounded abrupt on the phone and his gut told him not to ask questions. Perhaps the dinner had not gone well.

"Good time, huh?" he asked as she clung to him in the Arrivals Hall. "Or are you just pleased to see me?"

"Of course, I'm pleased to see you, you fool. It's been a tiring trip, that's all."

"And the party?"

"The party's over. I don't want to talk about it."

He didn't pursue the matter. He took her home instead and that night for the first time, she invited him to stay.

"Sweetheart, are you sure you're ready for this?" Chris kissed her gently. "I don't want to feel as though I'm rushing you or taking advantage."

"Chris Harris, are you turning me down?"

His stomach churned at the anguish in her eyes. It made him want to hold her tight. "Are you kidding me? I'll never turn you down. I just wanted to make sure…"

"Shut up and kiss me."

She grasped him tightly as though trying to melt into him. His aroused response was immediate and very apparent. She led him to her room, shutting the door quietly before turning to face him. With eyes fixed on his, she slid down the zip to her dress. Dropping it to the floor, she stepped out of it and grasping his face between her hands, reaching up to claim his lips.

With a soft moan, he slid a hand down her back to grab her butt and press her as close as it was possible for two people to be with their clothes still on. Opening her mouth to him, their tongues engaged, a gentle journey of exploration— teasing and tasting. He could feel her nipples, trapped in their lacy harness, hardening to pebbles and pressing against his chest. His arousal strained in response.

Pulling back, Melissa undid the buttons of his shirt, baring his skin beneath her fingers and darting quick licks across the hollow of his neck. At the same time, he unhooked her bra, dragging it off and casting it aside. He took one breast in his hand, caressing the peachy tip between the finger and thumb and causing her to throw back her head with mewls of pleasure.

The remainder of their clothes were discarded with mutual haste. With a gentle shove, she pushed Chris onto her bed, her legs entwined with his as they began an exploration of each other's bodies.

It was a tender sweet coupling, driven by tentative exploration as much as anything, after which she clung to him and silently wept. She soaked first his chest and then the sheet with which he tried to wipe away the torrent.

"What did I do wrong? Tell me—what did I do?"

She clung to him, her face still buried in his chest.

"Nothing. You've done nothing at all. Just hold me, Chris. Promise you won't change."

"Of course, I won't change, sweetheart. I'll hold you as long as you want me to."

The next morning, they made love again with Chris rousing her to wakefulness at first break of day. Her drowsy response gave way to a sense of urgency as her body reacted delightfully beneath the explorations of his fingers. This time it was a more passionate affair, as Chris took the lead and directed proceedings, ensuring her response was enough to make her forget everything except the moment.

CHAPTER 9

DAYS, WEEKS AND months settled into an easy pattern. Chris loved his job and the variety it entailed. One day he would be flying for the traffic report and the next he would be flying to the site of the latest news event. Sometimes he flew the owner of Channel Nine to his country property and on occasions took well-known celebrities out there as well. He and Melissa socialised with Joanna and Bruce occasionally, and Bruce had taken Chris under his wing during the first days of employment with the station. After that, Chris's natural charm took over and he forged his own work relationships.

Melissa printed the photos from her father's birthday party and then put them aside, except for sending prints to Pete and Tania, and also to Jenny of the photos that she had taken of her. There were regular contracts often working with Angela and Eduardo, and on one occasion they travelled to New Zealand, working on a winter collection.

There was no pressure to her relationship with Chris. It was something to be nurtured and given free rein to grow and develop without expectation. For now, they simply enjoyed each other, with the unspoken understanding that in time, it might become much more.

Sometimes their days off coincided and then they would explore Sydney together; the Art Gallery, trawling The Rocks, or getting a ferry to the other side of the harbor and finding somewhere for lunch before making the crossing back again.

It was on one of those excursions they stopped off at an art exhibition in Newtown. Russell happened to be there, as exuberant as ever and campishly delighted to see Chris again. He was wearing suede pixie boots and a flowing over-shirt of green and gold over black slim-fit jeans. He made a beeline for them as soon as he spotted them hovering at the entrance.

"Melissa! How wonderful to see you and you've brought that fabulous flying man."

"Hands off. He's mine." Melissa linked her arm through Chris's.

"Pet, I knew that, before you I think, but you can't blame a boy for wishful thinking. Why haven't you been to visit me?"

"Well, you haven't invited us for one thing, and we've been busy getting settled for another."

"You have a standing invitation, you know that. Now have you been working on an exhibition of your own, as we discussed?"

"Not really. To be honest since relocating to Sydney, I haven't given it much thought. I've been too busy with the fashion work to have time for my own stuff. Anyway, I don't have the contacts here to organise anything like that."

"But I do. Chris, you must make sure this woman gets her act together. She doesn't promote her talents and from what

127

I've seen she's got enough material to put on a fabulous show. I know your fashion work pays the bills, but you need to exhibit all those stunning prints from around Alice. What do you think of this exhibition, by the way? Sam's one of my protégés."

Sam, an edgy young man, was engaged in animated discussion with a couple of visitors, evidently analysing the deep message behind his work. His gestures were so dramatic a splash of his red wine landed on the tiled floor, creating a puddle reminiscent of a Pro Hart painting.

"The exhibition? It's challenging. I need some time to think about it." Melissa gave up on diplomacy and referred to her own work. "I'm not sure my prints would be of interest here in Sydney, certainly not a marketable interest. Exhibitions cost money so you need to be reasonably sure of achieving some sales."

"That's true, and the smart thing to do when you're establishing a presence is to team up with a couple of others and then you can share the costs and of course they promote the exhibition through their contacts as well. That's wider publicity for nothing and everyone wins," Russell said.

"So, who would I team up with? It would need to be compatible work."

"Leave it to me, Pet. I'll comb through my networks and see who I come up with. There are a couple of galleries I can chat to about staging the event. You'll have to be able to show them samples of your work of course before they'll take you on so while you're reviewing your portfolio, think about which signature pieces you'll use to promote yourself."

"Go for it, Melissa," Chris interjected. "I'm not sure how I can assist, but if there's anything I can do I will. I can stick posters up at Channel Nine at least."

"Don't be silly. They won't let you stick up posters."

"Wait a minute," said Russell. "You're working at Channel Nine, Chris? But that's fabulous. I can see it now, cameras at the exhibition, Lexie Ferguson doing an onsite interview with you, and all sorts of spin-off benefits. You can't lose with this one, sweetie."

It was overwhelming. Russell was building up to full-on exuberance and in that mode, he swept everyone with him. Melissa knew this. He was likely to get excited about this project and then when something else caught his attention might transfer his enthusiasm to that instead, leaving her high and dry.

Despite her reservations, she promised to consider the suggestion further and Russell committed to helping with the logistics. As they left the venue, he was engaged in animated discussion about Sam with other patrons. Melissa turned at the door and looked back. Russell was gesticulating dramatically, his voice indicating his level of excitement. They continued strolling up King Street before Chris took her home.

Not having done anything like this before, the thought of being stranded and making a fool of herself terrified her. She might also lose money she could ill afford. She and Chris were seated in the lounge room in Annandale with a cup of coffee. Angela had made a polite withdrawal.

"I know what you mean. He's unpredictable, that's for sure. I think you have to put together your own organisational strategy, pick up what knowledge you can from Russell but

129

expect that in the end, the organisation is up to you." Chris was comfortingly pragmatic. "The important thing is to get your work out there. I think you've got talent and only need support demonstrating that to others outside of the fashion industry. Take this opportunity and look on it as a learning curve. Even if you only break even financially, you'll benefit from the experience."

Melissa chewed her lip pensively. Failure was not a word in her vocabulary. To her that was losing face and Melissa Gilbert never lost face.

"I need to consider the risks carefully," she said after a while. "If I get the planning right, there's a better chance of success."

Just voicing this started to shift her perspective. "I need a focus and for that I need a name. Have any bright suggestions? I want to show people that Central Australia means more than photos of Uluru, or stockmen in boots and check shirts."

"Centralian Explorations? Sunrise on the Centre? Central Relations?"

She winced. They were not quite what she had in mind. "Perhaps we'll work on that later."

Chris shrugged. "Why don't you assemble some likely prints for inclusion and a name might naturally suggest itself when you review them collectively?"

"That sounds like a plan. I'm still looking for suggestions though." She threw him a quick kiss on his cheek. "I feel better knowing I've got you at my back."

"Always, sweetheart," he said, grabbing her and returning the kiss with slightly more intensity and an affectionate grab to her butt. "Always."

He had an early start in the morning and so didn't stay. As he left, he called out that she mustn't forget the dingo. He had a fondness for that animal, given its role in bringing them together.

After he'd gone, Melissa dragged out a box of prints from under the bed and started laying them on the living room floor, shuffling them in order and shuffling some right back into the box. She'd brought them back with her after the dinner party for her father.

"What are you doing?" Angela had emerged from her room and stepped carefully around the floor display to better see the images.

"It's probably a crazy idea, but Russell has talked me into staging a photographic exhibition, focussing on Alice Springs and the surrounds."

"Wow! That's exciting." Angela was most impressed at the news. "You should have some stand-out photos in your collection. That country is so evocative—what I saw of it anyway. If you need a good framer, I can put you in touch with one. I've used him a few times to frame some promotional work, and I'm sure he'd do you a deal for a bulk consignment. Something simple, don't you think? You don't want to detract from the images themselves. Do you have any idea what you'll select to exhibit?"

"Not really. I'll lay them all out and start short listing. People have this idea that the centre of Australia is one big desert, always hot and full of sand and red dirt. Sometimes that's true but I want to showcase the colour and form that's there and to present the diversity in the animal and plant life as well."

"What about the people?"

"I'm not so sure about that. I'm not really a people person. Most of the photos I have of people are focussed on activities at Plenty River; daily life and that sort of thing. They're not representative enough."

"You'd be mad not to. Adding people helps the viewer to make some sense of an unfamiliar environment—a sort of window into their lives. It helps them get to the heart of the story."

"Hmm… I'll think about it." Melissa pondered the window analogy.

"What about *Desert Heartbeat* as a name for the exhibition?" Angela suggested.

"Desert Heartbeat." Melissa listened to the sound of it. "I like it. Simple but sums it up." She smiled at her friend with relief. It was somehow easier to plan around a name. They shuffled a few more prints, adding some and detracting others.

"So, changing the subject, you and Chris seem to be getting quite serious." Angela sat down on the sofa with the air of someone settling in for answers.

"Well, we're more than 'just friends', but taking things slowly. These are early days."

"I think you've got a keeper there, but he strikes me as a decent human being. Don't mess this one up."

"Mess it up? When have I ever done that?"

"You've mastered the Ice Queen act to perfection. One look from you in one of your moods can make a bloke's vital bits shrivel and shatter. Anyone who doesn't measure up gets frozen out very quickly."

"I don't know what you're talking about."

"Yes, you do. At college the guys were taking bets on who could break through that icy reserve. They were drawn to your looks and terrified of your reactions. You had them alternatively enthused and confused."

Melissa didn't bother denying the comments. It was true she cut people down quickly if they didn't measure up. It had taken her a while to realise who she was measuring them against, but to anyone who knew her intimately, it would have been blindingly obvious. Alex Woodleigh was her benchmark. He was a man who was competent, had presence, and of course, was good-looking to boot. It also helped that he owned a station and understood the environment in which she had been born and had grown up.

The men she met in college and in Sydney never had a chance. That was what made her relationship with Chris more surprising. He didn't match the template. He had an open and friendly nature though. His was a natural charm and he was attractive without having the rugged good looks Alex sported.

She put aside pondering the nature of attraction and turned back to the pictures. There were a couple of those dingo prints, but also landscapes of wild flowers; wallabies drinking from a rock pool at sunset; a goanna in sand dunes; and various small critters. She was particularly attached to a magical grotto at the base of a gorge, and a series of sunrises and sunsets that were a blaze of colour and intriguing outlines.

In a separate pile were the photos that did feature people. She wanted to think more carefully about those. There was Pete on a horse, picking his way through a creek bed with one of the station dogs at his heels. Another was of her father, hands on hips, back to the camera and watching a mob of cattle as they passed through a gate in a cloud of dust. She included some shots of the Harts Range Races, with the horses pounding past the winning post and the reactions of those who were watching. Then she contemplated a couple of the prints from the fashion shoot; models displayed against the reds, browns and ochres of rocky outcrops in the early morning sun. She would have to get permission from the client to use those.

She sat back on her heels surveying the selection. Angela nominated her favourites and there was a little more shuffling that took place. They debated over the feature print to be used in publicity. Angela wanted the picture of her father with the cattle, but Melissa thought that it was too much along the lines of what the public might expect and she wanted an alternative image. It came down to a toss-up between a carpet of wild flowers as seen from the air, and the grotto in the gorge – a scene that was green and lush and hinted at hidden spaces and discoveries.

The photo she didn't show Angela was one that she had of Chris. She'd taken it during a quiet moment at the Vaucluse party, while he was standing, drink in hand and looking out over the water. In his borrowed tux, he looked incredibly dapper. He didn't know she had taken it, and she'd not shown him the print. It was the only image she had of him. She wasn't ready to share it.

CHAPTER 10

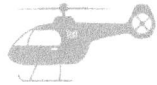

IT DIDN'T TAKE long for arrangements to be made, but at times Melissa thought it was happening too fast. She made lists, and then lists of the lists and checked off the tasks to be completed. She was up early on the day of the opening and drove Angela crazy until it was time to leave.

"Have you got the glasses… the guest book… the flowers… the…"

"For the last time, yes we have them all. The car's packed, everything's under control. You look stunning by the way. Take a deep breath, get out there and slay 'em."

Angela had supported Melissa through the preparations for the exhibition and an important part of that had been calming the nerves and banishing self-doubt.

"C'mon—it's time to go."

Melissa took a deep breath and looked around the room for one last time, checking she hadn't forgotten anything. Now the time had finally arrived, she was reluctant to leave for the gallery. What if nobody came? What if nobody bought anything? What if the reviews were bad?

For goodness sake, she told herself, *don't be so wet.* More than anything, she was determined not to let anyone else see she was anxious or nervous.

She planned to meet Chris at the gallery. He had a work flight that day and wasn't sure what time he would finish. She hoped there were no major news events requiring him to ferry the reporters and camera crew to site. She wanted him by her side.

Melissa and Angela arrived at the same time as the other exhibitors, and she recognised the same undercurrent of nervous energy. They each had a lot riding on this event. Russell had been true to his word as he found two other people to share in the exhibition. Myah was a jeweller and Warwick worked with glass. They were each exhibiting work that complemented the outback and Centralian theme, whether by form or in colour. They were all there early allowing time for setting up the catering and having one last look at lighting and placement. Myah offered Melissa a necklace to wear, an example of her work. They were all doing what they could to support and promote each other.

The flowers were Australian natives and Angela filled the vases with water and distributed the arrangements strategically. This was a budget do-it-yourself exhibition. None of them had the money to engage assistance or to book a venue where everything was laid on. Joanne knew more about these things and had freely offered advice. She'd sent out press releases to various print and media outlets and had arranged for a couple of final year students from the Diploma of Photography course to circulate and take photos of the event. Angela acted as general factotum.

With everything done, all they had to do was wait. Where was everyone? Melissa mentally ran through her list of invitees. Surely, they wouldn't let her down? She felt sick. This had been a stupid idea. It was a disaster before it had even begun. She had invited Jason Lombardi, the winner of this year's Australian Photographic Awards to open the event and now she was going to be humiliated in front of him. How would she live this down?

"Myah, have we got the right night? We did put the venue and the time on the invitations, didn't we?"

"Of course, we did. You know people never come on time. It's just not done. Everyone will be here soon. You'll see."

The door to the street opened and a couple of people ambled in. They were friends of Myah's, and she moved to greet them. The door opened again and a few more people trickled in, and then Russell swept in, full of colour, noise and exuberance. Melissa seized on his presence with relief as he planted a kiss on each cheek.

"Melissa, you're looking stunning as ever. I need a drink, then take me on a tour of your fabulous prints."

She was happy to be diverted. She couldn't face the idea of a drink herself. Her stomach was too churned up for that, but she fetched Russell a glass. Taking him by the hand, led him through the display. She'd arranged it to tell a progressive story. He carefully reviewed and commented on each, noting the subject, the composition, the lighting and the striking features. He was knowledgeable and discerning, and Melissa valued his input and support.

"So—what's the verdict?"

"You're fishing, Pet. You don't have to. There's some brilliant work on those walls and you know it. You just need more confidence in yourself. Stand back and watch the reactions of the spectators. That will tell you all you need to know."

The venue began to fill. Melissa noted with relief that quite a few of her friends had arrived. People picked up the catalogues and consulted their copy for details about the prints on the walls and of course the glasswork and jewellery. She hoped that included looking at the price and making decisions about a purchase. She'd dropped a bit of money for this exhibition, and desperately hoped she would at least break even. Purchasers could order numbered copies of the prints, or the framed exhibits, which were available to be collected at the end of the display period.

"Look Pet, Jason Lombardi's just arrived. You'd better go and look after him. He'll want to have a look around so he knows what he's talking about during his opening speech."

Russell squeezed her arm in a gesture of support and moved on to chat with Myah and Warwick. Melissa looked at her watch. Where was Chris? He should be here by now.

No time to ponder. She took a deep breath to steady her nerves, applied a smile of confidence and moved to greet Jason.

The first thing she noticed was his height. She had to look up to him and as she did, she observed appraising eyes beneath a mop of unruly hair. It was a tousled look that complemented the cool persona he presented. He was an attractive man, and Melissa felt the charge of current that passed between them. She hadn't met him before, but was aware of his reputation. His work was acclaimed, as evidenced by the award. His reputation as a lothario was also well known, particularly by the female students at the technical college she'd attended. He was charismatic as well as attractive, and that ensured he maintained a level of interest with members of the opposite sex. Melissa knew all of this, and as he turned those dark molten orbs in her direction, she understood why so many women melted in his path. It was a captivating look of pure heat.

"And you must be Melissa," he purred. "Your photograph doesn't do you justice. You need a better photographer my dear. If you drop in to my studio, I'm sure I can produce a magnificent portfolio for you. People will be just as interested in you as in your work, you know."

He leaned forward and deposited a soft kiss on her lips, his eyes never once leaving hers. It was as blatant an invitation as she'd had in a long time. She experienced a tingle of response, but she wasn't going to let him see that. "Thanks for the offer. I'll keep it in mind. For now, I rather like the photos I've got. Shall I show you around?"

She swiped a drink off the tray that Angela was carrying and offered it to him. If he was holding that, his hands would be occupied. That was the theory.

As she manoeuvred him in the direction of the first print in her display, she glanced around and was startled to see Chris standing watching them. She flicked him a quick smile and a wink, hoping he wouldn't misinterpret what he'd just seen.

Initially he was stony-faced, but then she got a small nod in return. Phew. He had her back.

Keeping an eye on the time and their schedule, she walked Jason through the display, telling him a little about the background story as she did. She also made a point of introducing him to Myah and Warwick, indicating the necklace she wore as an example of Myah's work. He reached out and touched the silver creation, his hand brushing her breasts as he did. Quite deliberately. She was sure of that. The man needed two drinks, one in each hand. She executed a soft shoe shuffle that would have been a credit to Fred Astaire and positioned herself out of arm's reach. If Jason noticed, he didn't comment.

"Lexie—how wonderful to see you!"

Russell's greeting intruded on her murmured explanations. Melissa turned around to see who he was addressing.

The woman was the centre of attraction, and for good reason. She was immaculately groomed and wearing a suit that decreed both class and style. It was her air of assurance that made her stand out as much as anything. She both commanded and expected attention. She was also a very attractive woman and stood close to and proprietorially with Chris. It was Lexie Ferguson, the television reporter from Channel Nine. Russell moved to greet her and as he did, glanced around as though checking if any television cameras were there.

Russell wasn't the only one who noticed the new arrival. Jason was quick to spot her presence. He completed the rest of his inspection in record time before also making his way to the woman's side.

"Welcome, welcome. May I introduce myself? I'm Jason Lombardi and I'll shortly be opening this exhibition, but I can give you a quick personal tour if you would like to look around. Can I get you a drink?"

Melissa gaped. The man was incorrigible. She'd never been dropped so quickly in her life. She wasn't sure whether to laugh or cry. Russell likewise looked bemused as Lexie was bustled from his side. It wasn't often he was sidelined in that fashion. Melissa gave Russell's arm a quick conspiratorial pat. If Jason did a good job of the opening, it probably didn't matter who he chatted up. With a quick wink in the direction of Myah and Warwick, who had also witnessed the episode, she pushed through the crowd to Chris and gave him a greeting kiss. He was still wearing his flying uniform.

"I thought you weren't going to make it! I see you brought a friend with you. How did you manage that? I think Russell was hoping there would be a full media crew. Instead, it was one glamorous woman hanging off your arm."

"And hello to you too. Wasn't that a strange man I saw perving over your body and getting way too close for my liking?"

"He *was* pervy, wasn't he? He also happens to be Jason Lombardi, the man who is doing the honours in opening the exhibition—very soon, I hope. Grab a drink before the supplies disappear!"

"Only something soft for me. I'll be flying again early tomorrow. Lexie was with me on the last flight, having done a series of interviews down at Nowra. I'd been telling her and anyone else who'd listen about the exhibition and when I asked her on the flight home if she'd like to come, she agreed.

I'll introduce you when the opportunity arises. Make sure you two get a photo together. Did you notify the paparazzi? This will become the exhibition that everyone has to see."

"I thought it already was." She smiled artfully, more relaxed now he was there and the event was in full swing. The gallery had a satisfactory number of people clustered around each of the exhibits and not just focussed on the refreshments. She noticed a couple heading in their direction.

"Look, Joanna and Bruce are here."

Her smile in greeting threatened to split her face. "I'm so glad to see you. I really appreciate your support." She and Joanna did the cheek kiss thing, while Chris and Bruce exchanged manful grins and handshakes.

The couple had already done a circuit of the venue and were appropriately effusive.

"We've picked out our favourite, haven't we?" said Joanna seeking confirmation from her partner. "We'll put that one in the entrance hall but we're just debating if we'll get one for Bruce's office at work as well."

"You mean you want a print?" Melissa felt faint with excitement. "Look I don't expect you two to buy one. I'll give you a print."

"No, you won't. This is a business venture. Anyway, Bruce can probably claim a tax deduction for his, so you ought to charge him double. He'll value it more that way as well. Where do we place our order?"

Hoping desperately her friends really liked the prints and were not just purchasing to support her, Melissa directed them to the desk where Angela was primed, ready and waiting. Her first sale; it was unbelievably exciting, but she didn't have time to dwell on it. She needed to get the official part underway and then she could properly relax.

"Chris, can you keep Joanna and Bruce company? I need to round up Jason and get this show on the road."

"Sure sweetheart. You look fabulous by the way."

That lop-sided smile was reassuring. It gave her a warm glow of confidence as she nodded to Myah and Warwick indicating that it was time to start the speeches. She pushed through the crowd to Jason and taking him firmly by the arm, steered him to where the microphone was set up.

"It's time for the official opening now, if you're ready Jason? I'll get the music turned off and we can start."

Out of the corner of her eye, she saw Eduardo arrive. Typical. He couldn't be punctual for anything that wasn't about him, rather preferring to make an entrance at a time he saw to be advantageous. She resolved to make him buy something before he left. He owed it to her.

Melissa caught his eye and blew him a kiss before focussing on Jason. She turned a hundred-watt smile in his direction, having realised that to this man, the attraction of a woman was everything. If that was what it took to get a brilliant opening speech, so be it.

She took a deep breath. The butterflies rampaged at maximum wing power. It was usually others who were the focus of attention, not her. At least Chris was there to support her and that made it easier. She felt personally judged along with her work.

Jason rose to the occasion and spoke with knowledge of the photographic techniques, admired the subject matter and used humour appropriately. He also introduced Myah and

Warwick's work and in short, was impeccably behaved. People laughed at his jokes and applauded his speech and Melissa was relieved that he didn't chat up the nearest female mid-performance. It finished without incident and the crowd resumed their inspections of the works.

A few people clustered around the sales desk. It was hard to tell if they were just picking up catalogues or negotiating purchases. Melissa was too anxious to look over their shoulders and anyway, it would be crass to do so. Instead, she focussed on presenting an air of cool nonchalance. She caught up with Eduardo and gave him a brief tour, pointing out which prints she thought deserved special attention.

"These would be a fabulous memento of your trip to Alice" she said, indicating some that had been taken on the morning of their shoot on the station. "I'm sure this one would also sell your talents as a director. Perhaps you'd like this one as well."

"Mellie, you're a marvellous saleswoman as well as a brilliant photographer. I've always admired your fashion work. You have this knack of bringing out the best in the models, but you know, you should do more in this vein as well." He grabbed a glass from a passing waiter. "My God, I need a drink. I'll do another circuit and think about it. Leave it with me, Darl."

The rest of the evening passed in a flurry of circulating and chatting and at the end she couldn't quite remember who'd been there or who she'd chatted to.

Chris introduced her to Lexie Ferguson.

"So pleased to meet you, Melissa. I've heard such a lot about your work. Congratulations. I hope the exhibition is a big success."

Her smile appeared genuine. Melissa repressed her instinctively prickly emotions and extended her hand. "It was good of you to come, especially after a long day at work. Chris must have provided an enthusiastic sales pitch for me."

The other woman laughed. "He's such a sweetie, isn't he? By far the best pilot we've had in ages. Great sense of humour and a good listener. He helps me unwind when we've had a demanding day."

Melissa fixed a smile on her face and kept it there while the photographer captured them together. *She's his colleague. That's all.*

Russell appeared at her shoulder, and as he and Lexie meandered off into conversation, she turned back to Chris and slipped her arm through his.

Chris walked Lexie out to her car later. "She liked it sweetheart," he said on his return. "She bought a necklace from Myah and said she would try to mention the exhibition on the morning show tomorrow."

"Did she really like it or are you just kidding me?"

"Since when have I ever done that? I tell it like it is. Haven't you learned by now?"

He kissed her lightly and she smiled before turning back to the last of the guests and then focussing her attention on cleaning up. It didn't take long as everyone pitched in.

Then came the moment of reckoning. Angela totted up the results. They had each made some sales, and with delight Melissa realised costs had been recovered and then some.

Even Eduardo had made a purchase. The exhibition was on display for another two weeks so there were still sales that could dribble in over coming days. How fabulous it would be if Lexie Ferguson could mention it on live television as well? That would be such a seal of approval and a tremendous publicity boost.

"Come on," said Russell. "I think a small celebration is in order. I know a great little wine bar down the street. Why don't we all adjourn for a glass of bubbles?"

"Chris?" she asked. "Can you join us? I know you have an early start."

"Yeah, I'll turn into a pumpkin shortly, but I'll join you for one mineral water before I shoot through. I reckon we can push the boat out on this occasion."

Melissa linked her arm through his as the group walked down the street. She would have been disappointed if Chris weren't able to come. As they opened the door, the noise spilled out of the venue. Pausing to adjust to the dim lighting, they spotted a couple of tables, which they pushed together to accommodate the party of ten. Russell summonsed the waiter.

"My good man, could we have two bottles of Grant Burge Pinot Noir Chardonnay, and a bottle of your very best mineral water for my flying friend."

"Is that on your tab, Russell?" Melissa asked, with the wide eyes of the ingénue.

Chris threw an arm around her shoulders. "I think this one's on me. My girl's proved herself to be a great success tonight, and so have Myah and Warwick. Well done to you all."

My Girl. She tasted the words and found them to be sweet. Nobody had ever said that to her before. On the one hand, she was nobody's but on the other, that connection with someone else felt good. It gave her a stronger glow than the wine.

Now Russell's fright over the wine had subsided, he could be expansive again. "A toast to the three most talented people I know—after me of course. May you all achieve the financial and professional recognition you deserve."

They debriefed the evening—who came, who didn't, what was said, and what was sold. There was even discussion about what they would do differently next time.

"For a start, I'd know what to expect when Jason Lombardi walked in the door," said Myah. "What a smooth operator. At least he rose to the occasion when he had to."

"Looked like that wasn't all that was about to rise," muttered Warwick, resulting in a couple of snorts around the table.

"So, Melissa—when are you taking your show on the road?" Russell asked.

"What do you mean? I'm not going anywhere."

"If I remember rightly, Belinda indicated she would be interested in hosting the exhibition in Alice. Have you put plans in place?"

"No. I was too focussed on this event. I didn't think she was serious. It's one thing to organise something like this where I can control it and everyone pitches in to help, but quite another to take it interstate."

"That's what Belinda is for, to organise things like that. She was brilliant when coordinating my exhibition. Give her a call. You've got the advantage of knowing people in town. You're bound to be a success."

"I'm not so sure. My relationship with the town and the locals might not be what you think. I'll give it some thought."

"He's right Sweetheart. You should think about it. You'd be surprised at the support you'd have in Alice, especially with your subject matter." Chris pushed back his chair and stood up. "Anyway, I must make a move. This is witching hour for me."

Melissa reluctantly moved her chair, allowing Chris to make an exit. She was going home with Angela but probably not for a while. She walked a couple of paces with him away from the table.

"I'm glad you could stay for a little while," she said softly for his benefit. "Having you here made all the difference."

"Sweetheart, I've been thinking..."

"Sounds ominous."

"No, hear me out. We've been keeping company for a while now. I wasn't looking for or expecting a relationship but what has evolved has been good—better than I might have expected if I *had* been looking."

"Oka-a-ay. I guess I could say the same."

"You don't have to give me an answer now but what do you think about us getting a place of our own and moving in together? No more going home to our separate houses and separate beds."

"But you often stay over."

"I know I do, but it's not the same. Just think about it and we can talk about it later. Right now, I need to be going."

With a kiss and a proprietary pat on her butt, he was gone, leaving Melissa with a head that was buzzing. So much to think about—the events of the evening, an exhibition in Alice and now a new phase of her relationship with Chris. Was she ready for any of it?

There. He'd put it out there. Surely Melissa could see they were good with each other. Life in Sydney was turning out well. He had a job that kept him engaged, and Melissa was growing in confidence and expanding her options. This was different to how he'd felt about Sarah, though he'd always be fond of her. He'd changed a lot since leaving Alice. Being with Melissa had pushed his boundaries as well, and that had been good for him. He liked to think that in various little ways, he'd been good for her as well.

CHAPTER 11

BELINDA WAS JUST as enthusiastic as Russell predicted when Melissa rang her. "Melissa, you know your work would be well received here. I'd love to arrange an exhibition—I told you that before."

"I know you did, but I wasn't sure if you were caught up in the heat of the moment after Russell's success. How did his event finish up by the way?"

"He did very well. The bulk of the sales were on the opening night, but they remained steady after that. He received some good publicity via the local press, and I arranged an interview for him with Joel Pemberton, the station manager from Radio Alice. I believe you know him?

"We're not bosom buddies but we've met."

"Great. I'm sure he'd organise an interview for you too— local girl hits the big time."

"I don't know that anyone would really be interested. In fact, I'm not sure I want to promote myself in that way. Can I be anonymous?"

"No way. It's all about you, Melissa. Your work will be fabulous I'm sure, but the attraction will also be you. You're a local, you grew up here, you're successful and you're a role model."

"I've never thought of myself in that light."

"Well you are. Just because you've grown up in a small town in the middle of Australia, doesn't mean that you can't establish a successful career that reaches beyond the MacDonnell Ranges. This is a duty you have really, showing the young people in the town what is possible if they put their mind to it. I reckon I could interest the Northern Territory Tourist Bureau in your work as well."

There was a pause during which Melissa could faintly hear paper rustling.

"Have you got your diary out?" Belinda asked. "These are the time slots in which I could accommodate you." She reeled off some dates.

Thoughts were swirling in Melissa's mind. Flying her kite in her home town was pushing her boundaries. "Okay, if you're sure about this, I'll make a booking, but I don't want to promote myself as Melissa Gilbert. I don't want to trade off my father's name, or to even bring him into it. This is all about me and my work. If I do this, I would just like to present myself as Lyssa. Can I do that?"

There was a moment's silence while Belinda digested this proposal. It was a spur of the moment suggestion but the more she thought about it, the more Melissa liked the idea.

"I don't see why not," Belinda said. "You can call yourself whatever you want. People will soon put Lyssa and Melissa

Gilbert together, but it might be a good promotional name. Sounds intriguing."

"I'm not interested in the marketing ploy. I just want to be accepted for myself and not Dan Gilbert's daughter."

They settled on a date and discussed the practicalities: how many prints, the marketing and what arrangements Belinda needed to make. Some of Myah and Warwick's work would also be exhibited. Melissa felt she owed it to her new friends to help them expand their reach, and it rounded out the event, being a better offering than just her prints. They could decide later if they were able to travel to Alice for the launch.

She rang Jenny later that day to let her know what was in the pipeline. She knew her best marketing tool would be the bush telegraph that Jenny tapped into, although that wasn't the reason for her call.

"Missy, that's wonderful news. I knew you'd do well. I'm sorry that I couldn't get down to Sydney to support you. It's been busy here lately and it wasn't the best time to get away."

"You have a standing invitation to visit me any time Jenny, but as far as the exhibition goes, you don't need to fly to Sydney. I'm bringing it to Alice."

"But that's fabulous. I'll tell your father."

"No, don't do that."

"Not tell him? But he'll want to see it."

"I don't want him there, Jenny. When I left Plenty River, I wasn't only leaving my home, I was leaving him as well. He never wanted me throughout my childhood and so it can't be a surprise that I don't want him now. He's never supported my photography anyway."

"He's bound to hear about it, Missy, you know how it is."

"I'm sure he will, but he won't hear it from me and I'd rather you didn't tell him either. Enough about him. Tell me what else has been happening. Have you been to town lately? What's the local gossip?"

She was homesick for Plenty River. Despite what she had said on her last visit, it was her home. She missed the space, missed Jenny and her mare Cleo. The conversation moved to safer ground and Melissa filled Jenny in on her general news. All the time, she was wondering what she should say about Chris, if anything. If she and Chris moved in together, then Jenny would find out about them soon enough, especially if she came to visit in Sydney.

"Um, did you know that Chris Harris lives in Sydney now?"

"Yes dear, I was aware of that."

"I've been seeing something of him lately."

"Yes, I knew that too."

"I might have known. There's not much gets past you is there? Why didn't you say something?"

"The local grapevine works very well, as you must be aware, and I knew that you would tell me when you were ready. So, it's serious then?"

"Sort of. Chris has asked me to move in with him."

"And?"

"I'm still thinking about it. I've told him I need to focus on this exhibition but when it's over we can talk about looking for a place of our own. We're spending a lot of time together, so it makes sense. I just need to decide if I'm ready to take that step. You know me Jenny; I've spent my life as the lone ranger. Chris has brought a lot of changes and for the better I think, but this is one big commitment."

"It is, but don't lose something good out of fear. I don't really know Chris but from what I've seen he's a decent man. If he doesn't do the right thing by you though, your father will kill him."

"My father wouldn't care less."

"Never under-estimate him, Missy. He cares for you more than you know."

This time, Melissa had an idea of what was required in organising an exhibition. For Belinda, it was a routine part of her job. Between the two of them, they wrote lists and ticked items off. It wasn't too difficult. The logistics of travel and the required insurance were the most challenging aspects and even they weren't such a problem. Belinda had contacts she used on a regular basis.

"Is there anything we've left out?" Melissa asked. "It almost seems to be coming together too easily."

She was making one of her regular phone calls to the woman who was fronting up as her new best friend, they were speaking that often.

"Nah. We've got it well under control. Trust me, it's a cinch. All I need now is a stunning headshot of your good self. If you have one of yourself in an outback setting, that would be brilliant. Looking pensive while balancing on a red rock and bathed in the setting sun—something like that."

"Not a chance, sister. I'll give you the most straight-up studio shot I can find." She changed the subject. "I think I've got the hang of this exhibition business now. Perhaps I've found a new calling. Exhibition Organiser."

"No, that's my role, amongst other things. Still, I can always call on you when I have future exhibitions with artists based in Sydney."

"Well, I was only joking but always happy to help. I think I owe you heaps for your assistance. You're making this process less painful than it could have been. I'll buy you a drink when we're in the same space again."

"I'll keep you to that. See you soon."

The only glitch from Melissa's perspective was the fact Chris couldn't join her in Alice. She would be doing this one on her own, except for Belinda of course.

"I'd love to come sweetheart, not just to support you but to catch up with Mark, Sarah and Kathy and a host of other people, but it just can't happen. Not this time anyway. For me, the timing's all wrong. The station is sponsoring some big events around then and I know the boss will want me on call for his VIP guests. I'll call you every day though, and I expect regular updates."

"I won't be away very long. Really it will be no different than if I had a contract on location. I'll be there a day before to set up, and the day after the opening, I'll fly home again."

"Aren't you going to make the trip out to Plenty River?"

"No. There's no point. I've asked Jenny to come to the opening, so that's all I need. I have no intentions of catching up with my father."

"Okay. That side of your life is up to you. I'll miss you."

155

"Me too."

Later that day, she reviewed their conversation. *How did I manage to let this caring person into my life? It wasn't like me at all.* If she were honest, Chris wasn't the sort of man to whom she was normally attracted, but she was glad she had been on this occasion. Life was working out just fine.

Jenny drove into Alice the day before the opening and met Melissa's plane. The two women exchanged an emotional hug.

"Have you lost weight? I hope you're eating properly in the big city."

"Of course, I am and it's good to see you too! Ooh, it's so nice to smell the fresh air again. I love living in Sydney but it's great to be back."

"I've missed you, Missy. Do you want to go to the town house now or straight to the Cultural Centre?"

"If it's okay by you, I'd love to go to the Centre first. I've been on tenterhooks wondering how well everything travelled. Once I've supervised the display, I can start to relax. I know Belinda will have matters well in hand, but you know me…"

"Yes, I do. I thought you might say that. We'll go there first and then we'll find a nice coffee shop and you can fill me in on all the news. I want to know everything."

When Jenny and Melissa arrived, they found the prints were already hanging, and Belinda was in the process of supervising the display of Myah and Warwick's work. The two artists were relying on Melissa to ensure that their pieces were well presented, but Belinda had that task under control.

They ran through the check lists of what needed to be done and basically it was all taken care of. Invitations had been sent, flowers ordered, catering organised.

"Belinda, you're a marvel. You've carried out all my instructions to the letter." Melissa was relieved.

"It's okay Melissa. I've done this a few times before, you know."

"And you're brilliant at it. Thanks for all your help." She applied a coercive smile. "There is one more thing I'd like you to do. Stand over there."

"Why?"

"I'm taking your photo, that's why. I'm a photographer in case you haven't noticed and that's what I do. Jenny, you too. I want a record of the people who've made this possible."

There was some prerequisite grumbling, but the two women did as directed after patting a few stray hairs into place, and sucking in bits they felt were too wobbly. In supporting Melissa, they were more than happy to oblige.

It might have been her second event, but there was still that familiar unsettled feeling in the pit of her stomach as the first of the guests started to wander in the following evening. Melissa knew many of them and stood just inside the entrance doing meet and greet duty. Some of the invitees were on Belinda's regular mailing list and probably some people had seen the event advertised and had decided independently to come along. The crowd was a good mix.

She overheard some interesting comments from people who didn't know her and didn't realise that she was in hearing range.

"… yes, local girl—sort of … never saw much of her … did you hear about the mother? … very sad really … she's always been distant, you know? … never liked to mix much with town people … thought she was a cut above us I think."

It was interesting to know how people perceived her. She couldn't dwell on it for long as there were people to greet, cheeks to kiss and polite conversation to be made. She mingled, conscious of the comment that she didn't mix much. True, she hadn't while growing up but there hadn't been much opportunity either. Plus, she'd been incredibly shy.

Kathy was sporting a baby bump when she and Alex showed up. The two women were polite but reserved with each other. With their history, they were never going to be bosom buddies. Knowing she had Chris at her back allowed Melissa to be uncharacteristically expansive.

"How good to see you both, especially under the circumstances. Are you still flying Kathy?"

"I am while I can fit behind the controls and have medical clearance. I don't flaunt my condition though. Some of the passengers find it challenging enough dealing with a female pilot let alone having the aircraft under the control of someone they think is about to go into labour at any moment."

It was Alex's turn to greet her. As she raised her face for his kiss, she took in the appearance and demeanour that used to make her heart miss a beat. She was still attracted to him— he was an appealing man after all—but with a jolt she realised the pain had abated. There wasn't the anguish there had been

158

in the past. As the couple moved on to do their tour of the prints, she had an overwhelming desire to speak to Chris. There was still time before the official business started. She could squeeze in a quick call. She dashed to the privacy of Belinda's office.

"Hey sweetheart. I thought the exhibition was on now?"

"It is. People are coming through the door. I just wanted to quickly hear your voice before it all gets too crazy."

"Crazy in a good way, I hope. You'll slay 'em, kid."

"I like your confidence."

In the background, she heard a woman laugh.

"Where are you? Is someone else with you?"

"Only Lexie. I had to take her and the film crew to do an interview up in Newcastle and it was a long, drawn-out day. We stopped off for a coffee after finishing up. I'll say hello to her for you, shall I?"

"Yes, do that."

As she hung up, Melissa felt that familiar ache in the pit of her stomach. It was happening again. Just when she let her guard down, life turned around and bit her where it hurt most. Would Chris be the next one to let her down?

CHAPTER 12

MELISSA'S FEARS OF failure and rejection in her home town were unfounded. The exhibition was a creditable success. The fact it coincided with school holidays meant there were a steady stream of tourists visiting the Arts Centre in the days following the event, and quite a few departed with mementos of their visit to the region. Arrangements were also made to post prints overseas to some of the international visitors.

She decided she would stick with the name Lyssa in the professional sphere. Initially chosen as a shield she could hide behind, it gradually grew on her. Melissa Gilbert had baggage and a reputation that wasn't always complimentary—in Alice at least. She knew her nature was often perceived as being aloof and condescending, rather than shy and inadequate which was what she really felt. As Lyssa, she could be a different person, someone who wasn't in her father's shadow and wasn't responsible for the deaths of her family. She was free to be herself.

Jenny and Belinda both provided her with post exhibition updates over the phone.

"They were impressed Missy. Tom Daly from Jinka Station even dropped in and I've never known him to visit a gallery before. Everyone told him about his photo taken at the Harts Range Race Weekend, so curiosity got the better of him. There was a good review in the Centralian Advocate, and I cut that out for you."

"Great, and I didn't even have to pay them!"

"What?"

"Just joking. Of course, I don't pay for reviews. The readership of the paper isn't huge, but I'm relieved they didn't slate it just the same."

"Your father liked it too. He was in town for a medical appointment in the week after the opening so dropped in to have a look for himself."

"It's a free country so I can't stop him from attending. Did he have any comments?"

"I thought you didn't care about your father's opinions?"

"I don't care. I just wondered, that's all."

"For your information, he was impressed. He thought from a conservation perspective that some of the photos were very important."

"Conservation!" She hadn't expected that comment. It didn't equate with her understanding of her father's conservative views.

"Your father cares about this country Missy. If you don't know that by now, you should."

The conversation with Belinda was on more practical matters.

161

"I think Myah and Warwick should be pleased. The jewellery was a big hit with the international tourists as it's light and portable. We had steady sales of Warwick's pieces as well. If they're happy to leave the remainder here, we should sell it progressively for them."

"I'm sure they'll prefer that to the hassle of shipping it back to Sydney. I'll let them know."

"And as I predicted, your work was very well received. We even had a group of photography students from Alice Springs High School come through on the last day. Their teacher was using it for illustrative purposes, showcasing technique, framing, subject matter, and the like."

"Wow. That was something I didn't expect. It's probably the biggest compliment."

As she reported later to Chris, she never expected her work to be held up as an example. "I'll be really conscious of that in future."

"So, you're planning future exhibitions then?"

"No... no I'm not, but then I didn't plan these last two either. They sort of happened in spite of me."

They had caught up for a meal—a cheap and cheerful noodle soup at one of the local Thai restaurants.

Melissa expected the issue of searching for a unit to be raised, and she agonised over her feelings. It was difficult to quell the voice of doubt that was trying to assert itself. Ever since hearing Lexie's voice in the background of that phone call, she had been fighting the urge to cut and run. She knew it was a silly reaction—it had only been a work thing—so why did she feel so threatened? It wasn't rational.

"You're quiet tonight sweetheart. Is everything okay?" Chris tore basil leaves from their stems and sprinkled them over the surface of his soup.

"Sure. Aside from trying to work out how to eat my noodles elegantly, I'm in the let-down phase. Just tired, that's all." She carefully blotted around her mouth with the serviette.

Chris nodded. "I'm not surprised. It's been a busy time. Great it was successful. You'll be making a name for yourself."

"I don't think I can give up my day job just yet. Speaking of which, I've got some studio work to do over the next few days, and then I have a quick overnighter in the Blue Mountains. I'm doing a shoot with Eduardo."

"My non-favourite person! Is Angela going too?"

"Yes; we'll drive up together. She was the location scout on this job and is overseeing logistics for the event. Usual thing. What's coming up for you?"

"More of the same, I think. Morning traffic reports, picking up the boss, carting the crew around. It depends really on where the news happens and who needs to be there."

"You seem to be happy in the job. Any regrets about leaving Alice?"

"I miss the people of course, but no—it's been great to have a change in direction and I've met some of the rich and famous. That's always interesting, seeing what they're like in person. I'm working with a supportive group of people and that helps."

Melissa placed her chopsticks carefully across the bowl, contemplating her choice of words. "It's good you've

163

developed that connection. Bruce was able to pave the way of course, but Lexie seems a really nice person."

"Yeah. I've been watching her. She's so good at her job. She does her homework and asks all the right questions. She comes across as all demure but underneath there's a sharp intellect. I've seen people—mostly men, I have to say—underestimate her based on her gender or her physical appeal and not comprehending she's reeling them in before aiming for the jugular. She's amazing."

"Makes a habit of reeling people in, does she?"

"Not unless the situation warrants it. She does all the good news stories too. She's a pro; she handles whatever the day throws at her."

Everything Chris said was reasonable. Lexie was experienced and professional. She wouldn't have lasted in her industry if she wasn't. It had been good of her to attend the opening and to buy one of Myah's pieces. Get over it. After all, Chris was going home with her, not Lexie.

They crept into the Annandale terrace quietly, not wanting to disturb Angela who was already asleep. With unspoken agreement, they headed straight for her bedroom. She had missed him. It had been a long time between drinks.

Chris was in no hurry. He seemed to sense her need for reassurance and kissed her gently, massaging her shoulders. After a long and demanding day, she carried the stress in those muscles. His magic fingers brought blissful results. Melissa moaned in soft ecstasy as Chris worked on the knots, kneading and teasing them into compliance.

"You're wasted as a pilot," she muttered into the pillow. "You should be a masseur. Come to think of it, I like having my personal masseur, available at my command."

"Why don't you roll over?" he whispered seductively. "There's a lot more of you that might respond to my touch."

She thought about it for all of half a second and then rolled over. He was right. It was amazing how well she slept that night. She stretched leisurely in the morning, feeling the warmth of Chris's body pressed along hers. A soft snuffle indicated he still slept. Raising herself on one elbow, she looked at him. The movement disturbed the sheet and exposed his chest. It was covered in soft golden hairs, and she had a sudden urge to run her fingers through them. The hair on his head had a scruffy, little boy look and his lashes fanned across his cheeks with amazing delicacy.

It was almost voyeuristic to watch him like this when he was at his most vulnerable. He wasn't the man she expected to end up with and she couldn't help wondering if Alex would have put her needs first as often Chris had done for her. Realistically not. There would have been the implicit expectation that her life would revolve around his and station life. Now she could review the prospect from a distance, she realised she didn't want to spend her life baking scones for station hands, or to sublimate her needs to the vagaries of station fortunes and cattle prices. She wanted so much more.

Melissa and Angela drove up the highway leading to the Mountains on a crisp, clear morning. With the radio tuned to popular music, they sang along, unrestrained by the need to be in tune or to know all the words. It made the early start more tolerable.

They were first on site, allowing time to review the location before the minibus and support vehicles arrived carrying the models and crew. Angela had seen it before of course as she did the location work and negotiated conditions of access.

Eduardo sprang out of the lead vehicle. He strutted around checking the location and muttering under his breath. The others exchanged glances. He was always like this at the start of a shoot.

"Right everybody—synchronise your watches. I want you all though hair and make-up in record time today. We'll do what we can this afternoon and then the rest in the morning."

"Eddie sweetie," Angela said, taking him by the arm and drawing him to one side. "Come and look at the location options I've chosen while the others get themselves unpacked and organised."

Appreciative glances were thrown her way as the crew scattered to make their preparations. The location was a grand homestead with rolling gardens, one of the first in the area. Melissa admired it briefly and then turned attention to her equipment and getting set up. She would have time later to explore and perhaps photograph her surrounds. The views were stunning.

Despite Eduardo's opening histrionics, the afternoon went well. The weather held out and there were no major incidents, at least none that couldn't easily be handled. There was even time for Angela and Melissa to explore the local village and indulge in coffee and a pastry before checking into their motel. They found a café featuring home-baked treats and with a free table in the sunshine.

"I don't know how you manage to keep that figure of yours," Angela grumbled. "It must be all the nervous energy. You just burn it up."

"I'm not nervous!"

"I didn't say you were. It's just you never seem to sit still for very long. Whenever you've got something on your mind, you pace the house. I always know when there's an issue. If it were me, I would retreat to a comfy chair with a block of chocolate."

"It might be the block of chocolate that makes the difference."

"I suspect you're right," Angela laughed wryly, her face becoming more serious. "You've been twitchy since you got back from Alice. Is everything okay? I thought you'd be basking in the glory of it all."

"Oh, I'm pleased with how everything has worked out. The exhibitions were more successful than I expected so they've been a tremendous confidence boost."

The waitress brought the order to their table, and they paused until she left again.

"So, what's eating you then?"

"You'll think I'm being silly."

"You, silly? Never. Spill."

"Chris works with Lexie Ferguson. They spend quite a bit of time together."

"Yes, I saw she came to the exhibition. That was fantastic, wasn't it?"

"Yes, but then when I spoke on the phone to Chris from Alice, Lexie was in the background. They were having a coffee after finishing up for the day."

"You don't seriously think there's anything between them, do you? Chris is bonkers about you."

"You think so? I need to know I can rely on him, Angela. If he lets me down, I'm not sure how I'd cope."

"But he and Lexie are colleagues. It's no different to you and Eddie having a meal after a shoot, which you do all the time. You can't expect the situation to be different for Chris and his workmates."

"Of course, you're right. It's silly. It's just something I'm hypersensitive about." Incredibly silly. Melissa told herself that again as she nibbled at her pastry. The afternoon was too nice to be side-tracked by paranoid thoughts.

&

Voicing her fears diminished them. As she stepped under the shower after checking into her room, Melissa felt the streaming water washing away the stress and self-doubt. It was blissful relief. She knew she had to learn to trust. In this instance, she had been working herself up over nothing. By the time she towelled herself dry, she had resolved to start looking for an apartment on her return to Sydney.

Making her way into the dining room, she felt refreshed. It was a casual affair, so a blue-lilac tunic over skinny white pants was adequate in the dress department. The crew spread themselves over two tables in the dining room. Angela, Eduardo and Melissa sat in a quiet corner, leaving the models and the hair and make-up people to another larger table. They tended to be noisier and talked about people Melissa didn't know. She was happy to leave them to it.

"Anything special on the agenda for tomorrow, Eddie?" If they had been at the table with the others, Melissa would have called him Eduardo

"More of the same, Mellie. There are a few more outside shots I'd like to do, especially down by the lake but that staircase inside will be a fabulous backdrop."

"Sure. Stairs can be tricky with lighting and choreography, but I'll see what I can do."

"You'll do brilliantly. You always do. Speaking of which, have I mentioned Ibiza to you?"

"Not to my recall. What about Ibiza?"

"I've been asked by the House of Rubens to produce the content for next season's promotions and the specified location is Ibiza. How about you come and do the photography?"

She was rendered momentarily speechless. Did he really suggest she go to Ibiza? "Are you for real?"

His expression was earnest. "I'd be so much happier with someone I knew. I know that I can rely on you to produce work that will meet or exceed the client's expectations. We'd be away about ten days."

"When is this supposed to happen? I'll have to see what else I've got on."

"Melissa!" Angela remonstrated. "This is a fantastic opportunity. Now is not the time to prevaricate. Clear your diary and go. Think what this will do for your portfolio, plus—

Emily Hussey

it's Ibiza! When else are you going to have a tax-deductible holiday there?"

"You're probably right—as usual. Eddie, can I think about it overnight and give you a decision in the morning? I'll check a couple of things in the meantime."

"Sure. Get back to me. If you're not available, I'm sure that Jason Lombardi could free up his calendar."

"Eddie, if you think Jason Lombardi might be better than me, I won't stand in your way. He doesn't have fashion experience, but after all, he does have a way with the ladies." She smiled sweetly.

Eddie just rolled his eyes. "Don't give me a hard time, Mellie. Get back to me asap—okay? This one's a rush job. Another team were booked but there's been a visa complication and they've had to cancel. We're stepping in at the last minute."

"Surely you need a location scout as well?" Angela asked. "I can clear my diary, no problem."

"Leave it with me, Ange," said Eddie. "We probably do, but I need to speak to the client first."

She squealed with delight. "If anyone can swing it, you can. Ibiza, here I come."

Melissa and Eddie's eyes met, and he shrugged. She knew Angela wouldn't let up until her name was added to the team.

Melissa's head buzzed with the possibilities. There was nothing stopping her from going. She had a few commitments but nothing major. She wanted to discuss it with Chris first. She'd become so used to him being a sounding board that for a big decision like this, it felt a logical thing to do.

170

Angela and Eddie were ready for a nightcap, but as soon as she could politely do so, Melissa excused herself and hurried back to her room. She put a call through to Chris.

"Hi Sweetheart. How did your day go?" he asked.

"Fine. It's a beautiful location. We should spend a couple of days here when we can coordinate some free time in our diaries."

"Can't think of anything I'd enjoy more."

"Speaking of going away, I've been offered a contract on Ibiza. It would mean being away for a week or so—perhaps more. We haven't discussed the finer details yet."

"Ibiza? But that's…"

"Off the coast of Spain, yes."

She paused, listening to a faint background conversation that the phone was picking up. A woman's voice was foremost.

"Who's with you?"

"It's a work thing. Lexie had to attend a work promo event and Harrison Fletcher, her on-air partner wasn't available, so she asked if I'd accompany her instead.

Her thoughts tumbled, an assault on her comprehension. The image of him attending an A-lister function with Lexie on his arm was not welcome. "You've gone to a station promo as Lexie Ferguson's partner?"

"Yes, but it's not…"

"It hasn't taken you long to adapt to city life," she interrupted bitterly, "and all the side benefits with it. I might have known you'd be no different. If you're looking for me, I'll be in Ibiza. Or in Barcelona. Or wherever."

"Melissa!"

She slammed the phone down. She wouldn't hang around to be humiliated a second time. There was no need to wait until morning to give Eddie her answer. Her mind was made up.

CHAPTER 13

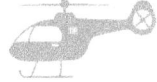

THE SEA WAS an incredibly beautiful shade of azure. As Melissa soon learned, the Island was all about beach culture—beautiful beaches and beautiful bodies. She was glad not to be paying for accommodation, which was at peak tourist prices. She couldn't have placed herself further from Plenty River if she'd tried.

She liked observing human behaviour and found plenty to keep herself and Angela occupied when not working. They had a rental car at their disposal and managed to leave the prime tourist spots behind as they explored the rest of the island. They explored D'Alt Vila (the Old Town) on foot, as necessitated by the cobbled roads. The early history fascinated her.

The team often met in the hotel bar after dinner. Angela progressively worked her way through the cocktails on offer, trying something different each evening. Of course, it could have had something to do with the alluring Spaniard who made them. He worked in the bar most days and was as practiced in flirting with the female customers as he was at mixing a mean martini.

"I don't know why it is," Angela said as she sipped her strawberry daiquiri, "but this tastes so much better than back in Australia. I can't decide if it's the local strawberries or the magical touch behind the bar."

"Hmm. Perhaps both. I don't know really." Melissa slumped back in her chair, massaging her brow. She'd hardly touched her own drink.

"Are you okay?" Angela asked. "Are you missing Chris? You seem quiet this evening."

"Not at all," Melissa lied. "It wasn't really working out. You'll have to know some time so I may as well tell you now. It's over."

"What! How come? I thought you two were a perfect match."

Yeah, so did I. How could I be so wrong? She gave Angela a synopsis of what had happened.

"Give him a chance, Melissa. If you want to drive him into some other woman's arms, you're going the right way about it."

Melissa's lips quivered with barely suppressed fury and indignation. Not many people would have seen this side to her. "Angela, I will not tolerate being second best or any suggestion that my trust has been misplaced. I will not be abandoned again."

"If you don't mind my saying so, you sound like your father's daughter."

"Well, perhaps I am."

There was an uncomfortable silence and Angela wisely changed the subject. "I need to discuss some aspects of tomorrow's shoot with Eddie. I'll just grab his attention before he drifts back to his room."

Seeing Melissa on her own, with a pretence of wiping down the bar, the barman stopped in front of her, cloth in hand. "So, senorita—your friends have left you by yourself. A beautiful woman like you should not be alone in Ibiza Town."

"Are you saying it's not safe?"

"No, no—not at all. If you are with someone who knows their way around, it is perfectly safe. I would not go walking outside by yourself at night. The men, they would be overcome by your beauty."

Melissa laughed. "That's okay. I wasn't planning on going anywhere."

"But why not? You cannot leave Ibiza without exploring the night life. I know all the best places." The low-lidded look he gave her smouldered, and unexpectedly she felt the heat. Looking into those dark pools of intensity regaling her, she almost melted.

He reached across the bar to take her hand. "I am Mateo. Soon, my work here will be finished. Come with me. I will show you a fabulous time and we can dance until the sun comes up."

Why not? What do I have to lose? When else will I can spend the night with a hot Spaniard?

His thumb brushed a circle on the back of her hand causing electric tingles to radiate up her arm. At that point, a man at the other end of the bar rapped on the counter, calling for service.

175

"Mierda," Mateo muttered. "Senorita, I will return." He released her hand and moved down the bar to take the man's order.

Mierda indeed. What was I thinking? The spell broken, Melissa slipped off her stook and headed for the door. An image of Chris came to mind and was quickly repressed. She didn't need anyone, and she particularly didn't need Mateo. It was safer that way.

"Hola, Signorina, there is a message for you."

Melissa took the note from the hotel receptionist and scanned it.

Melissa, please call ASAP. Chris

She screwed it up and gave it back to the woman at the desk. "Could you put this in the bin, please?"

She headed to her room to finish her packing. The contract was over, and she'd just slipped out to make a last-minute purchase for Jenny. Rather than return to Sydney immediately, she'd decided to make the most of the long journey from Australia and do some sight-seeing while she could. First stop was Barcelona and then she would roughly follow the coast of the Mediterranean, travelling north to Montpellier, Marseille and Cannes in France. She would make a small stop in Monte Carlo, just so she could say she had been to the Casino as much as anything. From there, her journey would take her into Italy and the cities of Genoa and Milan. After that, she wasn't sure. Probably down to Rome and then to catch a flight home. The idea of not being fixed to an itinerary was appealing. It was a hedonistic freedom she hadn't experienced before.

They were all checking out that day, but most of the crew were flying back to Australia. She returned her key to reception and joined Eddie under the portico at the front of the hotel. They had agreed to share a cab to Aeroport d'Eivissa. Angela had taken an earlier flight as she had a work commitment back in Sydney.

"Signorina! Wait, signorina. There is a phone call for you."

She hesitated at the door of the cab. Her luggage was already stowed in the boot.

"Take it, Mellie." Eddie said. "I can hold the taxi. We're not rushed for time."

At a reasonable guess, it would be Chris. He might try to persuade her to come home and she wasn't ready to do that. She didn't want to be talked out of her Mediterranean tour. She wasn't ready to talk to him either.

"Tell him I've gone. You weren't able to catch me."

The receptionist didn't look surprised. Probably guests in this hotel often manipulated their situations to suit themselves.

Eddie was the one who looked at her in confusion. "Was that Chris? I thought you two were tight."

"Yeah, we were. Sometimes things change. Shall we go?"

"Sure thing, ma'am," said Eddie. "Get in then. Tell me again—where are you going?"

"Following my nose really. Just going walkabout along the Riviera. Who knows where I'll end up?"

"You're not going to run out on me, are you? Having a break is all very well, but I expect you back in Australia. I

177

wouldn't have brought you over here if I thought you weren't coming back."

"Of course, I'll come back. I just need some time out. If I don't come back, you'll have to call on Jason Lombardi."

"Petal, don't you dare. Jason Lombardi will never understand me like you do."

"I dare say he won't. The two of you are prima donnas. There would be the most god-awful rows between you both. It's almost worth staying away just to see what happens."

"Insolent woman! I'm envious but I have commitments back home. I had a fabulous time when I explored that region a couple of years ago. If you get to Monte Carlo, you might like to stay at Villa des Fleurs. It's a bed-and-breakfast on the coast and is a welcome change from both major hotels and budget accommodation. The views over the sea are fabulous and you can take your breakfast on the terrace, pretending for a while that this is how you always live. Madame Sabine is a real gem and a wonderful host. She can give you tips on where to go and what to see."

"Thanks for that. I'll keep it in mind."

They shared a flight to Barcelona, and then parted ways. Eddie travelled back to Australia and Melissa spent a few days in the Spanish city before heading up the coast. Her initial thought had been to hire a car, but on realising that train travel was an option, decided on that instead. It meant she didn't have the task of navigating and driving and dealing with the complexities of driving on the wrong side of the road.

To be travelling through the Riviera was so exciting. It would have been a fabulous itinerary for a honeymoon, or at least with a companion. She experienced a pang of loneliness
178

and in that instant, wished Chris had been able to accompany her. Even Jenny would have been good. It was a while since she had spoken to her favourite person and Melissa missed her sorely.

Her first stop was at the local post office where, after checking the time difference, she was able to place a call through to Plenty River. It was so far away. It seemed bizarre that a simple phone connection could reach her childhood home. Jenny's clipped tones responded on the message bank.

Nobody is available to take your call. Please leave a message and your call will be returned as soon as possible.

It was disappointing but not unusual. Jenny and her father could be anywhere on the property, or even in Alice Springs. Melissa left a brief message.

"Hi Jenny. It's me. Would you believe, I'm heading for France. Wish you were here with me. I'd love to share the experience. I'll call you again when I can. Byee."

Of course, Jenny wasn't the only companion with whom she could have shared this journey. Her thoughts strayed to Chris as the train carried her north. It would have been so special to explore this area with someone close. Just thinking of him brought a tightness to her chest.

The city of Montpelier combined the old and the new. She wandered the lanes, and a couple of museums and galleries, absorbing a sense of the local history. Her French was minimal, based on very rusty school lessons but she could read and understand most of the directional signs. Grasping the spoken word was more challenging but sign language went a long way. When things became too confusing, she retreated to a café and took stock over a coffee and a small pastry. She fell back on her personal mantra. *I can do this on my own. I don't have to rely on anyone.*

Familiar accents caught her attention on the train between Montpelier and Marseille. The two young women in her carriage were clearly Australian. The flag emblems on their backpacks would have told her that if she hadn't been able to hear them. One of the women caught her eye and smiled.

"Hi. We heard you muttering to yourself earlier. You sound like an Aussie. I'm Diana and this is Emily. We're doing our version of a grand European tour."

"You've guessed right. I'm glad it was the accent and not any ockerish behaviour that gave me away. You've chosen a lovely part of the world for your tour."

"Fabulous, isn't it? We're loving the scenery and the food, and just everything." She winked. "And even some of the men. Are you travelling alone? Why don't you join us?"

It turned out that Diana and Emily were also headed for Marseille and Melissa was grateful to have the company. They had already researched suitable accommodation and had information on what to see during their stay.

"We've booked ahead in a small boutique hotel. Why don't you see if there's another room available? We can share a cab from the station."

Accommodation was quickly sorted on arrival and they shared an evening meal at a small bistro in the Old Port area. The sounds of the harbour could be heard from the restaurant and the seafood on the menu was said to be obtained from the boats and served fresh. They dined by candle-light, and the waiter judiciously flirted with each of them. They sipped their wine, watching other tourists and locals who were either dining or walking by.

"I can't think of anywhere I'd rather be," drooled Diana as she caught the eye of a passing example of Gallic masculinity. "Has anyone tried a French lover?"

It was a rhetorical question and Emily rolled her eyes and raised her shoulders in an open-palmed gesture as though to say, "You see what I have to put up with?"

"So, what's brought you to this corner of the world?" Emily asked instead.

"I'm a fashion photographer. I had a photographic assignment on Ibiza and decided that given I was already so far from home, I should take advantage of the opportunity to see more of this region. I don't know when I'll have the opportunity to come back."

Emily's eyes widened in admiration. "That's a cool job. You must have some fabulous experiences, and of course you would meet some gorgeous men on a regular basis."

Melissa thought briefly of the men she knew in the industry and laughed. "They are all either self-absorbed, prima donnas, gay or already taken. There are some great friends amongst them but none that classify as relationship material."

"So, there's nobody special in your life?"

Melissa's pause was telling. She looked away, avoiding eye contact. "Not really."

She caught their glance at each other, eyebrows raised in doubt.

Emily Hussey

"Well there was, but I thought he was two-timing me while I was away from Sydney on a contract."

"And was he?" Diana looked sympathetic.

"Well… I wasn't absolutely sure, but I wasn't prepared to take the chance. I've been let down before and was determined it wasn't going to happen again."

"So you walked out based on a suspicion? Wow, you're one tough, uncompromising woman."

Melissa flushed uncomfortably. She had only mentioned it to Emily and Diana because they were so far from home and she probably wouldn't see them again after these few days. Explaining the situation to somebody who didn't know her did make her flight appear an over-reaction.

"Like many things, it's complicated. What are your plans for tomorrow?"

The women took the hint and discussion turned instead to potential tours that they could take. They decided to have breakfast in the markets in Canebière before signing up for a guided tour of the highlights of the town. Marseille had a gritty energy, based not only on its history but the contribution of migration from neighbouring countries and northern Africa. There was a lot to see but the tour would give them a taste for the areas that they may like to explore in greater detail.

The following evening, Melissa tried to call Plenty River again, but once more only reached the message bank. It was disappointing, but hopefully she would catch someone home on the next call. She longed to give an update on her travels. She had sent some postcards, but it would be ages before they reached their destination.

She spent the next day exploring galleries, and another evening with her new friends, before setting off via train the next morning for Cannes. Diana and Emily were staying longer in Marseille, but they promised to stay in touch after they all returned to Australia.

Cannes was a totally different experience. It was an intriguing mix of old and new. Melissa expected it to be full of the beautiful and the glamorous, and it was. She explored on foot, looking at the mix of private and public beaches, and the impressive boats in the harbour. She felt very much the voyeur, somehow naked without the protection of her camera lens, though she did take some pictures. It made her realize how much she used the camera as a protective barrier against the world.

Watching all the couples was an odd feeling. Everywhere she looked, there was evidence of togetherness. There were couples in cafes, strolling down the boulevards, occupying adjacent sun-lounges on the beach. She put them from her mind. What she was going to do was go for a swim. She would be able to say she had been bathing on the French Riviera with all the beautiful people.

Melissa was pleased she'd brought a swimming costume and wrap with her. She was able to hire a towel on the beach, along with the sun lounge and a sunshade. What she really wanted was a cocktail with a decorative umbrella and cherry hanging off the edge, and someone to take her photo. One of those 'wish you were here shots'. As it wasn't a private beach with full waiter service provided, the cocktail was out of the question, but she did manage to buy a bottled drink from a beachside kiosk and persuaded another tourist to take her photo. That would have to do.

It was only a short bus ride from Cannes to Monaco, so she opted for travelling by road instead of by rail. It gave her more opportunity to see the coast. She followed Eddie's advice and booked in advance at Villa des Fleurs, successfully using her school-girl French to converse with Madame Sabine. The attraction in Monaco was principally the Casino but she also wanted to see the tomb of Princess Grace. She and Prince Rainier had been interred in the Saint Nicholas Cathedral, where they had been married many years before. The princess had been an intriguing woman, with an impeccable sense of style. Now she was here, Melissa thought she ought to pay her respects. That was on the agenda for the following day.

Her immediate task was to find a cab, then find the Villa and check in. She wanted to offload her luggage, and to think about what she would wear that evening. Perhaps she could slip back into the main part of town and cruise the shops for some hopefully inexpensive glamour.

The Villa was everything she'd hoped. Positioned on a hillside, it had fabulous views over the Ligurian Sea. A terrace extended to the front of the white building, framed in burgundy bougainvillea. A kidney-shaped pool sat one level lower than the terrace. She was glad she hadn't opted for a cheap pensione in perhaps a noisier part of town.

As she paid the taxi driver, a woman came out of the house, no doubt having heard the approach of the vehicle.

"Mam'selle Gilbert?" She extended her hand.

"Please, call me Melissa. You must be Madame Sabine.'

"Welcome to my 'ome. Please to com' inside. Le soleil is so 'ot."

Picking up her suitcase, Melissa followed her host into the cool of the lobby area. It was elegantly furnished. As she produced her passport and completed the formalities, Sabine handed her a note.

"Zis man, he rang and left ze message for you. Please to call 'im immédiatement."

Melissa unfolded the paper and read the words. It didn't make sense. Why was he calling her here? How did he know where to call?

Urgent. Call as soon as you get this. Chris.

He gave a phone number and that really puzzled her. It was the number to Plenty River.

Jenny. Something must have happened to Jenny.

"Madame Sabine, may I make a telephone call and add the charges to my account?"

"Mais oui. Le téléphone is through here."

Madame Sabine showed Melissa to the alcove in which the phone was located and discretely withdrew.

This time, the call was picked up on the second ring. Chris answered.

"Melissa! You got the message."

There was an echo on the line and a slight delay, making conversation difficult.

"Chris—what are you doing there? Is Jenny okay?"

"Jenny's fine. She's in Alice. It's your father I'm calling about. He's had a stroke. Melissa, you have to come home."

Chapter 14

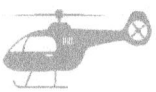

MELISSA PUT DOWN the phone and looked out over the bay. The blue sea and the white yachts framed by the colourful bougainvillea over the deck presented a stunning sight. It wasn't the same as home though. The pang caught her by surprise. She missed the smell of the bush, the call of the crows and the strong Australian colours. She missed her mare Cleo. It was so long since they'd been riding together. She hadn't expected to be homesick, but she was; not just for Australia but for Plenty River.

Melissa consulted Madame Sabine on how she might connect with an international flight, fighting the emotions that threatened to overwhelm. If only she had responded to Chris's message in Ibiza or taken his call, she would have known of her father's condition days earlier. It hadn't occurred to her that anything like this could happen. When she'd last seen him, he'd looked fighting fit. She'd always thought of him as indestructible.

She would have to travel to the airport in Nice and from there fly to a major city and then pick up a flight to Australia. With Madame Sabine's help, she located a travel agent and booked the flights. She could fly to Dubai and get a connecting flight to Sydney. After that, it was a case of organising a local flight to Alice Springs. It wasn't possible to leave for another day.

"What a catastrophe! Your poor father. Come; you sit on ze terrace and I bring you a cup of coffee. Per'aps you prefer ze cup of tea?"

"Madame Sabine, a cup of tea would be perfect. You've been so kind."

It was good just to sit for a while and take stock. She hadn't had any down time since leaving Australia. Her heart wasn't in sightseeing, but she had nothing else to do and hours to kill—hours she didn't want to spend worrying. She would still like to visit the Cathedral and Princess Grace. Madame Sabine had given her directions.

She needed to call Chris again. If she did that before visiting the cathedral, it would ease some of the worries. She wanted an update on her father's condition and there were a few other questions Chris needed to answer. Like what was he doing at Plenty River and how had he known where to contact her. Fortunately, the line was clearer this time. She missed that smile. She missed him. She pictured Chris in her father's study. It was not somewhere she had ever expected to find him. Nor she suspected had her father.

"How is he?"

"Not good, but stable. There have been some signs of improvement, but it will be a while before the long-term

187

effects are known. He's paralysed down one side. His speech is not coherent, but he seems to understand what's said."

"You know my father—he doesn't tolerate less than one hundred percent effort from anyone, and that attitude applies to himself as well. If he survives this, he'll be fighting to get back home again and back onto Caesar. He won't just lie back and accept it."

"I don't know him as well as you, but I suspect you're right."

"So, tell me again—I didn't take it all in before—how did you know where to find me?"

"It's a round-about story. When Jenny found your father, he was in a bad way. They were a long way from medical help. She rang the Flying Doctor, who flew out and gave immediate treatment before bringing your dad back to hospital in Alice."

Melissa could imagine the anxiety Jenny must have experienced. She must have felt so alone. "Thank God for the Flying Doctor Service. Dad has always donated to their fund raisers, and it seems with good cause."

"I reckon. Alex Woodleigh heard the radio chatter and he flew over to Plenty River to see what he could do, arriving just before the medical crew. Jenny accompanied your dad in the aircraft, but before she left, she asked Alex if he could contact you. He managed to track down Angela via a number that Jenny gave him. Angela gave him my number. I tried contacting you on Ibiza, but you must have already left."

"Umm, yes—I guess I must have." She didn't want to own up to ignoring him. It now seemed an incredibly petty thing to do. "I've been to lots of places since Ibiza. How did you know where to find me?"

"Believe it or not, I had a sudden brain wave and tracked down Eduardo. I asked Angela for his number."

"He's the last person I'd have expected you to call."

"I never thought I would have to do it," Chris agreed. "Just shows how desperate I was. He repeated his last conversation with you, and I took a punt on whether you would follow his advice. I looked up the contact details for Villa des Fleurs and left a message. Beyond that, I'd run out of ideas."

"It's a lovely place; you ought to see it. For all of five seconds I was able to pretend I was living the life of the rich and famous. It's still going to be a couple of days before I can get all the connecting flights and get back to Alice, but I'll be leaving here early tomorrow morning. You still haven't explained why you're in Plenty River and not flying for Channel Nine in Sydney."

"Alex gave me a contact number for Jenny, so I rang her to let her know that I was tracking you down. She said there was another muster about to start and she knew your father would be fretting about it. It seemed like an opportunity to help out and get some country air back into my lungs. I took some leave and here I am."

To say she was astonished was an understatement. This was her family's problem. She didn't expect Chris to be involved. Their relationship was, or rather had been, quite separate to her family affairs and it had ended so abruptly. To have somebody go out of their way to this extent was surprising. It was in keeping with what she had come to know of Chris.

"I'm sure my father will compensate you for your time," she said awkwardly.

"Do you honestly think I was looking for compensation? Melissa, what sort of person do you think I am?"

"I'm sorry; I didn't mean to be offensive. I just don't want you to be out of pocket."

"Sometimes Melissa, people help each other simply because they see help is needed. When I got here, I found Pete had things more or less under control, but he appreciated some extra support. I'll hang around here until you arrive and then I'll get out of your hair."

There was a strained silence. *Damn. I messed that one up. Now he'll think I'm treating him like the hired help again.* She bit her bottom lip, not knowing how to retrieve the situation. "I'm on the house phone, so I need to go. I'll let you know when I expect to arrive in Alice. Give Jenny my love."

"And your father?"

"Just tell him I'm coming home."

Something kept her from adding anything personal for Chris. The words stuck in her throat.

Have I made a fool of myself coming back to help? That was a weird comment. The Gilbert family could be autocratic in their dealings with contractors, but this was him, not some stranger. Did she really doubt his motivations? Melissa and her father were more alike than she realised. This trip back to Alice had been a welcome break from city life, but the phone call left a sour taste in his mouth. It made him start to question some of the recent decisions he'd made.

He thought again about Mark's offer. Perhaps he'd been mad to pass that up. It might not be too late. He would store that thought away for later dissection.

"You there, Chris?" Pete had stuck his head in the kitchen door. "I'm finishing up for the day. I'll feed the horses and then be off home. Did you want to join us for tea? Tanya said to ask you."

"That would be nice, mate, if you're sure it's not too much trouble."

"She wouldn't ask if it was. Come on. Better than eatin' on your own."

You're not wrong there. This is one night when some company would be welcome. "Thanks Pete. I'll be there after I clean up."

❧

Melissa was incredibly tired but relieved on touchdown in Sydney. It felt as though she had been in the air forever. Conflicting thoughts consumed her during the flight. How would she feel if her father died before she returned to Alice? Why would it trouble her, given the fractured relationship they had? The answer she realised was that deep down, she had always hoped he would acknowledge her with respect as his daughter; that he would stop comparing her to William and blaming her for the past.

On the one hand, she was apprehensive about going back to Alice because he could die and never give her that recognition she craved. On the other hand, he might not die, and nothing would change except that his health and ability

191

might be compromised. In that situation he would be terrible to live with and she couldn't leave Jenny to deal with that.

Her relationship with Chris was an added complexity. Did he travel back to Alice because of his past contractual relationship with her father or because of his personal relationship with her? She might have over-reacted about his association with Lexie Ferguson, but she wasn't prepared to suffer the humiliation again of being rejected in favour of another woman. She wouldn't give Chris that opportunity.

First, her father had thought that as a daughter, she was not good enough. Williams's death compounded that situation. Then, Alex Woodleigh had rejected her in favour of blow-in Kathy Sullivan. It didn't matter that deep down she knew life as Alex's wife would have been stifling. The real knife in the guts came from knowing Alex preferred Kathy.

She had a short stopover in Sydney before catching the flight to Alice, long enough to exchange a suitcase full of dirty clothes for those that were clean, and to give Angela a brief synopsis on recent events. As always, her response was grounded.

"You over-think things, that's your problem. Just make the most of today and don't worry about things that might not ever happen. Did I mention I saw a photo of Lexie Ferguson in the social pages on the arm of some elite golfer? It's not my scene, but I gather he's a hot catch. Do you need a lift to the airport?"

A hot blast of air rose from the tarmac as she paused at the top of the aircraft stairs. She could see the MacDonnell Ranges in the distance and drew solace from the fact she was home, even though Plenty River was a couple of hours away.

Jenny picked her up. "Missy—am I ever glad to see you. Give me a hug. I was so worried when I didn't know how to contact you."

"I'm so sorry you've had to deal with this on your own. How is he?"

"He's tough, Missy. It would have been much worse if the delay in getting help was any longer but he's responding to treatment. I've been warned improvement will be slow and he'll need physiotherapy. It's impossible to know at this stage to what degree he'll recover."

Her etched face indicated the stress Jenny had experienced over the past week. The weight of worry had been heavy on her shoulders. Understanding this, Melissa could see she needed to take on some of that responsibility.

"You're looking tired. Let me guess; you've not had a decent night's sleep since Dad's collapse, have you? Why don't you drop me at the hospital now, and then slip back to the townhouse and have a nap or at least take some time out. Go for a walk, get a coffee or get your hair done. Get some Jenny time is what I'm saying."

"Are you sure you're all right on your own?"

"Jenny! I'm a grown woman. I think I can cope with my own father. It's not as if he's able to do much, is it? I'll be fine."

It was a lie. Her footsteps echoed as she walked down the passage towards her father's room. Part of her wanted to turn and run. She was nervous of what she might find, and what her father's illness would mean.

She opened the door and peered into the room. The figure on the bed was smaller than she remembered. His pale complexion didn't look like one that had experienced years of outdoor working either. The sight was unnerving. There were cousins she rarely saw, but her father was the only close family she had; except for Jenny of course.

"Father?"

The eyes opened, sought her out, and then closed again. Whether through disinterest or tiredness, she wasn't sure. Melissa pulled up a chair and sat by the bed.

"I've brought you some Cognac—French. From Monaco actually but it's French anyway. I've just come from there."

There was an unintelligible grunt from the bed.

"I'll take it home to Plenty River. You'll be able to drink it when you get home again. If I leave it here it might disappear."

His eyes opened again and regaled her steadily. She assumed he understood her. "I'll be in Alice for a couple of days and then I'll drive out home. I gather that there's a muster happening. Chris Harris told me. I'll check on progress and let you know how it's going."

"Missa...go...home."

He clawed at the bedcover with the effort of making himself understood, his face screwed up in concentration.

"You go home or me? I think you'll be here for a while yet, Dad. Jenny says you're making progress, so once we've got physio organised, you can hopefully get out of hospital. It might be practical if you stay at the town house for a while, but we can sort that out later."

"You … stay."

"I can't make any promises on how long I'll stay. I'll relieve Jenny and will make sure the accounts are being paid on the station and things like that. I'll ring Chris later and get an update. I think he and Pete have it under control. I'll let you know tomorrow what they have to say."

A rivulet of drool collected at the side of his mouth and began a slow progression down his chin. Melissa reached over with a tissue and wiped it away. Never before had she performed such an intimate act for her father, but never before had he been so vulnerable. His eyes closed and after a while she realised he had fallen asleep. It was time to go.

She waited until evening to call Chris, choosing a time when she knew he would be finished with the outside work. She smoothed her hair back as she waited for the call to be answered. He seemed just as far away now as he had when she was in Monaco.

"Hi. It's me. I'm in Alice."

"Welcome back, sweetheart. Have you seen your father?"

Sweetheart. He's still calling me sweetheart. "Jenny took me straight to the hospital after my flight arrived today. I didn't know what to expect, but it was a shock seeing him like that."

"I can imagine. You can tell him things are under control here. I've only just come in, actually. Pete and I brought a mob into the home paddock late afternoon."

"You must be pooped. You'll be out of practice for this type of work."

In her mind's eye, Melissa could see what he probably looked like; tired and sweaty with his hair pushed up into tousled peaks after taking his hat off and running his hands through it.

"It's been a long day, that's for sure, and tomorrow will be just as long." Even his voice sounded weary. "We've got another mob to bring in tomorrow, and others after that. Once we've got them all, we'll start trucking them into the sale yards."

"Is there anything I should tell my father tomorrow?"

"Only that it's all under control. We've done a bore run as well. No problems we can't deal with." He paused. "Pete and I have worked well together. He knows what he's doing."

"He should do. He's grown up on Plenty River. He's almost part of the furniture."

Chris sounded hesitant. "That's a strange way of putting it, but perhaps he is."

The conversation was sounding stilted. Melissa knew she was probably keeping him from a hot shower and a meal. *If I was there, I could have cooked for him.* "I won't keep you any longer. I really appreciate what you're doing for Dad, and what Pete's doing of course."

"Sure. I'll tell him, shall I?"

"If you like, but I'll speak to him myself when I see him next. I'll call you again tomorrow."

"Yes, do that. I'll update you again then. Bye, sweetheart."

The call left her feeling vaguely unsettled. There was no reason for that. Her father was improving, and everything was under control.

Her father was noticeably brighter when she saw him the next morning, though still having problems speaking. Melissa relayed a bevy of greetings and messages from neighbours and gave him a synopsis of the report she'd received from Chris.

Dan Gilbert listened intently to everything she had to say. It was clear where he would rather be, and it was not in hospital. The doctor made his rounds while Melissa was visiting and indicated he was happy with her father's progress. Dan's speech was improving and so was the movement in his affected side. He could start with basic physiotherapy.

"You must have had a beneficial impact," the doctor said to Melissa. "He's improved significantly in the last couple of days."

"I don't think it's due to me. He's just a stubborn old bugger."

"I'll take your word for that," the man said. "It will probably work to his advantage in coming weeks."

"Not…old," came the muttered comment from the bed.

Melissa drove out to the station two days after her arrival in Alice. She took the Land Cruiser, with Jenny assuring her she could manage with taxis for a few days or else could walk. Her first stop after rumbling over the cattle grid at the main gate was to stop off at the grave site for William and her mother. There were a few weeds around and she pulled them out and tidied up. In earlier years, she had tried planting flowers, but the kangaroos usually decimated them. Melissa could never figure out why they didn't eat the weeds instead.

The dogs met her as she pulled up at the house. They went crazy in fact. *She's home! She's home! Oh, this is so exciting, she's home.* Nobody else was. She went through the house, calling out, but Chris wasn't there. Nor was the station 4-wheel drive so he was obviously out and about.

Next stop was the horses. She grabbed a couple of apples from the kitchen. She couldn't go empty handed. They snickered their welcome, not as exuberantly as the dogs but an acknowledgement anyway. Cleo's foal shied away but looked on with interest as its mother hung over the fence.

"Missed me, have you? I've missed you as well. I wish I could take you back to Sydney with me."

The horses nuzzled into her as she scratched their necks, clearly enjoying the tactile attention. Melissa proffered the two apples, which were promptly devoured.

"Were you pleased to see me or just looking for what treats I might have?" she teased.

"They haven't been neglected but they could do with a ride. They're getting fat. Good to see you, Melissa."

"Pete! I didn't hear you coming. I can see they haven't been starved. They look like they should be on a diet."

"They haven't been ridden in a while. They're gettin' a bit lazy, I reckon. Still, if you take Cleo out now, she'll probably be frisky."

"You're right, but it might do us both good. I haven't had any decent exercise for a while either."

"So, how's the old man then?"

Melissa bristled. It was a disrespectful reference to her father. She knew Pete wouldn't speak like that if her father were around; in fact, he wouldn't speak much at all. She nearly reprimanded him, but let it slide. Her father could fight his own battles, when he was able.

"He's improving. I'm going to change into my riding gear. Pete, can you saddle Cleo for me?"

"Yes, ma'am" he said with a mock salute. He didn't hide the smirk. "I hear you're a famous photographer now!"

"Hardly. I held an exhibition here, but that doesn't make me notorious—outside of Alice, anyway." A thought struck her. "Did you see it?"

"Yeah, I was in town with your old man and we dropped in and had a look. We both found ourselves stuck up on the wall." He chuckled. "Does that make me famous too?"

"Nope. Neither of us are." *I should have known everyone would see it.* "I'm sorry. I should have sought your permission before displaying the photo."

"Don' be silly. Tanya really liked it. She wants a copy. *She* thinks I'm famous and I'm not gonna argue with her."

"Absolutely not. I'll print a copy for her."

It was good to be back in the saddle. She followed the creek bed skirting the water holes. It led her part way into the gorge before she broke out and cantered through the back paddock. Birds screeched either a warning or a welcome—she couldn't be sure which—and a couple of roos paused, watching her approach before taking flight. The track wound around a low hill. It was one she'd often ridden over, and that familiarity gave her the confidence in giving Cleo her head.

"C'mon girl. Time to go."

A small cloud of dust followed behind them. The ride was exhilarating. Out of nowhere, she saw a vehicle up ahead, coming her way. It was a narrow section of the track with trees on one side and large rocks on the other. There was nowhere to go. The driver jammed on the breaks, skidding slightly on the loose sandy surface. Melissa pulled hard on the reins, and Cleo reared in response. Amazingly, she kept her seat, though not without her heart nearly jumping out of her chest.

Chris was at the wheel. Of course. She should have known he would be somewhere close by. The car door slammed.

"Melissa! What in the hell are you doing out here!"

"I might ask the same."

Cleo danced sideways in agitation, snickering her displeasure, until she settled enough for Melissa to slide off.

"Dammit—we've got to stop meeting like this."

She rolled her eyes. "If that's supposed to be funny, it's not."

"I'm sorry. You have this habit of appearing where I least expect you. At least you didn't fall off this time."

She winced. There were some muscles that were letting her know she'd been too long out of the saddle. Chris caught the expression.

"Do you need a massage, sweetheart? You look a bit stiff there."

200

At his words, a flood of memories came back. Memories of Chris and her together; of his support; of him massaging her shoulders. Of Chris in her bed. *I'd forgotten how cute he was.* The sudden emotion was like a stab of pain. She drew an involuntary breath and looked away, not wanting him to see the raw emotion he'd evoked. Huffing out the breath, her eyes sought his again.

"I may need a massage but not quite where it hurts."

He grinned, a roguish, salacious grin.

"You're a wicked man, Chris Harris. Keep your thoughts to yourself."

He didn't answer but in two steps, reached for her and drew her to him.

"You're a stubborn, crazy woman Melissa Gilbert, but I've missed you."

"Of course, you have. I wouldn't expect anything less." *I've missed you too.* Probably her response when she melted into his embrace gave him some idea. She wasn't quite ready to take up where they'd left off but seeing him again reminded her of everything she admired in him. Like his integrity for a start; that and his strong fingers.

"I've still got a couple of bores to check. We're bringing a mob down here tomorrow and I need to be sure that there's enough water for them. I'll get that sorted, then see you back at the homestead."

"Okay. Cleo and I will finish our ride and head back in that direction too. I'll get a meal going. Oh, and Chris? Thanks again for stepping in to help."

Thanks. Melissa actually said *thanks*. Chris had a smile on his face as he swung himself behind the wheel again. She had a knack of surprising him, whether popping up when he least expected her or behaving in a most un-Melissa-like manner. It was good to see her again, no matter what the circumstances.

That didn't mean there weren't questions he wanted to put to her. He had a feeling tonight would not be the night but sometime soon they needed to have a serious talk. He didn't have that long in Alice, and he didn't want to leave without some answers. He had his own future to think about.

Mounting Cleo, she headed back in the direction of the homestead, leaving Chris to finish his chores.

After showering and changing into clean clothes, Melissa collected the financial records and a sheaf of unpaid bills to take back to Alice. She sorted out some of her old prints and negatives she wanted to take with her to Sydney, before wandering into the kitchen to make a cup of coffee and investigate supplies. It occurred to her she'd never cooked a meal here before. To be rummaging around without Jenny seemed to be intrusive. The kitchen was Jenny's domain.

The pantry and cool room were always well-stocked. She managed to find frozen vegetables and some chicken and thawed them in the microwave. A simple casserole should suffice. Jenny's kitchen garden provided the herbs and she raided her father's cellar for a splash of wine to go in as well. They could have the rest with their meal.

It felt like date night, when later they sat down in the dining room. With only the two of them, it would have been more practical to sit in the kitchen but on a whim, she set the table in the dining room with best crockery and cutlery and crystal glasses for the wine. Chris hadn't felt comfortable installing himself in the house, so he'd been staying in the staff quarters he had occupied previously.

He was surprised at the set up when he made his way into the house that evening. "Sweetheart, if I'd known it was going to be formal, I would have worn the tux. I'm feeling under-dressed."

"You're fine just as you are. Scotch?"

"Please. If I remember rightly, your father keeps a rather good single malt."

Taking the glass from Melissa, he leant forward and deposited a light kiss on her lips. "I just felt like doing that."

She smiled and sipped her Scotch.

"I promised Father an update on progress with the muster. What shall I tell him? It looks like you and Pete have got everything under control."

"We have. I've enjoyed it. I was already due for a couple of week's leave and strangely I needed a break to clear the head. Can't think why." The look he gave her over the rim of his glass was wryly accusing.

How do you think I felt? It wasn't a picnic for me either. There was some perverted consolation in knowing he had been as miserable as her. She hoped the flush she sensed wasn't betraying her feeling of guilt.

If Chris noticed, he didn't mention it. "I had to promise to keep an eye out for any newsworthy stories, but coincidentally the Channel Nine boss is coming to the Territory next week anyway so I 'll be commandeered for some flying duty as well. He's looking at an investment in the cattle industry. I've got to know him slightly during our flights together and he's interested in my local knowledge and experience."

"He must trust your opinion."

"I'm not sure I'm the best adviser he has available, and certainly not in a financial sense but I know a little about the local industry and how things should operate behind the scenes." He laughed. "It's a novel change to be regarded as an industry specialist."

They moved to the dining table. The ceiling light cast a golden glow on the mahogany table, reflected with a warm glow on their faces. The crystal glasses sparkled as Chris solemnly did the honours and filled them with the ruby liquid. He raised his glass.

"Here's to your father's improving health, and the quality of his cellar."

"I can see you've slotted right back into station life. No regrets about moving to Sydney then?"

"No, sweetheart. It was the right choice for me at the right time."

As they dined, Melissa gave him a run down on her travels and the different experiences. It was the first time she'd been to the Riviera and it had been novel and exciting.

"I look forward to seeing the photos. I'd love to see that part of the world for myself. Perhaps, we could do that one day." He gave her a quick uncertain smile. Melissa noted the reference to 'we' but let it pass. It would be wonderful to see it again with another person, and even better if it were with a partner, a partner like Chris even, but she was still hesitant about making that commitment.

It was Chris who changed the subject. "I saw the graves for your mother and young William. I see they died on the same day. If it's not too painful to talk about, what happened?"

Melissa played with her cutlery while gathering her thoughts. "It was a long time ago. William was just a toddler and was due to have more vaccinations, so Mum was taking him into the clinic in town. I was going too, but I mucked about instead of getting ready and that made Mum late. Later I learned she was driving faster than she should have. She skidded on the dirt road and rolled the car. She and William died, I survived with a broken leg. If I hadn't made her late that day, she wouldn't have been trying to make up time and she and William wouldn't have been killed."

Chris reached across the table to take her hand. "That's a big stretch Melissa. You were only a little kid. Dragging your feet getting ready wasn't your fault. That's what kids do. Maybe your mother should have started getting ready earlier. Maybe there were other things happening that day that you don't know about. You can't take that blame on yourself."

"I always have though, and my father has never indicated that there were other reasons. He wasn't happy when his first born was a girl and then I compounded the crime by causing the death of his only son. I've always known I've failed him."

"I'm sorry you had this happen to you." Chris paused, taking another sip of his wine. "What a complicated family. It explains a few things and sort of leads into something else I

205

wanted to talk to you about. I've got to know Pete better while I've been here. He's an interesting character. Do you know much about him and his family?"

'He's always been around. I remember him from when he was a little kid, but I didn't have much to do with him while we were growing up. His mother is a local Alyawarre woman. Her people have lived here since forever. I have no idea who his father is. We've not discussed personal matters."

"I don't think Pete knew who his father was, until recently. His mother has only just told him."

"You must have got into the deep and meaningfuls. We never really mixed much with the employees and station hands on Plenty. My father didn't encourage it. Jenny was different of course, but she's like one of the family."

"Hmm." Chris raised his glass to the light, observing the colour through the cut crystal. "Your father mixed sometimes."

"Well Dad was working with them so of course he mixed more than I did."

"Melissa, this will come as a surprise, but I think you should know. Dan is Pete's father."

"What?" Her stare was incredulous. "But that's ridiculous. What makes you say something like that?" *I would surely know if this was true. It's rubbish.*

"Pete has only just been told by his mother. She heard your father had suffered the stroke and feared he might die before there was any acknowledgement of Pete's parentage. Prior to that, Pete had no idea. He wondered if he should speak to your father about what his mother had told him and asked my advice one day while we were boiling the billy. I didn't
206

know what to tell him. I don't know your father that well and it's nothing to do with me really. I thought I'd handball it to you instead."

Her eyes widened. "But that means Pete's my half-brother! But how? When did this happen?"

"I'm not the right person to answer those questions. The how is kind of obvious but no doubt there's more to it than that. You'll have to speak to your father."

Questions tumbled over themselves in her head. How could she not have known? Why hadn't her father said anything, done anything? Was Pete always going to be just the station hand? It was difficult to take it all in.

"He's never been treated any differently to any of the station hands and hired help."

Chris looked at her, one eyebrow lifted questioningly.

"I didn't mean to infer… I didn't… I don't know what I meant. This has all been confusing. I'll speak to Pete in the morning. God knows what I'll say but I want to hear this for myself." She paused. "I know his mother. She used to help around the house years after mum died." *What else did she help with?* "I think I need another drink."

She broke off. Perhaps the *how* was apparent after all. Chris poured her another drink and reaching over, massaged the back of her neck. The muscles were taut and rigid. She hadn't realised how much so until those fingers started to work their magic.

"Is the hired help allowed to stay?" he asked softly, the lopsided smile more of a question mark.

"Absolutely. I think you need to finish what you've begun. I might even have missed you—a little bit." *Maybe a lot.*

She took him back to her room, and then to her bed. It was a fierce coupling, driven by her need for comfort and reassurance, and to make sense of her world which was changing around her. As she ran her fingers over his chest and felt the firmness of his thighs which were intertwined with hers, she drew solace from the innate strength and virility. Wrapped in his arms, she found the security she craved.

~

She went looking for Pete the following morning and found him in one of the sheds, servicing a motor bike. She stood watching him. He didn't acknowledge her presence initially, but she knew he was aware of her.

"Going riding again?" Pete asked.

Melissa propped herself against the side of the ute, awaiting its turn for attention. Pete was working with the confidence of someone who knew what he was doing.

"No Pete. I wanted to talk to you. Chris told me what you said—about who you think your father is."

"I have no reason to doubt my mother. It seems my father has been here all along."

"Did you have any idea before? Why didn't she tell you earlier?"

He put down the spanner and straightened up, wiping his hands on the back of his jeans. Only then did he turn and look at her. She found herself looking for signs of similarity.

"It was all news to me. She never talked about my father and with the disinterest of a kid, I never thought to ask. We have lots of family around here—lots of uncles. Anyway, Walter was always around, and I think I sort of assumed that he was my dad. A father never seemed particularly necessary, you know? I learned the ways of my people and that kept me going."

"But it seems *my* people are also your people," she replied.

"That's going to take some getting used to—Sis." At this point, he fell about laughing. "You and me—I never imagined anything like this."

She bristled. "It's not funny. I think my father has some questions to answer. What did he think he was doing?"

"He's not the first white boss to take advantage of an aboriginal woman. Look around you. There are lots of half caste and lighter-skinned aboriginal people around. That didn't come from washing too often."

Melissa didn't appreciate the inference.

"Perhaps your mother was the one who took advantage. Have you thought about that?"

"No. What advantage was in it for her, either then or since? You think about that."

There was a frosty silence and Melissa had the good grace to look embarrassed. She looked away while trying to calculate dates. How old was Pete? He was younger than her but was this before or after her mother died? She had no idea.

"Mum told me she worked in the big house for a while and looked after you before Jenny arrived. After that, she wasn't needed any more. She never said anything about her pregnancy, not even to the old man. Jenny arrived and she just went back to her people and got on with it. She went walkabout

209

for a while and came back after I was born. By that time, she was with Wally, who also worked on Plenty River until he died a few years back. Your dad gave me a job working here too."

"Kind of him," she said bitterly. "He must have had some idea."

"Yeah, well—you'll have to ask him."

"I will. I'm going back to town today. He's not able to talk much but he's going to have to talk to me about this."

There was nothing more she could learn from Pete. She left him to finish his work with the bike and walked back to the house. She had more questions than answers. Did she even know her father? It seemed not.

She cleaned up the kitchen and loaded the car. Before leaving, she drove out to where Chris was working, taking morning tea with her. They sat in the shade of a lemon-scented gum, having checked first for ants and other uninvited critters. Somehow, a cup of tea in this environment tasted incredibly good. So did the scones she'd found in the freezer. They just had to swat away the flies that seemed to think they'd been invited to the party.

"Sweetheart, we haven't talked about us."

"No, we haven't." She swept the hair from her eyes as she turned to look at him. The knot in her stomach tightened. "Chris, I know I fly off the handle a little quickly. I might have been hasty. The thought that you were getting close to Lexie just tore me apart. It wasn't jealousy but overwhelming insecurity that sent me running."

"Lexie is a colleague; you know that. I like her—I've told you that before, but I like lots of the people I work with. I like her partner too."

210

"You mean Harrison Fletcher?"

"No; her other half. I haven't met him as Lexie keeps her personal life reasonably private, though she's told me a few things about him. They've just become engaged, but that isn't public knowledge."

"Oh…" *I've been such a fool.* She licked her lips, which were suddenly very dry. "…I think I owe you an apology. I should have let you explain."

"Can we start again?" There was a note of appeal in his voice. "Not pick up from where we left off but wipe the slate and start again only this time with more trust."

"Trust! I don't know who or what to trust any more. You're such a good man to put up with me. Can I sort out this business with my father first? Then we'll talk, I promise. Right now, I appreciate your support. I'm not sure I deserve you." She swiped at a pesky fly that dive-bombed her face. "Nor does my father."

᷎

She went straight to the hospital on reaching Alice, and found Jenny sitting in the cafeteria. She looked more rested than she had a couple of days earlier.

"Nursing staff are tending to your dad, so I thought I'd leave them to it and grab a cup of coffee. How were things back home?"

"Interesting, very interesting. I'll grab a cup of coffee as well and tell you about it."

There was never much to recommend about hospital coffee, but Melissa needed support for the next conversation.

The queue at the counter was short, and she was back at the table in five minutes.

"Jenny, did you know about Pete?"

"Know what? Nothing's happened to Pete, has it?"

"He's fine. From what I've learned, he also happens to be my brother, or at least my half-brother. Did you know about this?"

"I didn't initially, but yes I learned about it in time."

How come Jenny was told about this and I wasn't? Is there anything else I don't know about?

"Why didn't you tell me?"

"It wasn't my place Missy. It was up to your father. It seems you've found out elsewhere anyway."

"Pete's mother, thinking Dad was about to die, finally told Pete. She thought he ought to be told. So how much do you know? What's the story?"

Jenny set her cup back on the saucer and paused before speaking. "Maisie, Pete's mother, used to help out in the house when your mother had two little kids to look after. After your mother and William died, she stayed on to look after you and do general housekeeping. I wasn't here of course, but as I understand it, your father was emotionally shattered, and evidently sought solace with Maisie. He was otherwise very much alone and at the time, grief counsellors weren't exactly the thing."

"Solace! That's one way of putting it."

"A few weeks after I was employed, she disappeared. Just said one day that she wouldn't be back tomorrow and that was that. Sometime later she was back with a little boy, one who was lighter-skinned than she was. Your dad may be lacking in social skills, but there is nothing wrong with his maths. He worked out that in all probability, the child was his."

"So, what did he do about that?"

"I don't know what conversations he had with Maisie, if any. He did make sure Pete had an education though. If you recall, Pete and a couple of other kids from the camp were given school of the air classes in your old school room. You were off at boarding school by then, but your governess was kept on to supervise the lessons. I think your dad thought Pete would be more comfortable if other kids were having classes with him. When it came time for high school, he sent Pete into Alice to boarding school. I don't know what arrangements he made with Maisie, or if Pete thought it was odd he was singled out."

"It wasn't exactly a prestigious school like I was sent to in Sydney, was it?"

"Do you think Pete would have been happy there?"

"Possibly not, but we'll never know."

Jenny looked at her sympathetically. "When you look at them both, there are similarities. Pete has the same walk as your dad and some of his mannerisms. They're both hard workers."

Melissa was quiet for a while, taking in what she had learnt.

"It's not right," she burst out. "He's been ignoring two of his children."

"He's never ignored either of you. He's just lived according to his own dictum. In his own way, he's been a very generous father. You've never wanted for anything, Missy."

"No, just recognition and affection, and it seems they're not things he's been able to give either of his surviving children. His behaviour is never going to bring William back. How pointless is that?"

"He expresses his love in his own way. That's never going to change now. You just have to recognise and accept that"

"So how is he now? I'd better go and see him."

"I think you'll find he's improving. Perhaps I'll stay here a while and read the paper. I'll let you have some time alone with your Dad."

Melissa pushed her chair back and dropped a kiss on Jenny's head. "Dear Jenny. I don't know what I would have done without you in my life. If you hear him scream, you'd better come running."

"Just behave yourself, my girl. Remember, he's not well."

Dan Gilbert was sitting up in bed supported by pillows and looking surprisingly improved. The physiotherapist was just leaving.

"You've made great progress, Dan. We'll have you up and about in no time. I'll be back tomorrow."

Dan grunted, in acknowledgement Melissa presumed. She waited until the woman had left the room before turning to address the figure on the bed.

"What I want to know, Father, is when you were going to tell me about Pete—my brother Pete."

He gestured towards her, then let his hand drop back on the bed. His looked away from her and sought the window.

"Father, what else haven't you been telling me? Is Pete the only one? Do I have any more siblings around the place?" She hadn't meant to sound so accusing.

214

"M'issa! You don't talk... me like that."

"You haven't answered my question."

The silence was more than frosty. Her father's face drained of colour. Against the pillow, he looked grey. *Oh god, what have I done?*

Melissa pulled the visitor chair closer to the bed and sat down. She fixed an intent look on her father. "I want to know why you didn't tell me." She spoke more softly. "And Pete— didn't he deserve to know who his father was?

Dan's chest heaved as he fought for breath and for words. "Not up to m-m-me. Never denied he was my son. Nobody asked."

"Why would they? That sounds like a cop-out."

"Maisie... his mother... respect her wishes."

Maisie; surely she would have wanted that acknowledgement for her child? Wouldn't she see it as an advantage? It dawned on Melissa she didn't really know how the situation affected Maisie. Perhaps she was the one who kept things quiet.

She thought back over Jenny's comments and let out the breath she'd been holding. "Dad, I know things get complicated sometimes, but I'm not a child anymore. If there are any more secrets like this, I should be told. It's the secrecy I mind more than anything. It makes me feel such a fool."

Dan moved his hand over the bed coverings towards her, his only acknowledgement other than his eyes moving towards hers.

"If it makes you feel any better, I'm happy to have Pete as my brother. Surprised; very surprised in fact, but he's a good man."

215

Dan's eyes closed and he looked exhausted. He attempted to speak, and Melissa leaned forward to catch what he was saying.

"Good man. Takes after his father."

CHAPTER 15

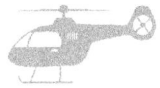

"HOW LONG ARE you staying in Alice?"

Pete was making awkward conversation as he and Melissa approached the main doors of the hospital. He had trucked a load of cattle into town that morning, and at Melissa's urging, had agreed to visit Dan Gilbert. He gave every indication of being unsure about the necessity of this meeting. Melissa declared his paternity needed to be acknowledged. He was not yet confident enough in this filial relationship to assert any opinion that differed to hers.

"I'll stay as long as Jenny needs me," Melissa said. "It depends on my—our—father's prognosis to some extent but he's better than was initially indicated."

"You mean he's still got his bite?"

"Probably not as deadly, but it's safe to say that yes, he's still got his bite. His teeth just aren't as sharp. I'm sure you'll be safe. He knows you know, and at some point, you have to face him so it might as well be now."

"Yeah—while he can't get out of bed!"

"You'll be fine. I won't go in with you. I think this is a conversation that needs to be between you and him. I don't want to intrude on that. While you go up to his room, I'll sit in the cafeteria and have a coffee. After you've seen him, you can come back to the town house for lunch before you have to drive back to Plenty. Okay?"

She had finished her coffee, read the complimentary newspaper and finished half of the crossword before Pete returned. His expression gave nothing away.

"Well? How did it go? Did he explain himself and his behaviour?"

"Fair go, Melissa; this was two blokes talking. It's a big change from discussing cattle all day to talking about ourselves. Nothing's going to change in a hurry, but he did acknowledge he's my father. I hadn't known before now that he paid for me to go to school in Alice. I'm not sure if that was out of concern for me or appeasing his conscience."

"We'll probably never know. C'mon, you must be hungry. Jenny will have lunch waiting for us back at the house. That reminds me; Jenny asked me to pick up some milk while I was out. Do you mind if we slip into the supermarket in the Mall?"

"Nah, go for it. I should pick up a couple of things to take back to Tanya as well."

They parted ways once inside the shop to search the aisles for their respective purchases, meeting up again in the line-up at the checkout. Pete looked at the milk that Melissa had in her basket.

"Pretty fancy stuff, this milk of yours. Perhaps the Old Man should've drunk more of it. Mightn't have had his stroke then."

A strident voice rang out.

"I saw that."

The shop assistant was pointing an accusing finger at Pete, indignation at the fore. Conversations in the line ceased and everyone looked from the assistant to Pete and back again.

"Saw what?" Melissa asked. She looked around but nothing was happening that she could see. Pete had a frozen look on his face, his lips pressed into a thin line.

"He pinched something from your basket. I saw him put his hand in there."

Now the looks were accusing. It appeared as if everyone took a step back, leaving Melissa, Pete and the assistant centre stage, though nobody had moved except to swivel their necks.

"Are you accusing my brother of stealing from me? Is that what you're saying?" Melissa's voice was as icy as the stare with which she fixed the assistant, and loud enough for everyone in the vicinity to hear.

The woman's mouth dropped open and she flushed. "Your brother... but..."

"Yes, my brother. Is there a problem"

"No; no problem. Sorry, I appear to have made a mistake."

"It's him you should be saying sorry to, not me."

The woman mumbled an apology and served them hastily, avoiding eye contact. Only when they were outside the supermarket doors did Pete speak. He had not uttered a word throughout the incident.

"Melissa, I'm not some banner to be waved about. If you want to make a statement, do it quietly. I don't need to be shoved in anyone's face. I'd like some time to adjust before I get 'outed' so to speak. Can we take the brother-sister thing slowly?"

"Sorry, I didn't mean to embarrass you. I hadn't thought what all this might mean to you. I just got cross at the assumptions being made about you, that's all."

"I can fight my own battles, thanks. Incidentally, this sort of thing has been happening to me my whole life. People just accept that sort of casual racism as normal. What would your reaction have been before you knew of our relationship?"

Melissa looked at him. She knew what would have happened. She might have spoken up because Pete was involved, but otherwise the incident would only have registered as an annoying hold-up on her progress in the queue.

Pete shrugged at her silence and started to walk back to the car. She was embarrassed. She knew Aboriginal inhabitants of the town often were subjected to racism but as it never affected her directly, had not given it much thought.

"Pete! Waddyer up to? How come yer in town?"

An Aboriginal woman stood in front of them, hands on hips. She wore a uniform that Melissa didn't recognise.

'G'day, Auntie. I'm just here for some family business."

"How's yer mum? She's okay?"

"Fighting fit. No problems there."

Melissa hung back, not wanting to intrude. The woman was casting inquisitive glances in her direction and Pete picked up on that.

"Auntie, this is Melissa. Her dad owns Plenty River." He turned to Melissa. "I went to school with Valerie, Auntie's daughter."

"So—you're Elizabeth Gilbert's girl." The appraising eyes looked at her more closely. "Yer take after yer mum. She was a looker too."

Melissa was startled. Her father never mentioned her mother, so nobody else did either. "You knew my mother?"

"In a round-about way. She use-ta do some voluntary work here in town at the Araluen Health Clinic, helping with the little kids on paediatric days."

"My mother! Are you sure?" Melissa had never heard that her mother did anything other than keep house on the station. She knew little of her mother's life.

"Course I'm sure. She brought you with her sometimes. You were just a little tacker then. Later, she brought yer brother too. I was real upset when yer mum died. She was a good woman."

Melissa's eyes prickled. She struggled to overcome the surge of emotion and was surprised by her reaction after all this time.

Pete shuffled uncertainly. "Auntie, we better be going, but it was good seeing you."

"You was going ter drop in at the clinic to see the work we're doing. When're you going to do that? Valerie works there now and I'm sure she'd like to catch up. Melissa can come too."

"I don't think we've got time today, Auntie. I'll visit sometime soon, I promise. Melissa's very busy—she lives in the big smoke now but she's just home because her dad's sick."

Melissa had a sudden urge to see the place where her mother had spent some time.

"Actually, I *would* like to come. We could do that this afternoon, couldn't we Pete?"

"It's up to you. If you want to, I can make the time. As long as I'm not too late driving back to Plenty. Tanya will give me 'what for' if I'm not home when she expects me."

~

Jenny had set out cold platters for lunch and made a pile of sandwiches for Pete to take with him on the drive back to the station. He was uncertain about sitting down to eat with the two women and Melissa realised he'd only ever been in the kitchen of the homestead at Plenty River, and the only time he'd have shared a meal with them would have been around a campfire while on the job. Would that change now? She had no idea.

They chatted to Jenny or rather Melissa did, and explained their plans for the afternoon. If Jenny was surprised, she didn't say, merely reminding Pete that he shouldn't leave it too late to head home. The roads weren't fenced, and there was always the risk of hitting cattle or roos if driving at night.

They all left again at about the same time. Jenny was visiting Dan and taking in clean pyjamas and some new reading material.

On the way to the Health Clinic, Pete asked Melissa not to say anything about their relationship.

"It's not that I'm embarrassed or ashamed or anything like that. I just want to handle this in my own way. Of course, the whole town might know by now after your outburst at the supermarket."

"Sorry." Melissa looked sheepish. "I won't do it again, I promise."

Auntie, whose name Melissa subsequently discovered was Marlene, welcomed them with enthusiasm.

"Glad you could make it. Come in and look around. Today's clinic is for kids from the town camps."

Noise and shrieks assailed them. There were little kids and big kids and general pandemonium reigned. There were some toys, but they were mostly broken and missing bits. Some kids were crying and clinging to their mothers and others were happily playing with each other. Marlene explained some were attending the clinic for vaccination updates, but that ear, eye and chest infections were common for these children.

"What we really need is a mobile clinic that goes around to the camps, providing initial treatment and assessment. There are a few kids who fall through the cracks and then we don't get to see them until their problems are chronic or severe. If we could see these kids early enough, they would have much better health outcomes."

"That sounds like a good idea," Melissa said. "Why don't you do that?"

Marlene looked at her, one eyebrow raised. "You have to ask? Really? It's all about the money. Everyone talks about improving indigenous health, especially at election time, but each year it seems we're being handed funding cuts rather than funding increases. We're forever trying to do more with less."

"That's terrible. Can't you hold fund raising events and get the community on board?"

"Who'd come? These people don't have any money to donate and as a cause it's not very sexy. The competition's fierce for available funds and there aren't many people giving money away in Alice."

Marlene was probably right. There were so many things Melissa had previously not considered. These were issues that had not intruded on her life before.

Marlene showed them around and introduced them to some of the staff. The clinic seemed to survive on the dedication and goodwill of those employed there. The tour didn't hide the fact that the facilities were run down.

"So, you said my mother used to come here?"

"Sure did. Not every week as she couldn't always get into Alice, but she'd trained as a nurse before she married your father. She wasn't registered any more, but she liked to help in a general way. She told me once that she'd go crazy if she didn't have these regular trips to town."

"I can understand that. I never knew her as a person. She was just Mum. Being here makes me feel closer to her though."

They didn't stay much longer as Marlene was busy, and Pete needed to hit the road. They made their farewells, and Melissa drove back to the town house where the truck was parked. Chris was bringing another load of cattle in the next day and so the truck needed to be back for loading and departure again early in the morning.

She was keen to see Chris, and the feeling was stronger the next morning. She'd had a restless night, with ideas tumbling around her head. What could be done to help the clinic? She'd never considered the welfare of Aboriginal people before, but now she had a link to the community through Pete, and knowing that her mother had taken an interest all those years ago gave her a different perspective. Not quite an epiphany but it made her realise there were so many years in which she could have done something, but never gave it a moment's thought. She'd been too busy focussing on her own problems.

Her mother was another issue. She needed to sit down with Rose Woodleigh. The two women had been young brides around the same time and would have known each other very well. If anyone could tell her more about her mother, it would be Rose. What sort of woman had she been? What motivated her? It was embarrassing she'd never asked these questions before. Jenny had come to Plenty River after her mother's death and had no personal knowledge of her predecessor. Her grandparents had died years ago, and her mother had been an only child, so there weren't many people who could fill in the gaps.

She raised both issues with Jenny over breakfast.

"I never knew your mother and as far as fund raising goes, I'm hopeless at coming up with ideas. Why don't you have a chat to the Country Women's Association? They probably have more experience with that sort of thing."

"Aren't they just focussed on cake stalls and making handicrafts? I don't think that will raise much money."

"Your ideas about the CWA are outdated Missy. You'll have to ponder this on your own. I've got some errands to run."

She heard the truck pull up outside late morning. The cattle had already been offloaded and Chris eased himself from the cabin, stretching his legs and shoulder muscles. "Give me

225

a chopper any day. Driving this crate in has been heavy work, to say nothing of the dust and potholes."

"Eww—you smell of cattle!"

"And hello to you too. I'd like to see what you smelt like after the sort of morning I've had."

"Come in and I'll make you a cup of coffee. We've probably got some cake somewhere but take your boots off first. I think you've been treading in it. I don't want eau-de-bovine in the kitchen."

Chris pulled a face but dutifully pulled his boots off at the door and padded inside in his socks. Melissa nodded towards the table while filling the electric jug. "Sit down; I want to discuss something with you."

"Yes ma'am. Anything else while you're at it?"

"Just listen."

Melissa gave Chris an overview of her visit to the Clinic with Pete and the impression it had left on her.

"Honestly Chris, that clinic is trying to make do with antiquated equipment. The whole place needs a facelift, and what they really need is a mobile clinic to treat the kids in the camp where they live."

"And let me guess—that needs money."

"I've been trying to figure out what I could do."

She ran through the options she'd considered, ticking each idea off on her fingers.

"Organise a quiz night? It's not really my thing and anyway I have no idea how to do that. I've never attended one myself. Perhaps a fund-raising dinner? That needs a good guest speaker and is a lot of work. Where could I hold it and who would come anyway? I'm a hopeless cook so couldn't run a cake stall. Perhaps a raffle is the answer. I would have to think what contacts I have who could donate something desirable, like a holiday or a car or something. How do these things usually happen?"

Chris slid another slice of cake off the plate and frowned as he considered the options.

"I'm confused by all of this. Is your life here or in Sydney? Why this sudden interest in Aboriginal health? I wasn't even sure you liked kids."

"I don't dislike them—I've never had much to do with kids to be honest. Other people's are okay. The point is, I never thought about it before, but now I've been made aware of the problems, I want to do my bit to help. My mother did, and I'd like to do something too."

"I see. This enthusiasm is commendable, but you're only a one-woman band. You need to think about your skillset and what you can most effectively offer."

"I know that, but what? I don't think t running photography classes is going to raise much money."

"No, but what about all that fashion stuff? You know about that and you've got the right contacts. Couldn't you organise a fashion show, parade thing and feature local models and clothing designs, or something like that?"

"That's ridiculous. No, I couldn't."

"Well sweetheart, I'm running out of ideas. What about an art show? Perhaps coordinate an exhibition of Aboriginal Art and get one of your art cronies to judge it. The winning entry could be purchased and exhibited permanently in the Araluen Cultural Centre. You could exhibit some of your local photos as well and donate the proceeds from sales. Would that be an option?"

He looked at her pleadingly. Decisions of this nature had not been what he was expecting this morning. He appeared relieved when after a moment's deliberative pause, she smiled.

"You know, you might have something there. At least I know now how to organise an exhibition. I'll talk to Belinda. If she thinks it's an option, I'm sure we can make it happen."

"We? What's this *we* business?"

"Didn't you say Channel Nine asked you to watch out for newsworthy events? I think you've just found one. The inaugural Territory Indigenous Art Show. Perhaps your boss would like to sponsor it. Tell him that it will give him greater acceptance in the local community. If he's on board, I might be able to talk Qantas into donating air fares as well."

Chris slowly shook his head.

"You were so unsure of yourself in your own exhibitions, but you seem more confident and directed on this issue. I'm impressed. The clinic must have made a big impact on you."

"I hadn't really thought about it but you're probably right. It helps to have some experience under your belt. I'll make myself a checklist today and work out who I need to consult to make it happen. If you could talk to your boss, that would be fabulous."

She rose to take the cups and plates to the sink, dropping a kiss on his head as she passed. In response, he grabbed her hand and kissed the inside of her wrist.

"I like you with this new confidence. It suits you."

"You mean you didn't like me before?"

"Now you're fishing."

She flicked him with the tea towel and laughing, he moved out of reach.

"Go and clean yourself up," she said. "I might see if Belinda can join us for lunch."

CHAPTER 16

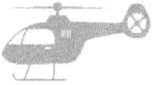

THE BISTRO WAS busy with lunchtime trade but the three of them secured a table in a quiet location. They placed their orders before Melissa outlined her plans.

"There's no stopping you now," remarked Belinda. "Next I'll hear of you staging events in London and New York."

"I doubt it, but what do you think of my idea? Will people get behind it? Do you have contacts within the Aboriginal communities? Most importantly of course; if we use the Cultural Centre, will there be an associated cost?"

"Starting with the first question, I think it's an interesting concept with a number of beneficiaries. There is public exposure for the artists and the opportunity to sell their paintings. Secondly, you'll have to do some spruiking to persuade people this is a viable and practical idea."

Belinda picked up her knife from the setting on the table and gestured towards Melissa.

"You'll need some local champions, especially Aboriginal champions and we can put some thought into that.

I would seek government support as well. You could approach the Minister for Aboriginal Affairs and the Minister for Tourism and Culture for grants. It would need a well-developed proposal but there's a fair chance you would get support."

Melissa sat up straighter and her raised eyebrows indicated her reaction.

"My goodness, there's a lot I need to consider. There will be more involved than the events I've organised before. I'd better update my notes. What about the cost of the venue?"

"I'll have to run that one past the Board, but if I recommend it, they'll probably agree."

At that point, Chris intervened. He'd listened to the two women talk, hands supporting his chin, elbows resting on the table.

"Sweetheart, this is going to be a lot of work. If you're going to raise sponsorship for this art prize, couldn't you just ask people you know for donations and forward them to the Clinic? Then you wouldn't have all the drama associated with organising this event."

Two pairs of eyes looked at him. Head tilted, Melissa raised one disdainful eyebrow. Belinda snorted into her coffee, but otherwise held her counsel. Chris raised his hands in mock surrender.

"Okay, okay—I gather that's not a popular idea. I don't fully understand your finance model, that's all."

"I haven't fully worked it out, but the idea is that indigenous artists are invited to submit their works for display and judging. There might be more than one judging category but that's the finer detail. I'll be looking for sponsorship for the prize or prizes. The judge of course will have to be someone of recognised repute. I'll have to consult my contacts on that one. Russell might have a suggestion."

The meals were delivered, and conversation paused in favour of the food. Melissa was quietly glad of the distraction. The objective was to raise funds for the clinic, and she hadn't figured out how that was going to happen.

"Salt? Pepper?"

She played for time, thinking quickly while she did. The exhibits needed to generate an income. maybe she could donate some prints as well.

"This is what I'm proposing," she said shortly. "The entries will be on exhibition for a defined period after the judging and of course will be available for public viewing. There will be an auction of all the pictures. Half the proceeds will go to the artists as compensation for their work. The other half will be donated to the clinic. Sponsorship will pay for the prizes and the costs of staging and promoting the competition. What do you think?"

"It's different to anything that's been done here before," Belinda said after a moment's thought, "but, it could work. I don't know if you'll generate enough to buy and set-up a van for the clinic, but it will certainly help."

"I'll take that as a vote in favour," Melissa said decisively. "With you and Chris behind me, I'm sure we can make it a success. I'll talk to Marlene next and get her support; then Pete, and perhaps Maisie. I'll let you know their response."

Belinda looked questioningly at Chris, but he just shrugged. Melissa was aware of this but chose to ignore it. They would each become more enthusiastic when they saw it all coming together. As she said, no-one else was doing anything to provide better health services to the kids from the camps.

It was still early afternoon when they left the bistro. Chris looked at his watch. "Sweetheart, I need to hit the road soon. I have to get the truck back to Plenty. I'll just tie off a few loose ends back there and then I'll leave it all in Pete's capable hands."

"So, you'll come back to town after that?" Her mind ticked over with possibilities. It would suit her to drive back to the station as well.

"In a couple of days. I'll be driving the ute back to town. The Boss is flying up from Sydney soon, so after that I'll be at his beck and call. I've booked a local chopper but need to organise a few things around that as well."

"Can you wait a little longer before you leave today? I need to speak to Marlene at the Clinic first, and then I might come with you. I'd like to talk to Pete and Maisie and get their input before I canvas options more widely."

"You mean drive back with me in the truck?"

"Yes. Is that a problem?"

"Not at all. It doesn't fit the image of glamorous Melissa Gilbert to be travelling in a truck with minimal suspension and which reeks of eau-de-bovine, as you so nicely put it. Aside from that, I'd love the company."

"In case you haven't noticed, I've never cared particularly what people think of me. I'd prefer to be travelling back in

233

your Merc, that's for sure, but for a couple of hours I can tolerate it."

"And I thought you were going to say that driving back with me made up for all the physical compromises."

"Now *you're* fishing."

For once, Melissa was the one who gave him a slow, seductive smile; one which started at the corner of her lips and spread to the glint in her eye, just showing behind a curtain of hair. Chris gave a hoot of laughter and planted a quick kiss on that seductive mouth.

"Just make sure you keep surprising me. Come on. Direct me to this clinic of yours before it gets too late."

Melissa was fortunate Marlene was working that day, as she hadn't thought to ring first. The scene at the Clinic was similar to her previous visit and she had to take a seat until Marlene was free.

"Marlene, I don't want to make any assumptions here. I need to know firstly that you and the Clinic are supportive of my concept, and secondly, that the local indigenous community will support it. Will they think it's a good idea, or just think here's another white person interfering in their affairs and not consulting them?"

"That's a good question. Before you get too carried away, you should speak to some of the old people. This is a matter of respect. After that, you can talk to some of the young'uns. As far as the Clinic is concerned, any funds are always welcome. There's no debate about that. I'll have to speak to the Board though about the idea of setting up a clinic van and taking health services to the communities instead of them coming to us. It's not just the van you know. There'll be additional operational costs."

"In my wave of enthusiasm, I hadn't considered that aspect, but you're right. Perhaps if the Art Exhibition is an annual event, the ongoing operational costs can be met that way? Do you think there's any chance that the government will meet fundraising dollar for dollar?"

"You'd have to tweak a lot of well-connected strings to pull that one off. Leave the Board to me. I'll have a word to others in management and we'll think about the best approach at that level. You'll have to speak to members of the community. I'll give you some names and put the word out that you'll be coming to have a chat."

Marlene fixed Melissa with a stern look. "Don't forget you're there to listen as well as talk."

Melissa took on board the advice, and after collecting Chris from the waiting room, where he was reading ancient copies of Reader's Digest, headed back to the house to pack an overnight bag and let Jenny know what she was doing.

"So, you're serious about this project then?" Jenny was bemused and it showed. "You do understand it will be a lot of work. People may say they'll support you but when there's work to be done you'll probably find yourself standing alone."

"I can't let that hold me back. This is a worthwhile cause and I'll just have to convince people. The Gilbert name and reputation must stand for something, surely?"

Jenny pursed her lips momentarily, but quickly smiled, handed over a parcel of sandwiches for their trip, and waved them off.

⌒

"Do you realise," Chris said, "this is our first road trip together?"

"A journey of a couple of hours between Alice and Plenty River hardly qualifies as a road trip."

"I know, but it's good to have some time alone with you, even if it is in a noisy, stinky truck. To show how much I appreciate it, I'll even let you choose the music!"

Music was one of the few areas in which their tastes differed, so this was no light concession, except as Melissa discovered, the only choices available were from an ancient collection of country music that resided permanently in the truck. The journey passed mostly in companionable silence, with occasional conversational interludes. Melissa recounted details of her recent travels and Chris described the highlights of his work with Channel Nine. Tactfully, neither of them mentioned Lexie Fergusson.

It verged on dusk as they rumbled over the grid and through the gates. Melissa dragged her eyes away from the graves set back from the entrance. The site was a magnet that drew her attention each time she passed. There was the comforting sense of coming home. The welcome from the dogs confirmed that feeling. The rays from the setting sun bathed the front of the house in golden light, giving it a softer almost magical perspective. Despite the intensity of her vow when she left after her father's birthday, this was home and would always feel that way.

***

"What are you plans for today?" Chris asked, gently kneading her shoulders. They lay in a comfortable cocoon, aware time to get up was fast approaching. The magpies warbling outside were better than any alarm clock.

"I'll speak to Pete and Maisie first thing, and then I'll slip over to Mulga Downs. I want to have a chat to Rose Woodleigh. Is it okay if I take the Land Cruiser?"

"Hey, it's not my car. The ute is here so that will do me. You won't be long, will you?"

"I'll be back by late afternoon. I'll be ready to drive back to town tomorrow."

She found Pete feeding the horses as he usually did first thing. The dogs had already been fed, and although they acknowledged her as she walked past, were not going to be distracted from their food. To look away from a bowl was to invite canine thievery.

Pete wasn't alone. He had rescued a joey from the pouch when its mother was hit by a car and had successfully hand-reared it. She was with him now, nuzzling his leg and watching out in case any treats came her way.

"You're like the Pied Piper with that little Joey following you around. I'm surprised she hasn't summonsed all her furry friends to join her."

"Nah, she won't do that. She thinks she's more human than kangaroo. I need to take her out bush where she might come across a mob and learn how to interact with them."

He straightened up, hands on hips. "I wasn't expecting to see you out here. The Old Man's okay?"

"Yes, he's fine. Improving every day. I wanted to talk to you actually—and your mum."

"Yeah? What about?" Pete sounded wary.

"After we visited Marlene the other day, I started thinking about what she said, about needing a mobile clinic so that health services could be taken to the kids in the camps. It was a sensible idea, but of course there's no funding for something like that."

Pete shrugged but didn't comment.

"It really had an impact on me. I admit I was probably influenced by learning that my mother sometimes volunteered there, but I started thinking about what could be done to raise funds for a van."

"You're organising a chook raffle then? Don't reckon there's much demand for one of those out here."

"Don't be silly, Pete. Just listen."

"Yes Ma'am."

Melissa paused long enough to take a deep breath. It was difficult unlearning some behaviours and she was still trying to find a footing for her new relationship with Pete. "I didn't mean to sound so abrupt. I'd really like your opinion on this idea. I'm thinking of staging an indigenous art show."

Pete listened intently while Melissa outlined the concept, and the anticipated benefits. He removed his hat and scratched his head before jamming it back in place. "Well if anyone can carry this off Melissa, it's probably you."

"I know that, but do you think the local community will get behind it? Will the artists submit their work?"

"Will there be an entry fee?"

"No. I'll get sponsorship to cover the establishment and promotional costs. There's no point in promoting it though if nobody wants to take part."

"And you're asking me because …?"

"Look, if you think it's a silly idea, just say so. I don't want to waste my time. There are plenty of other things I can do with my life. I just thought if it was known that you supported it, the art show might generate more interest and credibility."

"Settle down Sis. I was just getting my head around everything, that's all. As long as I don't have to do anything in public, that's okay. If it comes off, I'll put the word out to the mob. Don't expect anyone to submit their paintings on day one; in fact, you'll have to find an artist who everyone respects and persuade them to bring in a painting. Then the others will follow."

Her voice rose a notch. "How am I going to do that? I don't even know any indigenous artists. You've got to help me Pete. You could persuade them."

"Actually, you probably do know a few. You've just never looked or paid them any attention."

"Like who? Who would I know?"

"Well Uncle Albert for a start. He paints. If you go to see my mum, you can ask him. He's staying with her.

Although in the early years, the local people had led a nomadic life over their country, they now lived in a variety of structures in an area that was still referred to as 'the camp'.

Melissa paused outside the house in which Maisie lived. She hadn't spoken to Pete's mother in years and having some idea what had transpired between her father and Maisie, she felt a little uncomfortable. It had probably been a relationship with a strong power imbalance.

Melissa didn't have to knock, as Maisie sat outside, chatting with a couple of other people. The group silently watched her approach. The knot in the pit of her stomach tightened. If they hadn't already seen her, she might have turned and fled. Anyway, a Gilbert always stood her ground. She exhaled, put a smile on her face, and called a greeting.

The reason for her visit was absorbed in silence. There was a lack of eye contact and no invitation to sit down. Melissa had the feeling that they weren't comfortable with her being in their space.

Albert was one of the trio. At least that was a plus. In what was becoming a well-rehearsed spiel, Melissa outlined her idea and explained why she was seeking their support.

"Albert, Pete tells me you're an artist—a good one." She crossed her fingers behind her back because Pete hadn't said anything of the sort though he had inferred it.

"If you enter one of your paintings in the Art Show, other people will follow. It's so important that the event is a success if we're going to raise the funds for the clinic."

Albert shifted his gaze from Melissa to some point in the distance but didn't actually say or commit to anything.

It was Maisie who spoke. "How's yer father?"

"Recovery will be slow but he's improving every day. He doesn't like being in hospital much."

Maisie pursed her lips but didn't comment further about Dan Gilbert. "Yer mum use-ta help out in the Clinic sometimes."

"You knew my mother?" She sought confirmation as much as asked the question.

"Course I did. I use-ta help her with you two kids when you was little. She was a nice woman."

Melissa looked away, struggling to bring her emotions under control. Here was another person who had known her mother. "How long did you work with her?"

"I started helping in the house when she was expecting you, and then helped out until after the accident. I looked after you when you came home from hospital, until your dad employed that Jenny."

"I remember. I remember you looking after me then. Thank you for taking care of me."

"You were a very sad little girl. So was your dad. You both were. It was a real sad time."

There was a strained silence. Melissa didn't want to discuss the relationship between Maisie and her father. It didn't seem that important anymore, and after all, it was a long time ago.

Maisie broke the silence. "He'll do it."

Melissa looked around and then back at Maisie, eyebrows raised.

"Albert will put a painting in, won't yer, Albert?"

Albert nodded his assent, his eyes still focussed on the distance.

CHAPTER 17

NOT WANTING TO visit Mulga Downs empty-handed, Melissa headed back to the homestead after visiting Maisie. She'd bought a couple of current magazines in Alice and thought Rose would appreciate catching up with new recipes and gossip from the outside world. As she drew up at the homestead, Chris pulled in beside her, a plume of dust following him. The dogs jumped down from the tray of the ute and flopped into the nearest shade.

Chris shook his head in bemusement. "They think they've done a day's work already. I thought you were driving over to Mulga Downs?"

"I am, but I need to grab a couple of things first. I might have a quick coffee before I go, if you've got time to join me?"

"You've won me. It feels like morning tea time." Chris removed his hat and slipped off his boots at the back door. There were always protocols to observe.

"How did you go with Pete and his mum?" he asked.

"Fantastic—well sort of. They didn't exactly jump up and down with excitement, but I've got their backing and best of all, I've lined up the first entrant for the art show."

While boiling the kettle and laying out some biscuits, she gave Chris a run down on what had transpired. Her face lit up with more animation than usual.

Chris didn't hide his amusement. "Seeing you all fired up like this could give a man ideas. If I realised what was going to light a fire in your belly, I would have suggested a social justice project months ago. Do you have to rush off to Mulga

Downs so quickly? There could still be time for a little morning glory." He drew her to him, a hand planted suggestively on her butt.

"In your dreams handsome." She pushed him to arm's length. "I need to hit the road, but the thought will sustain me on the drive. Anyway, haven't you got things you need to be doing?"

"It's all a matter of priorities. Do I want to chase cattle around or do I want to make love to you? It's a hard choice."

"Idiot. I must get going if I'm to be back early enough for dinner. I think it's your turn to cook. I'll look forward to what culinary delights you might have for me when I get back."

"You're a demanding woman, Melissa Gilbert. I'll see what's in my repertoire. As you won't take me up on my tantalising suggestion, I'd better get back to the cattle."

Melissa made a quick call to Rose Woodleigh to check that she was home and happy to have a visitor. It was about fifty kilometres between the homesteads, so not an onerous trip but often slow because of the loose surface of the road.

Rose had held up lunch in anticipation of her arrival and emerged from the front door to greet her when Melissa pulled up. "It's so long since I've seen you, Melissa dear. It will be lovely to catch up with all your comings and goings. Freshen up in my bathroom, and then come and join us in the dining room."

Alex and Kathy were already seated. It was a simple but satisfying meal, with convivial company. She told them all a little about her recent travels, and then described in greater detail her latest idea. To her surprise, Kathy offered to help.

"I've got some time on my hands at the moment." She indicated her swollen belly. "I'm grounded now, thanks to this. If there's anything you think a beached whale can do, I'd be delighted to help."

"Thanks. I'll take you up on that. in the course of your work you must have met people who could be interested in participating. I'll chat to you later about reaching out to them."

With the meal over, Alex and Kathy politely excused themselves, leaving Melissa and Rose alone.

"I'm pleased to hear your father is on the mend, Melissa. He's the last person I expected to have a stroke."

"You're not the only one. In my mind, he was indestructible. As I explained on the phone, I want to talk to you about my family and in particular, my mother. I know so little about her and you're one of the few people who can tell me more."

"I'll tell you what I can. I only got to know her after she came to Alice of course. After you rang me, I went through my albums to see what photos I have. Here are your parents on their wedding day."

They bent over the photo, examining the detail it presented. A handsome couple looked back at them, no doubt full of anticipation at their future life together. They looked so young and to Melissa, they looked so happy together.

Rose smiled at the memories and placed her hand over Melissa's. "Elizabeth was a generous woman who loved children. She certainly would have had more if she could but there were complications at William's birth that put paid to that. It was one of the reasons she volunteered at the Clinic. She also had a strong sense of social justice and was concerned

244

about the health issues of Aboriginal children. She would have approved of what you are proposing."

"My parents must have been such opposites. How did they end up together? I don't really have any memories of family time, so I don't know what their relationship was like."

"Your mother was a nurse, newly arrived from the city. They met when your father was briefly in hospital with a badly broken arm. Came off his horse, I believe. Your mother nursed him. He was smitten by this bright, vivacious young woman, and she in turn was bowled over by this handsome man from the bush. He went out of his way to woo her."

"Doesn't sound like my father."

Rose sighed. "He changed after your mother's death. It was as though someone turned out the lights. He withdrew into himself; it was so very sad. He never really recovered emotionally."

Rose regarded Melissa intently, head to one side. "You know, you look a lot like your mother."

Melissa brushed the hair from her face and examined the photos critically. She could see the resemblance. It was reassuring—an indisputable link. "It definitely hasn't endeared me to my father."

"You take after your father in many aspects as well. You're both very stubborn and determined people. It's no wonder you clash sometimes. You each like to get your own way."

Melissa stared. Rose was probably right. It was an uncomfortable realisation.

Closing the albums, Rose continued. "My dear, I think you're doing a wonderful thing. If I may, I'd like to make a donation—to go towards a prize for the best female artist."

The radio blared in the back part of the house and she could hear Chris singing with more enthusiasm than talent. Clearly, great things were happening in the kitchen. Melissa opted not to disturb the chef but disappeared into her bathroom to shower off the dust from the road. On a whim, she slipped on a softly draped jersey dress, teamed with a gold belt, and pinned up her hair. She added a pair of pearl earrings which had belonged to her mother and had been given to her by her father on her twenty-first birthday. They had always been special to her, a link to the woman she could barely remember.

When she appeared in the kitchen some time later, she was met with an appreciative whistle and a hands-free kiss. "Wow! Sweetheart, I didn't hear you come in. You look stunning. I'll try not to get my messy hands on your dress." He nodded at a bottle which was waiting on the sideboard. "I'll open a bottle of wine in a moment, and you can tell me about your day. Give me two seconds to wash my hands and I'll join you."

"Whatever you cooked, it smells divine."

"Part of my strategy to woo you, my dear," he said with a lascivious smile. "After this, you should find my charms totally irresistible—good looking, gun pilot, short-notice cow wrangler and chef extraordinaire."

"Is that all?" Melissa cooed. "I was expecting a superb dancer and vocalist as well. I heard the singing when I first arrived home, and I don't think it wins any awards."

"You've got me there. I provide a good line in massages though."

"Ah yes—the massages. That might be what wins you the brownie points."

They relocated to the dining room, where to Melissa's delight the table was already set, complete with a vase of flowers and assorted greenery that he'd collected from the garden.

"I'm impressed. How did you get time to do all this?"

"I slipped in at lunchtime and got the meal started and scouted around to see where everything was kept. Easy really."

The meal was a slow-cooked casserole and was delicious. The meat fell apart easily, and it was bedded on clouds of fluffy mashed potato. He'd even found some garnishes from the herbs in Jenny's kitchen garden. The vegetables had been steamed at the last minute and it was an unpretentious yet satisfying meal.

Conversation turned to the coming weeks as they relaxed over coffee and a liqueur.

"What's going to happen here while your father is recuperating? It will be a while before he can return, and we've both got lives in Sydney though I'm not sure any more what your plans are. I've enjoyed this break and being able to catch up with Mark and some of the others, but I'll have to go back soon."

"I've been asking myself the same question. I guess Pete will keep running the place. He grew up here so he's more than capable and after all, he has an interest in the property now."

"How that plays out is up to your father. What does Pete want to do?"

"I haven't asked him. I assumed he would always be here. I'd better speak to him." She was silent for a moment, head tilted to one side as she considered how to answer his inferred question. "As far as work in Sydney goes, I've been able to refer a couple of contracts that came up to other photographers, and I've put the word out that I'm unavailable until further notice. I'll stay here until I get the art show under way. I haven't defined my plans after that."

Chris reached out and swept the curtain of hair from her face. He leaned forward to look her in the eyes. "What I really want to know is what are your plans for after the art show. Are you coming back to Sydney? What about us?"

There was a moment's silence that threatened to become uncomfortable. Her lips were dry, only made worse when she tried to moisten them. "Chris…"

"You don't have to answer me now. I don't want to put you on the spot. Take your time but set a date by which to tell me. By the time the show is over, you should have decided if you're coming back to Sydney and if you're coming back to me. Is that asking too much?"

"Chris, let me finish. I explained to you the other evening some of the issues from my family life and the impact they've had on me. I've never talked to anyone else about that time. I know it sounds silly, but I still blame myself for my mother's death, and at the same time feel so angry with her for deserting me." She could feel her throat constricting with tension as memories surfaced. "My father was never emotionally available, and that was my just punishment. I was desperately unhappy as a child, but never felt I deserved happiness. The big fear I have is that if I get close to anyone else, they'll abandon me as well."

"Sweetheart, I'd never do that to you."

"I know Chris, you've been my rock, but even my father nearly deserted me. I hadn't expected to feel the angst that I did when I heard about his stroke."

She paused while he refreshed their glasses.

"While I was on the road today, I had time to think about this art show and why I'm doing it."

"Isn't it to help the clinic and the kids in the camp?"

"Of course, it is, but I began to understand it's more than that. I've never really felt a part of this town. Perhaps if I'd gone to school here instead of boarding in the city, I might have made some of those connections. People look at me in the street, and in my head, they are saying 'There goes that Melissa Gilbert', but I'm not really one of them. In their eyes, my work doesn't measure up. Underneath, I'm scared I'll be exposed as a fraud, and that everyone knows this already."

Chris looked at her in open amazement. "But your exhibition here was a success. How could you possibly think you're a fraud?"

"I know—the tourists loved the prints, but as far as the locals were concerned, I was just another person from the city who was blowing in and blowing out again. Organising this art show is a way of justifying my existence I think--and proving to myself as well as everyone else that I'm part of this community after all.

"And what about your father? Isn't this also about gaining his approval?"

She chewed her lip pensively, a small frown creasing her brow. It was a moment before she replied. "I hadn't thought about that, but you're right. His opinion does matter to me. That's very perceptive."

"Dr Freud, that's me. Sweetheart, you're incredibly hard on yourself. Drink up. I think it's time for one of my healing massages."

They left early the next morning, driving back in the ute Chris had borrowed from Mark. He dropped her off at the hospital, before continuing to Mark's flat.

"Call me. I'll be at the Crown Plaza with the boss, so if I'm not around you can leave a message at reception. I hope your dad continues to improve. Let me know how your plans progress."

She leaned across and gave him a kiss before opening the passenger door and scrambling out. There was never an elegant way to get out of a ute. She had a couple or errands to run in town, but the only person she still needed to speak to about her plans was her father. Would he support her? With him, it was impossible to tell.

The hospital doors slid open at her approach. The air conditioning was a blissful contrast to the heat of the day. Just as Melissa was about to step into the elevator to go to the level accommodating her father, Jenny stepped out of it.

"Jenny! Good timing," she quipped.

"Hi Missy. You obviously made it back safely. Everything okay at home?"

"Running like clockwork, as far as I could tell. Chris and Pete seem to have things under control. How's dad today?"

"His speech and mobility are improving every day. I'm not sure if it's his determination or the standard of medical care he's getting. Sometimes he loses words or stutters, but based on what I saw just now, he's on the path to recovery."

Melissa shook her head. "Here I am, racing back from the other side of the world because my father has had a major medical crisis, and he's bouncing back already. Typical. He's such a contrary bugger."

Jenny laughed with her. "Bouncing back is an exaggeration, but you'll be impressed. He'll be happy to see you. He's driving himself and everyone else crazy. He's never had such a long period of inactivity. He's a rotten patient."

"I pity the ward staff. They're probably doing everything they can to get him better and out of their hair. I want to discuss my current plans with him, so I'll see you back at the town house this afternoon."

As she walked down the corridor towards his room, she rehearsed in her head what she was going to say. She wasn't looking forward to this discussion.

Her father, in dressing gown and slippers, was seated in a chair by the window. A book lay on the bedside trolley, indicating that he was managing to read again, or at least trying.

251

Facing him, Melissa perched herself on the end of his bed. "How are you feeling, Dad?"

"Be b-b-better when out h-h-hospital."

"You'll be pleased to know that Pete and Chris have got things under control with the muster. The cattle were trucked into sale earlier this week and Chris has gone back to his proper job, though he's still flying in this region for a few days."

"Hmmph."

Melissa decided she should assume this meant, *Thank everyone very much for me.*

"Dad, we need to talk about a couple of things. Firstly Pete. Are you planning on publicly acknowledging him? What role are you planning for him on the station now?

"I'll look after Pete. Jenny's b-b-been in my ear. He's a g-g-good man. Likely to make me a g-grandfather before you ever will. What's g-g-going on... you and Chris Harris?"

Melissa crossed her arms, feeling the heat surge in her cheeks. She hadn't rehearsed this part of the conversation. "We were talking about Pete not Chris, but since you ask, he and I have been close for a while. There's nothing more to tell you. Incidentally, it was his idea to come up here and help you out. I had nothing to do with it. You should thank him when you see him next. Getting back to my initial question, are you going to let other people know Pete is your son?"

"If they ask. There's no need to sh-shout from the rooftops. 's up to him; depends what *he* wants. He might n-n-not want me for a-a-a father. You don't."

She contemplated a couple of responses before deciding that she was not going to get side-tracked on that issue. "The
252

other thing I wanted to talk to you about is the Araluen Health Clinic. I heard that Mum used to volunteer there sometimes. I'm organising an Art Show for indigenous artists to raise funds for the clinic so that they can provide better services to kids who live in the camps. It was a combination of learning of mum's involvement and discovering some of the inequities that Aboriginal people face that made me think about it. I've got preliminary support for the proposal though I still have to approach the big sponsors." She tried not to sound wheedling. "Will you donate money for a prize? I think given the family connections to the indigenous community, raising funds for the clinic is the least we can do, don't you?"

"I thought your life was in Sydney now; finished with Alice and with me in particular. Now you want me to d-d-donate money to some local c-c-cause."

There was an awkward silence. Melissa looked critically at her father. He had more colour than when she'd first returned to Alice, but he seemed to have aged. The stroke had been a shock to him, just as it had been to everyone else.

She was conflicted. He had been an abysmal father, but Rose was right. They had very similar personalities. Through her feelings of guilt, she'd allowed him to intimidate her when growing up. It was time she stood up to him. She should have done so years ago.

"Father, you've controlled so much of my life. Everything I've done has been seeking your approval and that's something you've never been able to give me. It's not that I didn't want you as a father, but you didn't want me as a daughter."

He flapped his hands at her, opening his mouth as though about to say something and then closed it again, falling back

253

against the pillow behind him. Melissa paused, noting his pallor but her drive to say what she needed to say was stronger than her concern.

"As a parent you were emotionally absent. I know the deaths of Mother and William were tragic and you've always blamed me for that, but I feel as though I have been punished enough. This is one occasion when I'd like your support."

He shook his head, as though unable to take in what she was saying. "What … you t-t-talking about? H-h-how did I blame you?"

Tears threatened. She couldn't look at him. *Dammit.* She didn't want to break down now. Her throat tightened and the words came out in a rush. "Mum was speeding that day because I'd made her late, and then I survived, and William didn't."

"Missa, …not your fault. You hear me? Not. Your. Fault. The t-t-tyre blew and that's why she rolled."

Dan clawed at his knees, making a rumbling noise in his throat. Melissa wasn't sure if he was trying to get up or just express himself better. He finally got the words out.

"My fault… my fault. My blame not making sure tyres okay. Blame myself for their d-d-deaths." Moisture pooled in the corner of his eyes. "Grateful one child survived. Never, ever r-r-regret you were alive.

He was breathing heavily, his voice hoarse with emotion.

"Raising little girl not something I knew how to do. I was lost. When you came home from h-h-hospital, you were withdrawn." He looked at her intently. "We couldn't change what had happened. We both had to t-t-toughen up. Only the tough survive in the bush." He broke eye contact, rubbing the side of his face with a shaking hand. "As you grew older, you looked like your mother. You reminded me of the l-l-love of my life. It wasn't you I was withdrawing from; it was the g-g-grief."

Melissa could no longer hold back the tears which coursed down her face. They were tears for herself, tears for her mother and tears for an impossible situation. For the first time, she realised what the impact must have been for her father. He pushed a box of tissues in her direction and looked away while she mopped her face. Dealing with emotion was still not one of his strong points.

When she was able to speak again, her tone was more accusing than she meant it to be. "That didn't stop you finding solace with Maisie."

"I'm not proud. She was a c-c-caring young woman... provided comfort when I needed it. No idea she'd had a baby, not until years later. She had a partner by then—didn't want anything from me. She let me send P-p-pete to school in Alice but that's all. She was proud woman."

The blanket over his knees slid to the floor and Melissa suddenly realised he was shaking.

"Melissa--had enough for now. I might lie down."

She jumped up from the bed, assisting him to lever himself out of the chair and swivel his body onto the bed. The intimacy of helping him was a strange feeling.

"Dad, about the art show …

"I'll th-think about it, all right?"

CHAPTER 18

CHRIS MOVED INTO the Crowne Plaza in an adjoining suite to that occupied by his boss. He was expected to be on call and able to depart at a moment's notice. True to his word, he made an approach to the Big Man on Melissa's behalf for sponsorship. As he told Melissa later, it certainly helped that the reason for being in Alice was to inspect some cattle properties. Any proposals putting him in a good light with the local community were likely to be favourably received.

It wasn't that simple though. The boss wanted Melissa to put her proposal to him in person and she was invited to meet with him and his financial adviser, Matt Dawkins, at the hotel. She fronted up as requested.

"So, explain to me Ms Gilbert—why should Channel Nine sponsor this event? What benefit will it be to the community and importantly, what benefit will it be to Channel Nine?"

The Big Man leant back in his chair, arms folded. Melissa took a deep breath and then exhaled slowly before she spoke.

He was more intimidating in person than she expected. She had to stop herself from gabbling as she outlined the concept for the umpteenth time "… and I've already got provisional support from members of the indigenous community, and even my father is prepared to stump up with a prize."

This was a fib as her father still hadn't committed himself. She was assuming that he would.

"Your father, as I understand it from my pilot, owns a station near here?"

"Well, depending on your definition of 'near', yes he does. The family has owned Plenty River for three generations. He's recuperating from a health issue in the Alice Springs Hospital at the moment and is very keen to get out. He's not a man to tolerate enforced inactivity."

"A man after my own heart. Perhaps I should have a chat to him. He may have some useful advice. Yes, we'll support your Art Show. I'll discuss it with Matt here on what we'll offer and the opportunities we expect in return. He'll contact you to discuss the finer points and you can sort out the paperwork with him."

The Big Man levered himself out of his chair and Melissa got the message the discussion was over. She glanced at Matt, not having paid him much attention before. He had pleasing features, bordering on attractive. The cut and quality of his suit and his well-manicured nails indicated that his was an executive-level role.

The smile he turned in her direction was open and friendly. "Leave me your number and I'll call you in the morning. Will around ten be okay?

He offered his hand and his grip was firm, but his palm was smooth. She could detect a clean soap smell. It was oddly appealing.

"That sounds wonderful. I look forward to your call." She turned back to the Big Man. "Thank you for your time. I'll let my father know you might like to pick his brains. There's not much he doesn't know about the area, or the local properties and the people. He's a man of few words but he'll be able to tell you what you need to know."

I'd better get to him first before he lets drop he hasn't given me any commitments yet.

She got a nod in response and Matt showed her to the door of the suite, confirming he would call her the following day.

As she walked out into the street, her step was lighter than before. It stood her in good stead for that afternoon, as she was approaching the suggested government departments. Belinda accompanied her to these meetings, as she had the contacts within these organisations and also the credibility based on her current reputation.

Once again, it was not possible to get immediate answers, but they came away satisfied the door was open and initial responses were positive. They were keen to debrief over some well-earned refreshments and Melissa guided her friend to a window table in Marnie's Café. It had become a favourite of hers since the initial visit with Chris. They eyed off the cake display but managed to withstand the temptation. Melissa pushed the sugar bowl aside to accommodate her notebook.

"You were brilliant, Belinda. Knowing the right people and the approach to take made all the difference."

"You did your bit. Part of the discussion was about proving your credibility and experience. Government ministers don't like to support projects that are not reliably going to succeed. There's no turning back now. I think we got enough positive vibes that we can assume it's going to happen. Time for some serious planning."

The coffees arrived, which to their delight were accompanied by complementary bite-sized shortbread. As Belinda remarked, sometimes that was all you needed.

"I'll definitely be coming back here," she said, spooning the froth from the top.

Melissa let out a huge breath, settling back in her chair. "I'm just glad to be sitting down. This has been a full-on sort of day. You know I met the boss from Channel Nine earlier? He's intimidating in person. I wasn't sure how to take him but he said he'll provide sponsorship. I just don't know in what form or what he expects in return. I'll find out tomorrow when his sidekick calls me with the details."

"You seem to know people in the best places. Are there any other big-name sponsors to approach?"

"Qantas of course, to get assistance with air fares for the judges."

"Based on your track record so far you should be fine. "

Belinda opened her diary and reviewed the programmes and exhibitions that were already booked in at the Cultural Centre.

"This is the time frame available to you. Does that sound workable? You'll need to put together your promotional plan. I'll line you up with a local graphic designer and printer. Now, where's your list?"

They ordered a second cup of coffee before completing the outline of tasks. Melissa's head was spinning. She sat back, brushing the hair from her face, and threw her pen on the table. The list was lengthy. There was so much to think about. It would be more involved than she'd appreciated. She'd been so caught up in how wonderful it would be to help the Clinic that the reality of achieving that goal had been slightly obscured.

As she said to Chris that evening when she met him for a drink, it was potentially overwhelming.

"It's made me understand just what I've taken on. At least the responses have been positive. I should hear back from Matt Dawkins tomorrow with details of the Channel Nine offer."

"Didn't you outline to Matt and the Boss what you wanted?"

"No. I should have gone to them with a concrete proposal, shouldn't I? They'll think I'm such a novice."

"If they don't do the right thing by you let me know," Chris said, assuming an arms-folded masterful pose. "I'll drop them off in the middle of nowhere and they'll have to walk back to town."

"Somehow, I don't think that's going to help. Nice thought though."

"Watch out for Matt Dawkins. He's a smooth character."

Melissa was pleased she didn't run into him as she quietly slipped out of Chris's hotel room some time later.

~

Unable to sleep with ideas and tasks buzzing through her head, Melissa rose early. Jenny joined her for an early cuppa on the front veranda of the town house as they welcomed the dawn.

"I love this time of day," Jenny said as they sat in companionable silence, listening to the morning birds. "It's part of my thinking time, when I mentally sort out the issues of the moment."

"Mmm."

"Talking of issues of the moment, what's happening with you and Chris and when are you going back to Sydney?"

"What's this—my early morning interrogation?"

"Tell me to mind my own business, but as much as organising this Art Show is doing a wonderful thing, and I'm very proud of you, I also wonder what you're running away from. I can look after your father—you know that. I've been doing it for years and he's getting the very best of care in hospital. It seemed that your life in Sydney was really coming together and I thought you and Chris were a strong item as well."

"We are... we were. I'm just not sure what to think. He's been my absolute rock in recent times."

"So, what's the problem?"

There was a drawn-out silence. Jenny waited while Melissa collected her thoughts.

"You know as well as I do that Father always assumed Alex Woodleigh and I would be a match. It was such a deep-seated belief that I took on that assumption as well. I knew and understood this was my destiny—to marry a man of the land and live my life here on a station as our families have always done."

She sipped her tea while thinking about what she had just said. "I realise now I wouldn't have been happy with that life, but it has taken me a while to truly appreciate that. This recent

261

overseas trip has given me enough distance to put some things into perspective." Her look when she turned to Jenny was earnest. "I would have been utterly miserable and so I'm sure would Alex. He and Kathy are much better suited. It surprised me initially, but I recognise it now."

"I think you're right about that. So, what about Chris?"

Melissa gave a wry smile. "You don't need me to tell you Chris is as far different from Alex as you could get. He's at home in the city as well as the bush, he doesn't expect my life to revolve around his, and he's genuinely thoughtful and generous. He still manages to surprise me when I least expect it."

"Sounds wonderful to me. Am I sensing a *but*?"

Melissa glanced quickly at her companion before colouring and looking away again. "You'll think I'm silly."

"Try me."

"I've never been totally convinced that I deserved the sort of happiness Chris offered. I can't be sure I won't wake up one day and find that he's gone or found someone else he prefers instead."

"Oh Missy—I don't think you're silly; I fully understand where you're coming from, but do you seriously think that Chris would do that to you? I don't know him anywhere near as well as you do but my impressions of the man are that he is quite honourable. Your feelings are more the issue."

"I think he's the best thing that ever happened to me—aside from you of course—but something is holding me back from making that final commitment."

A morning jogger hove into view, a small dog panting at her heels. The two women watched her progress, pausing their conversation as she passed.

"Missy don't let life's opportunities pass you by. You have a long time to live with regret if you do." Her soft voice was tinged with sadness and instinctively Melissa took Jenny's hand and stroked it. She couldn't bear to think of the other woman being distressed. "God, Jenny, how insensitive of me. Here I am asking people questions about my mother, but I never asked about your life before you came to live with us. I never asked why. It must have been a big change to isolate yourself on a remote property, looking after a sad little girl and a taciturn man who rarely managed more than a grunt."

"It wasn't that bad and nor is your father impossible to live with. He was grieving of course, but he's always been fair and respectful. I knew where I stood with Dan Gilbert, and looking after you was never a chore. You've been the daughter I never had."

"But what enticed you to accept the job? It's all right to ask that question, isn't it?"

"Of course, it is. It's past history now, anyway. I fell in love with a married man and stupidly devoted prime years of my life to him. He had children and couldn't leave his wife while the children were growing up but promised he would when the youngest left school."

She was matter-of-fact in this telling, but that didn't disguise the underlying sadness. "It meant our time together was always stolen, and we never got to share Christmases or special birthdays or anything like that. I put up with it all because I loved him and believed one day, he would be free, and we'd be together."

"Jenny, how awful for you." *And then to end up at a loveless place like Plenty River. Was this how Maisie felt? Did she run away from a hopeless situation? What did she feel for my father?*

Jenny continued. "I'm a slow learner because I let this situation drag on for years. Then I discovered I wasn't the only one. There was another woman he was seeing at the same time, and of course he never intended leaving his wife for either of us. I was utterly devastated and so I ran away as far as I could. I fantasised about turning up at his house and creating a scene, letting his wife know what a three-timing pig he was, but I was emotionally shattered. I wanted to crawl into a big black hole and not emerge for a century or two. Instead, I came to Plenty River."

Melissa's heart ached for the woman beside her. Not for the first time, she was aware she had been so self-absorbed with the nuances of her life, that she'd given scant thought to the stories of those around her. She was embarrassed by how self-centred she'd been.

"Some people might say you did crawl into a black hole. I'm so sorry Jenny, not only because you had to go through that but because I've always selfishly assumed that you were there for our benefit and were happy to do so."

"Missy, I didn't tell you this story so that you would feel sorry for me. What I want to tell you is not to miss life's opportunities. Don't fall into your own black hole when you don't need to. I wasted all that time waiting for my life to start and it never really did. Not with him anyway. Whether Chris

264

Harris is the right partner for you, I have no idea. I don't want to see you make the wrong decisions, but I don't want to see you lose out through not making any decisions either."

CHAPTER 19

IT WAS LATE morning before Matt rang. Melissa had been busy with her own phone calls and the Channel Nine offer had momentarily slipped her mind, but he was very apologetic.

"I'm so sorry. I know I said that I would call at ten, but it's been a busy morning. We spoke to your father amongst other people. Chris Harris told us where to find him. He and the boss got along fine."

"Oh—that's… good." *What did my father say? Did he drop me in it?*

"Look, it's almost lunchtime," Matt said. "Would you like to join me and then we can discuss the sponsorship over a quick meal."

"Oh, there's no need for that. Can't you just tell me over the phone?" She pushed her hair behind her ears and reached for a pen to take some notes.

"Well, not really. There's a contract to sign so we need to do that in person. We both need to eat so we might as well kill two birds with one stone. Can you meet me in the Crowne Plaza Restaurant in about half an hour?"

It made sense. At least they would get the paperwork out of the way. "Okay, I could do that. I'll see you soon."

Disconnecting the call, she quickly looked at her wardrobe. This was not a casual diner to which she'd been invited. It was a little more salubrious, but on the other hand, she didn't want to be over-dressed for lunch. She selected a simple cotton dress in shades of blues and lilacs that was teamed with a white bolero sporting matching trim. She slipped espadrilles on her feet and swept her hair up into a loose knot. With a quick application of mascara and lipstick, she was ready.

Matt was waiting at the bar when she arrived at the restaurant and rose to greet her with a welcoming smile and a warm handshake, grasping her hand in both of his.

"Melissa—good to see you. Can I get you a drink?"

"Just a mineral water thanks."

"Sensible choice. Let's move to a table." He summonsed the waiter and organised the drink and table in quick succession. He was, as Melissa noted, a man who was used to taking charge. Probably that was why he was in his particular job.

They got down to business while waiting for the food to be served, reviewing the Channel Nine offer and what was expected in return. Melissa didn't feel she was in any position to bargain, being happy to accept whatever they suggested. There were a range of PR requirements of course, and an insistence that she work with their publicity department in relation to all advertising and promotions.

The contract also stipulated the size and frequency of promotional material being displayed. Her head spun and she desperately hoped that there was no conflict with requirements that other sponsors might have, but in true gung-ho fashion, decided she would cross that bridge when she came to it and add the experience to her growing list of learnings. The offer was too good to quibble over. She signed the paperwork.

"Now, tell me more about yourself. How is it that such a beautiful and talented woman is staging an indigenous art show in Alice Springs?"

Melissa shrugged off her discomfort at his choice of words and gave him a brief outline on growing up at Plenty River and subsequently living and working out of Sydney. He absorbed every word with a direct gaze that made her feel she was the most important and fascinating person in his life.

"I'd love to see examples of your work. When are you back in Sydney? We could catch up again when we each have more time."

My God, he's coming on to me. The realisation sent a tingle down her spine. He was a very good-looking man and incredibly charming.

"If you want to see my work, there's some featured on the walls of a local restaurant here in Alice, and I think there are still some prints on display at the Araluen Cultural Centre."

"I know I could go and look at those, but it's not the same as having the photographer talk me through each scene—what was happening at that time, and what influenced you to take that photograph. That's what I want to know. When I understand that, I'll have a better understanding of Melissa Gilbert and her artistic muse."

To have someone so intensely interested in her work was as heady as an aphrodisiac. *Is my work that good? What is he suggesting? Surely he realises Chris and I are more than just friends?*

When would she go back to Sydney? Perhaps she *should* start making some definite plans. Her work wouldn't wait forever after all. The fashion houses and shoot directors would look elsewhere. These thoughts flashed through her mind as he smiled at her again and reached across the table to take her hand.

"Do say you'll let me take you out to dinner in Sydney." At that point, his phone rang. He frowned, apologising for not having turned it off. "Do you mind if I take this? It's probably the boss."

"Sure. Go ahead." The boss wasn't a man to be kept waiting. That was the impression she'd gained anyway.

He rose from the table and moved to a corner of the room, engaging in animated but quiet conversation. Melissa decided to make the most of the moment with a quick visit to the bathroom. On her return, Matt was facing the window, still in conversation. The carpeted floor muffled her footsteps and as she passed by, she heard him say, "Sure honey, I won't forget. I'll pick up something special for the kids before I leave."

She had slipped back into her chair before he finished the call and returned to the table.

"Sorry about that. Work stuff. Never really stops." The smile that he gave her was pure charm, only this time she saw it for what it was. Pure con.

"Matt, this has been a delightful lunch, but I can see you're very busy and I mustn't keep you any longer. I have a host of things to do as well, so I should be going. Thank you for the sponsorship, and I look forward to this partnership with Channel Nine." She leaned down to pick up her bag. "I hope you and your boss can come back for the opening. Chris Harris will keep you informed of details. I'll make sure it's a noteworthy event."

She held out her hand, head tilted to one side, not holding eye contact for any longer than she had to. With a polite smile, she turned and walked out of the restaurant and into the afternoon sun.

Pulling up in the hospital car park, she sat for a while, basking in the warmth penetrating the car windows. She had dodged a bullet. Perhaps the naïve approach in requesting sponsorship had convinced Matt Dawson that she was naïve in other matters as well. Or perhaps this was just standard operating procedure for him. She should have known better than to be drawn in by that sophisticated charm. Chris did warn her. She hadn't understood then what he might have meant. With Jenny's story still fresh in her mind, she was painfully aware of the consequences of making such a mistake. Not that she would have made it. He would never match up to Chris.

He father sat again in the armchair by the window in his room. He appeared to be dozing but opened his eyes as she approached.

"Melissa! I had an interesting visitor today."

"So I heard. Were you able to tell him what he wanted to know?"

"I d-d-don't know if it was what he *wanted* to know, but I t-t-told him what I th-th-thought he *ought* to know. There's a difference."

Melissa thought that her father and the big man were an interesting match for each other. She suppressed a grin. "I hope he appreciated your expert opinion."

"He did. He's offered me a-a-a consultancy. He wants an… adviser to help firstly on his property acquisition, and then… on management of… his cattle empire."

There was a measure of smugness behind these words. The day was full of surprises. Melissa gave her father an incredulous look. He was still in hospital and in need of monitoring and physiotherapy.

"Dad, how will you manage that? You've still a way to go with recovery and then there's the station to run, though Pete has it under control. I suppose he'll take over greater responsibility for operations now."

"Well that's where you're w-w-wrong. Pete won't have much to do with the property at all."

"What do you mean?" Her indignation rose along with her voice. "You can't just abandon him. He's grown up there—it's his life."

"Have you asked Pete what he wants to do?" The raised eyebrows inferred a measure of accusation. "No? I have. Perhaps you should too."

Strange that Chris also had mentioned she should put the question to Pete, instead of making assumptions. Her father clearly revelled in knowing something she didn't. He was like a little kid with his barely suppressed glee.

"Okay, tell me. What does Pete want to do?"

"He wants to apply for medical school and move to Adelaide to go to Uni. He wants to be a doctor. You're not the only one who wants to improve indigenous health, you know. It must run in the family."

"But where has this come from? He's never mentioned it before." It was embarrassing to realise she'd never asked him any of those personal questions or invited any confidences. Why should he have mentioned it to her?

Her father shook his head, and she could see that underneath, he was as surprised about this turn of events as she was.

"We discussed it on his recent visit. I suggested he should take over running the property, as this health scare has made me realise I can't keep up the same pace that I have to date." This statement was punctuated with a sigh.

"He said he would help where he could, but what he really wanted to do was study medicine. He'd not thought it was possible before, but there's a special program available in assisting indigenous students who want to apply for medical training."

With the enthusiasm for his topic, Dan's speech improved. As Melissa realised, his improvement was significant.

"His school reports were always sent to me and I saw he'd done well with his studies but never thought any more of it. It never occurred to me that he might want to pursue a tertiary education let alone study medicine."

His shoulders shook with a brief coughing fit. It took a few moments before he regained his composure. "I've said if he puts in the work and gets accepted, I'll give him a living allowance. As for what happens in the future with the property, we'll just have to see."

Melissa propped herself on the edge of his bed. She shouldn't have been surprised, but she was. She had taken it for granted that she had the freedom to choose where to live and what to study. A few indigenous kids had grown up in the camp near the station. They either stayed there or migrated to the outskirts of Alice, but never went further afield. Many of them never finished high school. She hadn't questioned that. It was simply the way things were. Perhaps Pete would change that.

"What about the station? You're not selling Plenty River are you? That's our home. That's where Mother and William are."

"No, I'm not selling. It's been in the family for three generations now and who knows what the future holds. It's time for a change though. I've had plenty of time in which to think while I've been stuck here and there are things even I would like to do before it gets too late. You know I've never even been overseas?"

"I didn't think you were interested. You've never said as much."

"I don't tell you everything, my girl. It's time that Jenny got some travelling in as well. She's been here far too long."

This is an interesting turn of events. What else haven't you been telling me?

"I'll still be overseeing the property, but I'm going to install a manager. Pete's not the only one who has been raised on or spent a lot of time working on the station. There are more of his mob, and if no-one's suitable, I'll bring in someone from outside. Whatever, it's time for some changes."

"I don't think you've ever surprised me before Father. You've always been predictable to the extreme. This time, I think you've done it."

Dan Gilbert briefly nodded in acknowledgement, a hint of a smile visible to anyone who looked closely—very closely.

"I heard you talked your way into some sponsorship, too. Not only that, I heard I've donated a prize."

Her head lifted a fraction. The gaze that met his was defiant. "Well you haven't said no. I might have jumped the gun, but I needed something to produce as evidence there was local support for the Art Show; that people were already putting their hands in the pocket. It was strategic."

To her surprise, her father chuckled.

"There might be some of your old man in you after all."

The days that followed were taken up with following her plan, in consultation with Belinda and Marlene. She called on the Qantas Office in town and then participated in a phone conference with the PR and Strategic Communications Division in Sydney. She met with Joel Pemberton, the manager of Radio Alice and also the manager of CAAMA, the radio station servicing the local indigenous community. Both managers gave a commitment to publicise the Art Show to their listeners.

Melissa had to guarantee she would provide regular updates of progress and ensure that interviews were available with either entrants to the exhibition, or else the judges and others who were involved in some way with promoting the event. She had no idea how she was going to arrange that, but her philosophy was simply to agree. She would worry later about how to make it happen. There may be costs involved, but sponsorship would cover that.

"Girl, you don't waste time," said Marlene. "I reckon we can start choosing the colour of that new clinic van."

"Marlene, that's called 'counting your chickens'. We've a long way to go yet. We've got a lot of people promising support, but until we've got those paintings arriving through the front door and the town's people and tourists lining up to view the art show, I won't believe we've pulled it off. That reminds me—the auctioneer. He's the next one to see."

She scurried off to tackle one of the town's real estate agents and to persuade him to run the art auction.

"Melissa, give me a house or two and I'm fine. I know what I'm doing but I know nothing about art. I'm not sure I'm the right person for you." His frown of concern was accentuated by his open-handed gesture.

"Martin, you don't have to know anything about art—you need to know how to work the crowd and keep the bids coming. You do that most weeks of the year. It'll be fun—you'll see. Did I tell you Channel Nine are sponsoring the event? You'll probably be on television. Think what this is going to do for your reputation. I'm sure it will be good for business."

"Why do I get the feeling I'm being steamrollered? Okay, I'll do it, but don't blame me if the whole thing tanks." He gave her a pseudo coy look. "Just make sure they capture my best side."

"You're a good man Martin. You won't regret this." As she left his office, he was still shaking his head and muttering to himself. He would cope.

That still left the judges to be engaged and that was important as she wanted to feature them in the promotions. She rang Russell and got him on the case.

"Leave it with me, Pet. I'll get you the best in the business and if I can't, I'll do it for you."

"Russell, I was thinking of a panel of three judges; one indigenous and two of repute, probably from interstate, but you will have a better idea than me on the artists who live both in the Territory and elsewhere. Can I leave it with you for now and call you back in a few days to see who you've come up with? I can probably use local contacts to identify an indigenous artist, but I need help on the others."

"You've come to absolutely the right person. With me on the job, it's bound to be a huge success. I can't wait to come back to Alice and help you with your grand event. Did you say you've got sponsorship from Qantas? They'll come to the party for art consultants, won't they?"

"I don't know, Russell," she replied weakly. "I haven't discussed that level of detail."

She met Chris for dinner later that evening. "What have I done?" she moaned to him. "I've unleashed the prima donna in Russell."

"I don't think so sweetheart. From what I've seen, it was there all the time. He'll just add some of the colour everyone expects."

They were in the restaurant attached to the Crowne Plaza. It was on the top floor of the hotel and looked out over the bed of the Todd River. When there was rain, the river became a raging torrent for a brief period, before settling into sporadic waterholes and then drying up completely. It was now a sandy river bed, punctuated by tall eucalypts. It was a characteristic view and didn't need water to be appealing.

Melissa would have preferred they dined somewhere else, but by the time Chris got back from his flight that day, he was exhausted. She didn't want to run into Matt Dawson again, although she would have to liaise with him at some stage. This was not the time to think about Matt. Chris was flying back to Sydney in the morning. The big man had completed his negotiations and so the Channel Nine group were leaving town.

She was going to miss him, though their time together over the past few days had been fragmented. Chris had flown each day and was on call when he wasn't in the air. She had looked forward to the evenings when she could debrief the day and assess whether she was really achieving progress.

Chris listened carefully to her report of the day's events. "You don't need me to tell you; it's all coming together. Speaking of which, am I sensing a thawing of relations between you and your father?"

"Yes, and no. No matter what he says, he can't erase a couple of decades of poor behaviour, just like that. I'm not quite ready to forgive and forget."

The waiter hovered at their elbows, so they paused to place their orders. Chris reviewed the wine list.

"I'm not sitting in the cockpit tomorrow, so there's no reason why I can't enjoy a drink tonight. We'll have a bottle of Moët and Chandon Imperial Brut," he said to the waiter.

"You're going top shelf tonight!" Melissa said after the waiter had disappeared.

"Why not? It's my last night in town, and our last night together for a while. I think that warrants a celebration, don't you?"

"You mean you're happy to be leaving? How does that reflect on me?" Her eyes widened with indignation.

He gave a quick smile, but there was no warmth to it. "No, sweetheart, I'm not happy about that. Things are still up in the air about our relationship and our future. I'd rather be leaving with a different understanding."

Melissa flushed and dropped her eyes. She knew now that many of her fears making her hesitate to commit were not justified but couldn't bring herself to talk about it. Not yet. The knot in her stomach tightened. Her eyes wandered over the table setting before looking back to meet his. "Did you know that Pete wants to study medicine? He wants to be a doctor?"

Chris looked at her for a moment, then sighed and picked up his glass. As a topic-changing strategy, it was clumsy and obvious. "Yes, I did. We talked about it when we'd run out of other conversation. I told him to go for it."

"You never told me."

He rubbed his head, his hair sticking out at odd angles which was endearing in an odd way. "Sweetheart, I know you don't want to discuss 'us', but hear me out. Then we'll talk about other things. Okay?"

She nodded at him, twiddling the stem of her glass, not trusting herself to speak.

Chris reached across the table and took her hand in his, his thumb making a gentle caressing motion. "I have a better understanding now of some of the major influences in your life and why you respond the way you do. Just remember—I'm not your father. I'm not judging you and even if I were, you definitely wouldn't be found 'wanting'. I know the Melissa Gilbert who is clever, artistic, highly professional, and is one sassy woman. I love your independence and your strength."

The wave of emotion she felt took her by surprise. *What have I done to deserve this man?* She didn't trust herself to speak, instead focussed on the intensity of his words.

"I know things are happening here in Alice for you, but I have to go back to my job. When you're ready, call me. I may not come running, but I'll be there." He paused, still looking her in the eyes. "So… how was your day?"

Melissa was flooded with conflicting emotions. She wanted to tell him about her conversations with her father and how they both blamed themselves for her mother's death; that the ground beneath her feet was shifting and she was learning to look forwards and not dwell on the mistakes of the past. She also knew that she had thrown herself so enthusiastically into the Art Show, that she'd had little time for self-reflection. She knew what Chris meant to her and she didn't want to lose him, but she also needed to process some of the things she had learnt about herself and her family in recent days. It was important if she wanted to move on emotionally.

"Thank you," she said. "Thank you for what you just said. You've been incredibly patient, and I am so lucky to have you in my life."

She shuffled the cutlery on the table.

"As for my day, it was full-on as usual. I'd rather hear about yours. I know you can't talk about the confidential negotiations but tell me where you went and who you saw. I want to hear it all."

Melissa knew the places and people he described over their meal and enjoyed the updates and regional news. It was indicative of what she had missed while living in Sydney—being part of a huge community that spanned huge areas and rarely caught up in person but stayed connected anyway.

"Don't you miss this life?" she asked.

"I do and I don't. I miss the stimulation, the camaraderie and the sense of freedom I get from working out here. I'm enjoying city life as well and the opportunities that brings. It's not the location that challenges me—it's who I share it with that counts." With his elbow on the table and resting his chin on the palm of his hand, he gazed into her eyes. A smile lurked. "Can I invite myself to come and view your etchings?"

Melissa tossed down the last of her champagne. "I thought you'd never ask."

He pulled her chair back as she rose, and they made their way down the lift to his room. This time, she didn't care who saw them. The shared night was bitter-sweet. There was now that easy familiarity, with bodies that melded beautifully, anticipating reactions and singing in harmony. Melissa revelled in the feeling of security as she nestled against Chris's chest.

"Thank you" he whispered.

"For what?"

"For being you; for being here with me." He kissed her gently and fell almost immediately into an easy sleep.

Melissa stayed awake a while longer, studying him while he slept. His hair was scuffed into childlike peaks, but his physique exposed by the turned-down sheet was anything but. She was tempted to run her fingers through the soft mat of golden hairs on his chest but let him sleep. Plenty of time for that. Tomorrow, she would tell him. She no longer had any doubts. She belonged wherever he might be. She fell into a restful sleep, knowing her champion lay beside her.

CHAPTER 20

WHEN SHE AWOKE, the bed beside her was empty. A note lay on his pillow.

> *Sweetheart – got an early morning summons from the big man. My flight leaves at 11:30. See you before I go?*
>
> *C xxx*

She rose quickly and slipped home for a shower and breakfast. She needed to update Marlene on a few details so would drop in at the Clinic first, and then continue to the airport.

As usual, the Clinic waiting room was chaotic. An adult rather than paediatric clinic was in session, but there were still children adding to the level of noise and activity. Melissa looked around in confusion, before she saw Marlene engaged in conversation with an elderly Aboriginal woman. She made eye contact and waited until Marlene was free to speak to her.

"I can see you're busy, so I won't keep you. I just wanted to let you know what's happened in the last couple of days.

Everything's falling into place. I'm just going to need some help in identifying a potential judge from the Aboriginal community."

"Come into my office. It'll be quieter in there."

It took a while to make it into the office, as two separate people waylaid Marlene to tell her about their issues.

"Just take a seat, Rosy. The doctor will see you soon. You must wait your turn. I know your belly still hurts. Did you take the medicine you were given before? You'll have to tell the doctor."

She was everyone's friend, and everyone's go-to person when there was a problem, medical or otherwise. Shutting the office door behind them and sinking into a chair, Marlene rested her forehead briefly in the palm of her hand and heaved a deep sigh.

"What time is it? Is it home time yet?"

Melissa paused by the door. "You stay there; put your feet up for a while and I'll make you a cup of tea. You look as though you need it. Just point me in the right direction."

"Thanks luv. That's just what the doctor ordered. I can't sit long though. There's too much to do and it's pandemonium out there."

With a mug of tea in each hand, Melissa pushed the door shut behind her with her foot. Carefully balanced between the handle and the rim of one were a couple of biscuits. "I thought you might need some sustenance as well."

"You're an angel. While you were gone, I wrote down a couple of names of people you could approach. What would be a good idea would be to speak to the owner of the MacDonnell Ranges Gallery. He's been selling indigenous art for years, and he knows good work when he sees it. He's not indigenous, but he's local and people trust his opinion. Why don't you have a chat to him?"

"Thank you I will. I knew you'd point me in the right direction. I'll talk fast while you drink your tea."

Melissa outlined the successful interviews she'd had with Channel Nine, Qantas and the Government Departments.

"It's not a done deal in each instance, but the reception was favourable and I'm reasonably confident they are going to get behind us. I've even got my first guaranteed entrant. Albert, Pete's uncle, has promised he'll submit a painting. He needed some persuasion, but he agreed and that's the main thing."

"Like I said, you take after your mum. Once she got her teeth into an issue, she didn't give up either."

"It's good to know I take after her in some things. Look, I'll get out of your hair now. I'll make an appointment next time I come in, I promise."

The scene beyond the office door was as expected. The elderly woman Marlene had been speaking to when Melissa first arrived was standing near the front door with her walking frame, peering out at the street.

"Marlene! My taxi hasn't come. How am I going to get home?"

"I could take her," Melissa murmured to Marlene. "Where does she live?"

"Coral has a house on the edge of town, in the Racecourse area. If you've got time, that would be marvellous. She gets agitated if she has to wait too long." Marlene raised her voice.

"Coral, Melissa will drive you home. You have to tell her which house."

While Melissa brought the car to the front of the clinic, Marlene walked the woman out to the road. She gave Melissa directions and settled the old lady into the front seat of the car, and the walking frame into the back. Melissa checked her watch. She should have plenty of time to drive her home and get to the airport before the flight left, although Coral's address was on the opposite side of town.

She followed the directions that Marlene had provided. "I think this is the right street. Which house is yours?"

"Dat one. The green house at the end of the street. Dat's my home."

A car was already in the driveway, bonnet propped open. It looked like it had been that way for a long time. It meant Melissa had to pull up across the driveway. Jumping out, she pulled the walking frame out of the back and unfolded the sides. Then she turned her attention to Coral and getting her out of the car. That was not so easy. Coral was slow and arthritic and unsteady on her feet and there was no point in trying to hurry her. It was a major exercise for her just to swing her feet, first one and then the other, to the side of her seat. Melissa hovered uncertainly. Should she lift Coral into an upright position, or would that be unwelcome interference? She offered her arm and Coral seized it, dragging herself upright, panting with the exertion.

"Take your time, Coral. I'll move a few things out of your way."

285

Leaving Coral by the car, Melissa picked up a child's tricycle and moved it to one side and then moved the rubbish bin as well.

Coral overbalanced on the uneven ground, and she and the walker fell sideways. Melissa caught the movement out of the corner of her eye but wasn't quite quick enough to grab her.

Coral was a small slight woman, and it was more of a sideways slide than a dramatic fall.

"Coral are you all right? Let me help you up. Sorry, I shouldn't have left you."

"I'm not helpless, girl; just unsteady, that's all. Once I get inside, I'll be fine."

This time, Melissa did pick Coral up, and stayed by her side as she made her way towards the house, one small step at a time. When Melissa tried the door handle, the house wasn't locked. She pushed the door wide open and stood back to allow Coral to go first.

"Do you need a cup of tea? Shall I put the kettle on?"

"You're a good girl. I think I might just have a little lie down. Me daughter will be over later, and I'll have a cup of tea then."

Melissa didn't like to just leave Coral. She was probably shaken after her fall. The walker got parked in the hall and with the help of Melissa's arm, they made their way down to the bedroom. Melissa slipped Coral's shoes off and helped her to lie down on the bed.

"I'm fine now, girl. You get going. I'm just going to have a little nap."

Observing that Coral seemed both happy and comfortable, Melissa decided it was okay to leave.

It was only as she slid back into the driver's seat that she caught sight of the time. It was eleven o'clock. What she had thought would be a quick side-trip had turned out to be a major exercise. It was impossible to get to the airport in time. There was no point in even trying. By now, Chris would be boarding the aircraft and the doors would be shut. She hit the steering wheel in uncharacteristic rage and frustration. She was furious with herself and there was nothing she could do to change it.

On impulse, she started the car and drove towards Anzac Hill. It was a long time since she had been up there. The road wound around the hill, stopping in a car park near the apex. The last section she took on foot, climbing the stairs that led to the obelisk and the view that waited. She was lucky—she had the place to herself. The settlement spread out beneath her in neat ordered rows, framed by the MacDonnell Ranges in the background. It put the town into perspective and was a good vantage point from which to put her own thoughts into order as well.

She sat, quelling her inner turmoil. There was still a lot to organise with the art show, but plans were in place and she didn't have to do it all herself. Kathy, Marlene and Belinda were all available to varying degrees and with proper organisation, there would be others as well.

She didn't need to be on the station to be close to her Mother and William. The work she was doing had brought her closer to her mother than ever before. She would hold them in her heart no matter where she was.

Then there was her father. He was the reason she had returned to Alice after all. He was improving steadily and to her surprise, seemed to be planning adventures of his own.

They also seemed to include Jenny, although she had no idea what Jenny thought about that. So much was changing around her.

The greatest element of surprise had been Pete. With the benefit of hindsight, there were similarities in mannerism and tenacity between Pete and her father. She and Pete would probably never have a strong brother-sister relationship, but they had a shared history. She'd even acquired a sister-in-law and perhaps one day she would be an aunt.

A passenger jet passed overhead on the climb. She tracked it visually until it was out of sight. She had no way of knowing if it was Chris' flight, but even if it wasn't, he was in the process of flying out of Alice and he was leaving before she'd managed to speak to him. There was an ache in her throat and a single tear tracked part way down her face before she wiped it away with her sleeve. Melissa Gilbert didn't cry. If only she'd got to the airport on time. If only she'd told him how she felt.

Suddenly it was obvious. She knew what she had to do.

CHAPTER 21

AFTER DESCENDING OVER A vista of red rooves, the plane banked over Botany Bay, and lined up on the runway heading. The final approach was from the sea and she watched out the window as the aircraft sank lower over the waves before connecting with the runway projecting into the Bay. It was a scenario that had the power to thrill her every time she made this journey. This time, there was a mixture of anticipation and anxiety. She wasn't sure what her reception would be.

The key to Angela's terrace was in her bag. It didn't matter though because when her taxi drew up outside, the front curtains twitched, and Angela flew out of the house. "Why didn't you tell me you were coming? I would have killed the fatted calf!"

The two women embraced, emotion overwhelming them both before Angela pushed her friend at arm's length to better see her. "You're looking fantastic—as usual. Are you back for good? Do you have a contract? What's happening at home?"

"It's good to see some things never change. How about you make me a cup of tea and I'll fill you in?" Melissa picked up the handle of her suitcase and wheeled it towards the house. "You haven't given my room away, have you?"

"Don't be silly. It's waiting for you. Your return is timely—there are some fantastic jobs coming up. I much prefer to work with you. Eduardo will be pleased to see you; he's been fretting that you wouldn't come back."

The cup of tea was so good. Aircraft brew was never quite the same, and usually lukewarm at that.

"Angela, such a lot has happened—you wouldn't believe. I haven't even told you about Europe and touring the Riviera. I'll tell you everything I promise, but first, can I borrow your car? There is someone I really have to see."

"Well I don't need three guesses to work out who that is. Course you can take the car. Drive safely. Sydney traffic will be a culture shock after where you've been."

Angela was right, but Melissa managed to navigate safely to the cottage in Marrickville where Chris was living.

His car wasn't outside. Of course not—he'd still be at work. She'd just have to wait. She turned on the radio and flipped stations until she found something worth listening to. It was warm in the car and she was tired. Closing her eyes, she settled back into a corner of the seat. She could just have a little rest while she waited.

Damn. Someone was parked in his usual spot. He would have to grab a space further up the street. Not a problem really, but after the day he'd had, it was the last straw. As he pushed open the gate to the cottage, he looked back at the interloping car and was surprised to see someone asleep in the front seat. A woman. She looked like Melissa. He peered closer, careful not to get too close. It *was* Melissa. *What the hell?*

He rapped on the window. Melissa stirred, and opened her eyes. She looked befuddled and confused. He rapped again. She looked around, yawning as she did. Their eyes met. He saw the recognition reflected as she became more alert. She opened the door and extricated herself from the seat, wavering with stiffness after being cramped in the car.

"Melissa? What are you doing here?"

"And hello to you too. You said you wanted to see me before you left but things happened, and I didn't make it to the airport in time."

"You've come all this way to say goodbye? You could have rung me, you know." Perhaps he was being obtuse, but he was tired, and nothing really made sense.

She looked at him uncertainly. "I need to talk to you. Aren't you going to invite me in?"

"Of course—I was taken by surprise, that's all. Come here and give me a hug and then I'll know you're real."

She moved into his arms and melted against him. He felt damp patches on his shirt front. Was she crying? He could also feel the thud of her heart, against his chest.

"Sweetheart, your father's okay, isn't he? He hasn't relapsed or anything?"

"Father's fine, Jenny's fine, Pete's fine and I'm fine."

He pushed her back at arm's length so he could look at her. "And that's good news, so tell me—why aren't you back in Alice organizing the art show?"

"Is Ollie home?" she queried, looking at the front door of the cottage.

"Probably. Did you want to go for a walk? We can chat on the hoof if that suits you better."

"That sounds a great idea."

She looked relieved. She locked the car and they strolled down towards the Cooks River and the linear park at the end

291

of the street. Families milled around the electric barbecues provided by the local council and while the parents organised the food, the children hung off the playground equipment. The dog-walkers were out in force, and joggers were pounding the paths.

"So, Melissa; tell me what's up?"

Melissa took a moment to collect her thoughts. "You asked why I'm here. There are several reasons. Firstly, a lot of the organisation for the art show is in place and I suddenly realised that I don't have to do it all by myself. Others can help, but if there is an urgent issue, I can sort it out over the phone."

"That makes sense." His eyes asked the question, "… and?"

"And then there's Father. He's recovering well and doesn't really need me. The cynic in me says that he's never really needed me, but I don't want to dwell on that now. These decisions are about me, not him."

Chris had taken her hand as they walked, and he gave it a squeeze. "I'm pleased to hear you say that. It may surprise you, but I like your father. I always know where I stand with him and he's always been fair in his dealings with me."

"Lucky you", she murmured.

Chris was not deterred. "He's a black and white character—no doubt about that—but there's no bullshit either. I might not feel the same if he'd been my father of course."

"Quite possibly not. I can't be sure because nothing has been said explicitly, but I think something is happening between my father and Jenny. He mentioned them travelling together. I hope he's not making assumptions with respect to what she would like, but somehow I don't think he needs me hanging around."

"Knowing your history with your father, I think it's healthy for your relationship if you live independently. So, if I understand the situation correctly, you realised you can take some time off from the art show and also that your father doesn't need you and on that basis, you decided to make a quick trip to Sydney."

"No… I mean, it's not just that. I know while you were in Alice, you were hoping for answers that I couldn't give you. That wasn't because I doubted the depth of my feelings for you; rather that I needed to understand some things about myself first before I could let go of attitudes and beliefs that were holding me back."

She paused, looking around. "Can we sit down somewhere?"

The conversation was going down an important path and she wanted to give it her full attention. There was a park bench overlooking the water and they made their way to that. They sat for a while, watching a family of ducks that nestled in the reeds on the river bank.

Chris broke the silence. "I missed you so much while you were away, but I was knocked sideways by the assumptions you made about me and Lexie. You didn't even raise your concerns with me—just flew off the handle and out of the country. How do you think that makes me feel, knowing that you don't trust me? Would it always be like that?"

"I was wrong, I know that. I jumped to conclusions and there wasn't any justification. I'm not proud of myself." She pushed her hair back out of her face and swivelled on the bench to face him and look him in the eyes. "It's no great surprise that I've had commitment issues. It's not that I don't trust you, but it's my fear of abandonment that has driven me. It took a while for me to understand that, but I know it now and realise I've been allowing that fear to define my life. It's governed how I respond to people around me, even those who are important to me."

She looked back at the ducks, chewing her bottom lip. This was not easy. "I couldn't cope with the thought that you might abandon me. The thought of you spending time with Lexie Ferguson pandered to my fears. It was silly, I accept that."

"Lexie and I work together. Nothing more than that."

"I understand that now. While I was in Alice, I was able to put a few things in perspective. I don't want to talk about all of it, but I understood I had allowed my beliefs to be coloured by a child's perception of reality."

His slight nod encouraged her to continue. She dropped her eyes. "I had also become rather self-absorbed and hadn't appreciated how many good things were happening in my life."

Melissa swept her hair back behind her ears and looked up again. She didn't want anything coming between them. "One of those good things—the most important really—was you." She paused, gathering her thoughts. "Chris—what I wanted to tell you before you left Alice, is that I don't want to lose you. If you think that I'm too much hard work, I'll
294

understand, but… I'm looking to the future, not the past and the person I see in my future is you."

"Are you talking about commitment?"

"For me, commitment has been a four-letter word, and it still is, in the nicest possible way." She raised her eyes to his. "Yes, I'm talking about commitment; now and always. I will have to be back in Alice sometimes, and other times I will be working in Sydney or wherever the job takes me, but wherever I am Chris Harris, I will remain committed to you. You are my rock and my anchor and knowing you're in my life allows me to deal with everything else that comes my way."

He regarded her silently, his face unreadable. A wave of doubt engulfed her, and her stomach began to churn. She hardly dared breathe. Was she making a total fool of herself?

"If you'll have me of course," she whispered softly.

Scared of what she might read in his face, she dropped her gaze to the level of his collar bone. She could see a couple of those golden hairs peaking over the top of his unbuttoned shirt. Would she ever run her hands over his chest again?

"Melissa, I need to be clear about what you mean. Are you looking for someone to support you, to have your back when times are hard, and to massage your shoulders when you're tired, or are you looking for someone to love unconditionally, to give and equally receive?"

She raised her eyes to his. "Can't it be both? Can't it be someone who has my back as much as I have his, someone who returns my love in equal measure?"

"Am I hearing right Melissa Gilbert, that you love me?"

"What do you think I've been trying to say? Yes, Chris Harris, I love you and know you're the best thing that has happened to me. I'll take all the shoulder massages you can give and more, I'll vent at times and probably be self-centred, but I'll also give as good as I get and when you need support, I'll be there."

"Melissa, don't ever change. I love you just as you are. You're the best thing that has happened to me too and we have a fantastic life stretching ahead of us."

He kissed her lightly, then stood up, pulling Melissa to her feet, one of his lop-sided smiles teasing the corner of his mouth.

"Let's finish our walk. I like having you by my side. I think we've said what we need to say."

With a smile of her own, one that was both relieved and full of promise, Melissa felt the tight band around her chest begin to dissolve. Hand in hand, they continued their walk, following the path along the river as the day faded to a soft dusk and the colours that spread across the sky promised good times to come.

High enough as to be only a distant mechanical vibration, a chopper tracked on course to Sydney Airport. They followed its progress until it disappeared from view, then turned back to the path, following joggers and dog-walkers alike.

CHAPTER 22

IT WAS FORTUNATE the Channel Nine boss was sponsoring the art show, as that made it easier for Chris to accompany Melissa to Alice for the big day. She had coordinated as much as she could from a distance but relied on the team on the ground to pull the auction together under Belinda's watchful eye.

"I feel guilty having left the hard work to everyone else," Melissa said as their aircraft touched down. "I'm sure they've done a wonderful job, but you know…"

"Sure. You're a control freak and don't like to let go."

Melissa bristled. "Is that how you see me?"

Chris patted her hand. "In the nicest possible way, sweetheart. There's nothing wrong with being a perfectionist."

"Am I hearing a 'but'?"

"A paranoid perfectionist could be pushing it." He brushed her cheek with his lips and gathered up the hand luggage. "C'mon. The sooner you check out the set-up, the happier we'll all be."

Peering towards the arrivals areas as they walked across the baking tarmac, Melissa could just make out Jenny through the darkened glass. It wasn't until they pushed through the security doors and into the bliss of the air conditioning that she realised Jenny wasn't alone. Her father hovered a short distance behind. He supported himself with a walking stick, but his colour had improved from when she'd last seen him. Not ruddy, by any means, but a colour that placed him firmly in the land of the living.

He hung back as Jenny moved forward to embrace her. Melissa didn't remember him ever coming to meet her before—not even when she'd returned home at the end of school term. He seemed uncertain of what was expected of him.

Melissa stepped forward, unsure herself. "Father... good to see you." *Do I kiss him? Give him a hug?* She'd never done either.

Chris pushed past her. "Good to see you up and about, Dan," he said, extending his hand. "You're looking well."

"Better than I have been," Dan conceded.

Melissa caught her breath. This was the first time her father and Chris had connected since she and Chris had openly become a couple. Would her father behave? She recalled his earlier comments in relation to Chris. Dan nodded in Chris' direction and shook the proffered hand. "Good flight?"

Melissa picked her jaw up from the floor. She noticed Jenny regarding her with a hint of amusement. She nudged Melissa gently in the ribs. "Let's get your luggage. I know you'll be busting to get to the Arts Centre."

❧

Half an hour later, they pulled up in the Arts Centre car park. They found Belinda in the main hall, directing activities. It wasn't quite chaos, but there were people up ladders, fiddling with audio visual cables, others generally meandering, and kids shrieking and running around. Outside, clusters of people from the settlements sat on the lawn, patiently waiting until opening time, even though it was some hours off.

Chris, Jenny and her father hung back, looking bemused at the scene confronting them. Keeping clear of the workers, Melissa approached Belinda from behind.

"Need any help?" Melissa was almost too scared to ask in case her offer was accepted.

Belinda spun around. "Melissa! You made it. I think we're almost under control, but thanks for asking." She flashed a wry grin. "I know, it looks like mayhem, but it's coming together nicely. By opening time, everything will be in place. Come and look at the entries."

Melissa beckoned the others to join her. "We've got time for a quick advance tour of the exhibits. Belinda, you'll talk us through, won't you?"

They walked around the gallery, stopping to review the work on display. The paintings varied in style, from those which were reminiscent of the Hermannsburg tradition as painted by Albert Namatjira, to the stylistic Western Desert paintings that were sometimes seen in galleries.

"I don't know a lot about the paintings," Dan said scratching his nose as he peered at the labels identifying the artist, "but some of the names are well-known around here."

Belinda turned to Dan and extended her hand. "You must be Melissa's father. I can see the resemblance. Thank you for sponsoring one of the art prizes." Her smile was warm. "You're coming tonight, aren't you? The emcee will invite you up to present the prize."

His expression was one of pure horror. "I'll leave that to Melissa. She's used to the limelight. You'll find me up the back— *if* I come. This isn't really my sort of thing." He politely shook Belinda's hand and then took a step back.

Melissa almost expected him to bolt, except that Dan Gilbert didn't run away.

They didn't stay long. The others wandered back to the car while Melissa remained to check final details. It wasn't only Belinda who'd been busy. There had been a team of helpers working behind the scenes to make the event a success.

She kissed Belinda on the cheek. "Have I told you you're a miracle worker?"

"Not in recent memory, but you can tell me as many times as you like. You'll be back later?" Belinda glanced at her watch. "Look at the time! The judges are due in fifteen minutes. Russell supposedly has them under control. I'd better print out the judging forms."

Melissa threw up her hands. "I'm out of here. I'm sure Russell is doing a fabulous job. I'll catch up with him when I come back. I won't inflict him on my father just yet." She ran out to the car, not wanting to keep the others waiting any longer.

"What are your plans for the rest of the day?" Jenny asked as she opened the car door. "If you come back to the house for lunch, you can pick up the Land Cruiser. That leaves you free to do whatever you need."

"Thanks, Jenny. We'll check into our accommodation after lunch. We're staying at the Crown Plaza." Melissa rummaged in her bag for her itemized list. "I have a few errands to run and then I'll help Belinda with last minute tasks. I think Chris has plans of his own."

It was ages since they'd exchanged news. Over cold meats and salads, Melissa gave a run-down on her recent contracts, the locations and who had been involved. Chris joined in the conversation, mentioning the highlights of his job.

"Have you seen much of my boss, Dan?" he asked.

Until that time, Dan had been largely silent, listening but not contributing to the conversation.

"I have, actually. He's been here twice, and I've introduced him to some of the locals. I visited him on the property he bought and helped him employ a good station manager." Dan sat back, folding his arms across his stomach. "He'll be fine, I think. He's invited me to visit him at his property down in New South Wales. Jenny and I will probably fly down next month." He speared another slice of ham with his fork.

The day was full of surprises. Melissa noted an element of smugness in the remark. She didn't know whether to be more astonished at the invitation, or the comment that Jenny was going too. Jenny's expression remained sphinx-like. If she had anything to say on the matter, it wouldn't be at the lunch table.

"You'll enjoy the visit," Chris interjected. "I fly him out there regularly. He'll probably ask me to take you in the station chopper."

"That will be great, Chris," Jenny said. "We'll look forward to that."

It took all Melissa's self-discipline not to roll her eyes. This atmosphere of conviviality took some getting used to. "If you're ready, Chris, we should be going. I don't want Belinda and the others to think I'm not pulling my weight."

This time, it was Chris who rolled his eyes, but he pushed his chair back and transferred their bags to the Land Cruiser while Melissa had last words with Dan and Jenny.

"You are both coming, aren't you? Dad, you can't let me down now."

Jenny laid a hand on her arm. "Calm down, Missy. Of course we'll be there. Just keeping out of the limelight, that's all."

It was a short drive to the hotel after lunch. They only stayed long enough to drop off their luggage. Melissa threw back the curtains and peered out at the dry river bed she could see from the window. "This view makes me feel like I'm at home again. I'm sorry now I didn't organize a trip out to Plenty River." She spoke wistfully. "I'd like to visit Mum and William again, but there really isn't time. It's taken me a while to realise it, but Plenty River will always be home. It forever pulls at my heart strings."

"We'll be back again," Chris said. "We'll leave more time for it then."

She turned back from the window. "I guess so." Her voice was flat. *Why didn't I think of this earlier?*

Melissa pushed her thoughts aside and ducked up Todd Mall to take care of her errands. An hour later, Chris dropped her back to the Arts Centre.

"You sure you don't need me here, sweetheart? I can… if you really want me to."

"No. You do what you need to do this afternoon. I know Belinda will have it under control." She leaned towards him to deliver a quick kiss. "I'll call you when I need to be picked up. See you later."

Mark looked up from the chopper he was washing as Chris pulled up beside the hangar. He tossed the cloth into the bucket of water and strode over to greet his mate.

"So, how's the big smoke treating you?" The two men embraced in a man-hug, slapping each other on the back.

"I'm enjoying it—living the high life, but it's good to be back, even if only for a few days. You'll have to come and visit.'

"I would, but I'm too busy at the moment." Mark gave Chris a meaningful look "I don't suppose you've come looking for a job?"

Chris felt a twinge of guilt, followed by slight regret. He could have been part of this too. He hated to think he'd let Mark down. It would have been good, the two of them working together still, but... he'd made a different decision. "So how is business?" he asked.

"Booming. I've got another machine on order and I'm interviewing pilots next week." He shook his head, wearing an amazed look. "I knew there was scope for the work, but never expected it to take off like it has."

"You've earned it, mate. You've worked bloody hard. I'm pleased to see it turned out so well for you." He nodded towards the office "I'll go and put the kettle on, while you finish up here."

"I thought you were going to wash it for me!"

"In your dreams. That's what you get for starting your own business—you have to do all the grunt work too." He ducked, laughing as Mark threw a sopping wet cloth at him. Some things never changed.

By the time Mark joined him inside, the kettle had boiled, and Chris had made them each a cup of coffee. He still remembered how Mark preferred it. "So, give me the news," he said. "What's everyone up to—Sarah, Kathy? Is Brian still with StationAir?"

"I think you'll see some of them tonight. They're planning on coming to this event Melissa's organised. She roped Kathy in to help and in turn, Kathy told us all we had to go."

They raided the biscuit tin and sauntered back outside, sitting on a couple of plastic chairs and observing the various comings and goings while they chatted. Mark detailed the local aviation news, and Chris described the intricacies of flying in Sydney.

Chris glanced at his watch. "Gotta go, mate. Are you coming tonight?"

"I'll probably wander along. How long are you in town for? Are you heading out to Plenty?"

"We're only here for a couple of days. I couldn't get any more time off work. Melissa wanted to go back home, but we won't have time. She's disappointed but she'll have to give it a miss this time."

Mark scratched his chin reflectively. "You know, you two are the most unlikely couple I know. How you reeled in Melissa Gilbert, I'll never know."

"She was swayed by my good looks and charm. What else?"

Mark chuckled. "Well, it certainly wasn't your money." He drained the last of his coffee. "Look, if she really wants to
304

go, why don't you take this machine out there tomorrow? For once, it doesn't have any bookings, so it's available if you want. Just square me up for the cost of fuel."

"Mate, that would be fantastic. I reckon you've just earned me a few brownie points." He handed his empty cup to Mark. "I've gotta go. I've a couple of other calls to make, but I'll confirm arrangements tonight. Don't forget you need to come east one day. I'll show you what real flying's about."

~

The firstperson Melissa saw when she entered the auditorium was Marlene. The woman tore over to embrace her.

"You done real good, girl. Look at all these pictures. How you got everyone involved, I'll never know." She squeezed Melissa in a tight hug. "Yer mum would be so pleased."

Melissa's eye's prickled. She blinked furiously, not willing to leave the refuge of Marlene's shoulder until she had herself under control. Those few words meant so much.

Russell claimed her next, grasping her shoulders and planting a kiss on either cheek. "Pet, meeting you here is getting to be a habit. You're looking wonderful, as always."

"So are you, Russell," she responded. He always did. "I assume you coordinated the judging?"

"It's been fascinating. I enjoyed both working with the judging team and seeing the exhibited works. Some of the artists have a rewarding future ahead of them. If they're interested, I can put them in contact with galleries in Sydney."

"That would be fabulous. Make sure they get a good price for their work."

"Would I do anything less?" He turned a pained look in her direction, his baleful eyes speaking volumes. "I'll

305

approach them later. I want to see how the judging has gone. I didn't take part in that process, just organised the judges and got them focused. They're conferring now."

"I look forward to hearing the results," Melissa said. "I must check with Belinda to see what needs doing, so we'll catch up shortly."

Russell sauntered off, and Melissa found Belinda in her office, ticking off a list of to-do items. "Caterer's on track, musicians organised, seating in place, brochures delivered and checked…"

"Sounds like you don't need me at all," Melissa said. "I might as well go back to the hotel."

"Don't you dare. I'll find plenty for you to do. You can ring Martin Endersby for a start and make sure he has all the details he needs for the auction." There was an air of urgency about the normally unflappable centre director.

"Yes, ma'am." Melissa reached for the phone and took the number that Belinda shoved at her. She was still dialling when Belinda issued her next request.

"And when you've done that, you can check the media kits. Make sure nothing has been missed out or importantly, mis-spelled."

Melissa gave a thumbs-up of acknowledgement to Belinda as Martin answered her call. "Melissa! You're here!... yes, I think I'm under control. I was just practising the pronunciation of some of these names. I don't want to get them wrong this evening." He gave a mock sigh. "How did I let you rope me into this?"

"It's because you're a good man, Martin, and you have such a strong sense of community."

He laughed. "I'll keep telling myself that." His voice took on a hopeful tone. "Are you thinking of moving back to town? I've some great properties on the market at the moment. Won't take long to show you around."

Never one to miss an opportunity. "I'm not in the market. Martin but when I am, you'll be the first to know

He gave a sigh, verging on theatrical. "Well, I can't ask more than that. I'll see you tonight."

She moved on to the media kits. Details of the Araluan Health Centre were provided, and the need for funds. The names of contributing artists were featured, with a brief biography when one was available. The kit outlined sponsorship partners with relevant contact details. Dan Gilbert's name featured in the list. That wasn't what drew her attention. Listed was the Elizabeth Gilbert Art Prize, sponsored by Dan Gilbert.

He never told me he was naming it after mum. What a wonderful thing to do.

Her heart warmed towards this obstinate man. There was a lot she didn't know about her father. It hadn't been apparent before, or else she hadn't seen it. *Are all father-daughter relationships like this?*

There was no time to ponder the matter. Belinda had her addressing a range of tasks, before it was time to ring Chris and ask him to pick her up. She wanted to shower and change at the hotel before returning for the big event.

"So, would you still like to slip out to Plenty?" he asked as he navigated the streets to their accommodation.

"Well, yes, but like I said, there's no time this trip."

307

"What if I told you I'd had a chat to Mark this afternoon, and he's made a chopper available to us? We can slip out there tomorrow and be back mid-afternoon, if that suits you. I'm not sure what else you had planned." He flicked a quick glance away from the road to Melissa, his raised eyebrows asking the question.

"Really? You beautiful man. That would be wonderful."

He really is so thoughtful. I should make sure not to let this one go.

Chris amused her by donning the same black outfit he'd worn on their first visit together to the Arts Centre. They made it a quick turn-around, as Melissa insisted on being there early to greet the arrivals. The only difference this time was they didn't roll up in the Merc.

The same musicians who had played for Russell's exhibition were setting up—a flautist, violinist and didgeridoo player. The music was an invitation to those gathered outside to come from the grassed area and into the auditorium. Nobody moved. The groups on the lawn stayed tightly clustered, except for the children who roamed and noisily sought each other out.

Inside, the hall had all the vibrancy of a mausoleum.

"Where is everyone?" she wailed to Chris.

"Give it time, sweetheart. You should know by now how it works. They'll pour through the door soon. I'll get us both a glass of wine while it's still possible to drink it without your elbow being jostled."

Funny man. She loved him for it though. He kept her grounded when the panic started to rise.

A few people straggled in, but not the numbers she'd anticipated. Melissa looked at her watch. The auction would be a dud unless more people turned up. A couple with a pram paused in the doorway, looking around uncertainly—Alex and Kathy Woodleigh. She hurried over.

"Alex, Kathy! Great to see you. Congratulations on the new addition. Jenny told me the baby had arrived." She peered into the pram. A tiny human lay there, peacefully sleeping. Amazing, considering they had just walked past the didgeridoo player. "She looks beautiful." Looking up, Melissa realised Rose hovered behind them. "Must take after her grandmother." She embraced the older woman tightly. "Congratulations, Grandma," she whispered.

Rose responded by tightening her hold. "She's a beautiful child. Come and see us soon, Melissa. You can meet her properly then. Don't be a stranger."

It will be a while before I'm at Mulga Downs again, but maybe one day. "Perhaps we can catch up for coffee before you go back to Mulga? I'll call you." She reached for the pile of brochures on the stand behind her. "Here's a catalogue. Why don't you have a look at the exhibits before the crowds arrive?" *If* they arrive. It didn't look promising, based on current numbers.

They took her up on the suggestion. Another couple ambled through the door, and Melissa recognised Sarah Hartford and Joel Pemberton. Joel had given them a good deal on radio advertising at the local radio station. They greeted her politely, and taking a catalogue, hurried over to join the Woodleighs.

They're a tight-knit group. I'll never quite fit in, but that doesn't matter. At least they're here. Chris came back with the drinks, and she took the flute gratefully. "While you're playing

309

wine waiter, there are people over there who might like a champagne." She nodded towards the group that had just come in, noting how his face lit up. His association with them all went way back. "Go on," she said. "Go and catch up. I've already said hello. Martin Endersby has just arrived. I'd better look after him."

He gave her a quick peck on the cheek. "Love you, sweetheart," and sauntered over to join his friends. She followed him with her eyes, admiring the seat of his well-fitting pants before turning to greet Martin.

"Here's the man of the moment," she exclaimed on reaching him. "Glad you're here. I'll introduce you to Russell, our artistic consultant, and he can take you on a tour of the exhibits. You'll find him very knowledgeable." She waved to catch Russell's attention and signalled for him to come and join them.

For once, Russell had foregone his usual eye-catching colour, and was dressed as a clone of Chris in head-to-toe black. Against that, his white-blond hair was a stark contrast. He looked to be, and was, one cool dude.

Martin cast a bemused look at her over his shoulder as he was swept away on a wave of Russell's exuberance. Melissa smiled inwardly. He would cope. But where were the crowds?

People dribbled in. She tried not to keep looking at her watch. That made her seem anxious. She caught Belinda's eye from across the room, and in pantomime, asked, *Where is everybody?* There was a shrugged response. *How should I know?*

Pete and Tanya sidled in next. Just who she needed. She made a beeline for them.

310

"Hey, Sis," Pete said in greeting, his grin stretching wide at the reference. Tanya threw a quick glance at Melissa, as though unsure what her reaction would be.

"How are you, Tanya?" Melissa said. "I hope you're keeping this man in line." She turned to the still-grinning man. "I need you to do something for me."

A wary look crossed his face. "Oh yeah? And what might that be?"

"You need to go outside and round up the people sitting on the grass. Make them come inside."

"I don't reckon I can *make* them do anything. They're a bit shy, you know? I can ask them nicely."

"Pete, I don't care if you get down on your knees and beg. Just get them in here—okay? They'll come if you ask them."

"C'mon, Pete," Tanya said. "If you persuade yer mum and Uncle Albert to come in, the rest will follow." She gave her husband a shove towards the door. "Don't worry, Melissa. They'll be here soon."

Tanya was right. A short time later, Maisie and Uncle Albert came in from outside, with Tanya by their side. Pete was still talking to the groups on the grass. Melissa moved to greet them, drawing them towards the paintings, though only addressing Maisie. Conscious of cultural issues, she would not make direct eye contact with Albert unless he acknowledged her.

"Maisie—I'm so pleased you're both here. Come and look at the paintings. Albert's picture is over here." She stopped at the artwork, and they both looked in silence at the painting, framed, illuminated and hung and on the wall. An adjacent card advised the artist's name and gave the title of the work to be *Desert Dreaming.*

"Looks good, eh?" Maisie said, nudging Albert in the ribs. Albert nodded, not saying a word. To Melissa's astonishment, he turned and looked at her, and nodded again. That was all she needed. He was pleased. She didn't know why it meant so much to her, but it did.

As a strategy, sending Pete outside had been a good idea. The hall filled up with people she knew, some she knew by sight, and people she'd never seen before. Chris caught up with her, seizing her around the waist and drawing her close. "Told you they'd come," he said. "Don't you know by now not to doubt me—nor yourself, for that matter."

"You're sounding very smug," she teased. "I don't mind. Come and help me schmooze. You do that very well. If you can get my father onside, you can manage anyone else who might be here."

He laughed, but dutifully moved between members of the crowd, greeting people and explaining what was happening during the evening and when. By the time the speeches began and Chris returned to her side, the hall was at capacity.

It had been decided to keep speeches to a minimum, although the Northern Territory Minister for Tourism and Culture performed the official opening. Russell then took centre stage, giving an overview of the quality of the artworks, and explaining the process undertaken with the judging.

He clutched a series of envelopes. "This is the moment you've all been waiting for; the results of the judging that took place earlier today. I should also add that we are grateful to our sponsors, who have made the individual awards possible." The rustling in the room indicated the level of anticipation. Melissa glanced around her, looking at the faces of the various artists. *Enough rambling, Russell. This is not the crowd to tolerate delaying tactics. Get on with it.*

Perhaps Russell discerned her thoughts, for he summonsed the Channel Nine representative to stand beside him and tore open the first envelope with a flourish. There were cheers when the winner was announced and a cheque was handed over, creating a photo opportunity.

The winner beamed his pleasure but declined the opportunity to address the crowd. "T'ank you. T'ank you very much," punctuated with nods was the extent of his response. The woman who won the prize sponsored by Rose Woodleigh was enthusiastically supported by a group of other women. They were part of a painting collective on the settlement on which they lived and took the award to be recognition of them all.

Russell tore open another envelope. This was the People's Choice Award. Melissa glanced around at the exhibits visible from where she stood. *I couldn't select one single painting out of any of these. They each have something different to present.* She twisted back to where the room was focussed.

"And the winner is… Albert Dobson"

Albert! That's wonderful. Melissa led the applause followed closely by Pete who was standing just behind her. "I'm glad dad sponsored a different prize," she muttered to him. "It would have looked like nepotism to have a winner who lives on Plenty."

He laughed. "Not much chance of that. The people voting wouldn't have known who sponsored the prize, much less cared."

"You're probably right. I'm pleased he won though. I must have another look at it when the official stuff is over."

When the Elizabeth Gilbert Art Prize was announced, Melissa turned to look at her father, raised eyebrows asking the question. He shook his head decisively, indicating with a flick of his hand that she should do the honours instead. There was no opportunity to argue, particularly as Chris gave her a shove in the small of her back, directing her towards the front. Shoulders back, she stepped forward, said a few choice words and handed over the cheque to the delighted recipient.

It was time to move on to the auction. Russell introduced Martin Endersby, who stepped up to the microphone and outlined the terms of the auction. He'd done his homework. Melissa was impressed. His voice boomed around the room as he spoke about traditional and evolving art techniques and the aboriginal names rolled smoothly off his tongue.

"Did you bring your cheque book?" she asked Chris, slipping her arm through his.

"What, me? You're joking. I'm a poor chopper pilot, sweetheart, not an art connoisseur. I leave that to the Boss."

"Just teasing. I'm nervous about this part of the event. I hope the paintings sell. It will be such a downer if they don't."

"Shhh!" A woman in front of them turned and glared, holding her look for a pointed moment before turning back to concentrate on the proceedings. Melissa bit her lip to keep from laughing. It was even harder when Chris dug her in the ribs, all the while keeping eyes front.

"Ladies and gentlemen——this is a unique opportunity to purchase an award-winning piece of indigenous art. After tonight, the world will know the artist's name. Not only will you own a national treasure but proceeds from your acquisition will also go towards the Araluen Health Centre." Martin warmed up the crowd. He eyeballed the patrons towards the back who might have deep pockets and alternately cajoled and worked on the collective emotions.

One or two hesitant bids were offered. Heads swivelled to see who was in the market. Arms were crossed and faces remained impassive. "If this is the best you can do, I might as well go home," Martin chided. "I'm not going to give this painting away. I'd rather keep it for myself."

A flush of embarrassment threatened Melissa. She caught her breath. Surely someone would bid? What a disaster. The Chanel Nine cameras were recording everything. They'd never get sponsorship again.

"Just wait," Chris muttered. "It's all part of the game."

On cue, another bid came from the back of the room. Martin pounced on it, dangling the potential sale in front of rival bidders. A voice at the front upped the ante; by a lot. An appreciative murmur rippled through the crowd. Martin picked up the pace and waved his gavel around, threatening to knock down the painting. Another bid, and yet one more. The margins were closer, but the price still edged higher. The voice at the front spoke up loudly again. "Seventeen fifty." The room fell silent.

"Going once… going twice… Ladies and Gentlemen, this is your last chance…" BANG. The gavel came down and the crowd applauded, whispering to each other about the price and the buyer. Martin's assistants moved in to collect the buyer's details and to make arrangements for payment, while he moved onto the next item.

The auction moved swiftly after that, with the audience more confident of the process and less inhibited.

"Told you so," Chris said. "It was never going to be a failure."

"Hindsight's a wonderful thing," Melissa said drily. "I'm glad you were right though." She began to breath normally again. The next painting to be offered was Albert's. She turned to Chris. "Should we? I mean, it is Albert's."

"Sweetheart, it's up to you. If you want it, we can put in a bid."

She mentally reviewed her finances. How much could she afford? She should have thought about this earlier. Martin opened the bidding. Melissa glanced around furtively to see if anyone else looked like participating. There was no obvious activity. Tentatively, she called out her opening offer. Martin nodded at her and incorporated her bid into his patter. Other voices called out and soon the price spiralled.

"That's me done," she muttered to Chris. "I can't afford to go higher but at least I got the bidding started."

"I think we got the best result, sweetheart. Didn't you see who bought it?"

She raised her eyebrows in query. Not everyone called out. Some just raised their hands or nodded in Martin's direction. She hadn't seen where the winning bid came from.

"It was your father. He bought Albert's painting."

CHAPTER 23

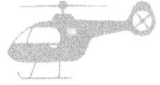

WITH CHANNEL NINE purchasing two paintings and the remainder selling well, the auction was deemed a success by those with a vested stake. Rose purchased the painting by the winning female artist, so Dan wasn't the only one they knew with his name on a sold sticker.

The crowd dispersed, with only organisers and stragglers left. Having farewelled several people she knew, Melissa turned her attention to Pete and Tanya. She hadn't spoken much to them through the evening. "Great you two were able to come into town as well. I was pleased to see you here."

Pete was his usual laconic self. "Yeah, well—we had to support Uncle Albert," he said. "We brought him and mum into town."

"Umm—Chris and I are going to dinner with a couple of others. Would you and Tanya like to join us?" She glanced at Tanya also to include her in the conversation. "We're going to a local restaurant where I know the owner."

"Thanks, sis, but we'll be joining the mob now, I reckon."

"Of course. I just thought..." She trailed off. What had she just thought? That they would all play happy families?

He picked up on her intention. "Melissa, not much is going to change, not really. What difference does it make who my father is?"

She stiffened. "It will make a difference with your future studies," she replied. "You couldn't afford to do that on your own." She expected some recognition of what he was being offered; some sign of gratitude.

"You know what? I reckon eventually I would have got there anyway, under my own steam." He now had a hands-on-hip stance that looked vaguely familiar. "Sure, it helped that the old man sent me to school. But I'm the one who has to make the effort to push myself. I'll get into med school in spite of Dan Gilbert, not because of him."

Melissa stared at him, astonished. He probably would. This was a side of Pete she hadn't seen before. "You know, you're more like our father than you possibly realise. That pig-headed determination might just get you where you want to go."

She smoothed away a strand of hair that had fallen over her face and turned to Tanya. "Don't let him get away with anything, Tanya. The men in this family have a way of trying to control everything and everyone around them."

The other woman laughed. "Don't worry about that. I make sure he knows who's boss."

She and Pete looked at each other affectionately, making it clear there was nothing lacking in their communication department.

"I'm pleased to hear it," Melissa said. "Enjoy your evening."

She looked around to see who else was left. Dan and Jenny were edging their way towards the door and Melissa moved to intercept them. "Father, you didn't say you were going to purchase a painting."

He pulled a slight face. "Are you saying I need to get your permission before I do anything?"

Melissa threw up her hands with a small shake of her head. "That's not what I meant. I'm pleased you bought Albert's painting. If I knew you were going to buy it, I wouldn't have placed a bid myself."

"To be honest," Dan admitted, "I didn't realise until the last minute that I *was* going to buy it. Someone twisted my arm."

Jenny smiled but refrained from comment.

Chris had joined them during this discussion, and he slid his arm around her waist. She knew what he meant. Just chill. Breathe in, breathe out. "I'm glad. Whatever the reason, I'm glad you bought Albert's painting. Where are you going to hang it?"

"I hadn't thought that far. Jenny might have some ideas."

"We've lots of time to think about that," Jenny said. "Right now, I think we need to go home." The home to which she was referring was the town house.

"A couple of us will probably go out for a meal," Melissa said. "Would you like to join us?"

Dan and Jenny shared a wordless look. "I don't think so, but thanks for asking." Jenny spoke for them both. "You'll want to review the event with your friends. We can catch up later. Why don't you drop in for breakfast in the morning?"

Melissa noted the complicit solidarity between them, but let it pass. She kissed Jenny on the cheek. "Good night, then. See you in the morning." She paused hesitantly in front of her father. "Good night, dad." She gave him an awkward hug. "I'm please you're looking so much better."

He reached out and wrapped his arms around her, patting her back with one hand as though she were a baby or a small child. It was a gesture of reassurance. She held herself rigid initially, before allowing herself to relax against him. Only for a while. She might have pushed herself back first or Dan might have dropped his arms. She wasn't sure. It was going to take some time to get used to this level of contact.

Russell and Belinda joined Chris and Melissa at the same restaurant they'd dined at after Russell's exhibition. As they sat down, Russell looked around, saying "Why do I have a feeling of déjà vu? I'm starting to feel like a local."

"Not likely," Melissa replied bluntly. "You're still a blow-in. Folklore says you're not a local until you've seen the Todd River in flood three times, but that doesn't really count. Some people will never be locals."

"Somehow, I think that's likely to be the case for me. I'll just have to assume de facto local status through you."

She frowned, shook her head and pursed her lips. "I'm not really sure that's possible, but if anyone can pull it off, it's probably you."

The remarks set the tone of the evening. Their mood reflected relief it was all over. The auction had been an undeniable success, although Belinda still had to do a financial reconciliation.

"It will take me a day or so, but I'll send you a report as soon as I've prepared it. I think the Health Centre will be very happy."

"They'd better be. It's been a tremendous effort from everyone involved."

"Will you do it again next year?" Russell asked.

Chris rolled his eyes in mock horror. "What, and go through all the angst again?"

Melissa chewed her lips pensively. It was too soon to think about next year. "I would prefer to be retained in a consultant capacity," she said after a moment. "The local community needs to decide whether this will be an ongoing thing and should control it. That way, they take ownership as well."

"That's a smart approach," Belinda said. "We can talk about it later. For now, here's to a successful event—yet again."

They clinked their glasses and the conversation moved on to Belinda's anticipated visit to Sydney. They all had suggestions for what she needed to see and do.

It might have been the long day, or it might have been the letdown at the end of an intense period of organisation, but none of them wanted to make a night of it. Melissa was glad when the evening came to an end.

"Send us your arrival details, Belinda." She turned to Russell. "Can we drop you off at your accommodation, Russell?"

They sorted the bill, and even Russell paid his share. That largesse didn't stretch as far as leaving a tip, but as Melissa said to Chris later after dropping their friend at his accommodation, you have to start somewhere.

Back in their room, Melissa kicked off her shoes and slipped her earrings out of her ears. She threw off her dress before heading to the bathroom to wash off her make-up and clean her teeth. When she emerged, Chris seized her from behind and kissed her bare shoulder.

"Hey, I can feel the tension in those muscles. Is this the right moment for a massage?" He nuzzled her neck and she arched back with a small moan of release.

Her eyes closed, and little shivers radiated from the points where his fingers now touched on either side of her spine "Is there ever a wrong moment?"

"This will go better if you're lying down," he whispered into her hair.

Leading her to the bed, Chris deftly undid the catch and slipped off her bra, allowing her breasts to fall free. They responded immediately to the cool breeze of the air conditioning, with each peak swelling with a rosy-coloured bud. He flicked a lick on each, causing her to gasp at the electrical sensation before he pushed her gently backwards.

"On your belly, sweetheart," he ordered. She flipped over and in a smooth movement he slid her knickers off, casting them aside before climbing on the bed himself and straddling her thighs.

"You've done that before," she murmured. She realised that at some point, he'd divested himself of his shirt and trousers. In her anticipatory state, she hadn't even seen him do it.

"Be quiet. You talk too much." Starting from her butt cheeks, he worked his way up her back, alternately stroking and kneading her flesh. She made small mewling sounds as he found the knots of tension and dug into the areas of sensitivity. In her mind, her body was melting and spreading over the bed in an amorphous puddle.

"Time to turn." Chris raised his hips, giving her the room to roll over onto her back, the tantalising sensations now focussed somewhere south of centre.

Her eyes flickered open, noting the boxers he still wore. "I've a feeling you're over-dressed."

"All in good time," he murmured, running his hands over her rib cage and easing around the side of each breast. His thumbs traced a deep line from her collar bone, and down and out to the sides of her chest, tracing the path of her ribs. "Did you know how much emotional tension is held in the chest?" he asked.

"I know where the tension is held now," she muttered, "and it's not in my chest."

Melissa reached for him, drawing his body close to hers, relishing the sensation of skin against skin. She began her own journey of exploration, working her fingers down the knobbles on his spine until his ministrations dominated her concentration.

Her fingers continued to work magic of their own, until mutual passion took over and resulted in a coupling that expressed more than anything a sense of belonging. All doubts aside, Melissa was where she needed to be.

~

"That was some massage," she murmured as he collapsed beside her, one leg still entwined with hers. His hand lightly trailed over her belly, his eyes closed as he savoured the moment. It was a while before he spoke. "I'd like to do this again, sweetheart."

"What, now?" Melissa propped herself up on one elbow to better look at him.

"No—tomorrow, and the day after, and the day after that. I want you permanently in my life. Will you marry me?"

Her eyes widened as she took in what he was saying. "You mean you want to marry me so you can have sex every day?"

"Now that's a wonderful idea. Of course, I'll be away flying sometimes so I can't guarantee every day."

He opened his eyes and met her fierce intense glare. He half-smothered a chuckle. "That look is priceless. Of course, it's not just about sex. Heaven help me, it's because I love you. It's not a sudden decision. I've been thinking about this for a while. Not the loving you part. Getting married."

"Ask properly."

He turned a wide-eyed look on her. "Has anyone ever told you you're a bossy-boots? I wonder where you got that from?"

"If you don't say it properly, my answer's no."

"Damn! I can't risk that. Melissa Gilbert, will you marry me?"

Tears sprang to her eyes, surprising them both. "Are you sure you know what you're asking?" she asked.

This time, he didn't laugh. He sought and held her gaze. "I have never been as sure of anything in my life."

Her voice caught. "You incredible man. You're either very brave or very silly. Yes, I'll marry you."

He rolled towards her, claiming her lips with his. "Sealed with a kiss," he murmured when he surfaced. This time, he wasn't smiling. "Our life together may be a rollercoaster, perhaps in Sydney, perhaps in Alice; who knows? We can go where adventure takes us—and you can request massages any day of the week."

If you enjoyed this book, please leave a review on my website, or any of the online book stores that you purchase from.

www.emilyhussey.com.au
emily@emilyhussey.com.au

Australia

Melissa was born on Plenty River Station, which was north-east of Alice Springs in the centre of Australia. She regularly travelled to Sydney on the east coast.

Don't miss out on your free download!

If you enjoyed this story, you might like to read a collection of short stories in **Romance In The Stone.**

To receive your *free* copy, click HERE or copy and paste https://bit.ly/3qQdbqR into your browser.

Emily Hussey

THE RED CENTRE SERIES

The Red Centre Series is set in and around Alice Springs, in the centre of Australia and also known as the Red Centre.

The Red Heart
Kathy Sullivan is excited about taking up her new job as a pilot in Alice Springs. She was surprised at the antagonism directed towards her by Alex Woodleigh, owner of Mulga Downs. She knew that it could be hot in the Red Centre, but Kathy had no idea how much heat she would generate. In the sky, she was in full command, but back on the ground she was in danger of losing her cool. Emotions peak when disaster strikes during a remote flight, forcing them to acknowledge the underlying cause of their conflict and antagonism.

Trust Your Heart
Embracing liquid refreshments a little more exuberantly than usual, Sarah falls off a table and into Joel's life. She introduces him to life in and around Alice Springs, but secrecy, for whatever reasons, gives rise to more problems than it hides. As water rises around him in the flooding Todd River, Joel is forced to question who he trusts. Is it too late for him to convince Sarah that with him, she has a chance for renewed happiness?

328

Follow Your Heart

Tragic events in her formative years colour a young woman's perceptions of her place in the world. Trust and commitment are not concepts she embraces. In a journey that takes her from a remote Australian station, to the high fashion world of Sydney and beyond, Melissa learns valuable lessons. She realises that family can be broader than you appreciate, and that she has choices to make in who she lets into her life, and who she loves.

Escape to
Sandy Bay

BOOK ONE IN THE SANDY BAY SERIES

EMILY HUSSEY

Escape to Sandy Bay

Alyssa needs to escape… from her job, her dreams, and her man. She flees to coastal Sandy Bay to lick her wounds. The town of her childhood holidays provides a job and a place to stay.

Her new-found sanctuary is shattered when she learns of a controversial proposal that will change the face of the sea front forever. With the sight of a man meticulously documenting soil samples and capturing images of the proposed site, Alyssa springs into action, determined to thwart the development.

Max's focus is on caring for his young son and building the reputation of his business. He's not looking for trouble, but in the guise of a lawyer who is quick to react, trouble comes looking for him. She stirs the emotions in ways he didn't expect, but when she neglects his son, he is quick to lash out.

Leaving the past behind is not so easy, especially with unfinished business back in the city. Should she forgive and forget, or forge a new life so different to the one she'd always imagined? The responses of the men in her life influence the decision she needs to make, but which choice is the right one?

Book 1 of the **Sandy Bay Series**. Available from your favourite eBook retailer.

EMILY HUSSEY

Having lived in several Australian states, Emily Hussey now lives in a coastal suburb of Adelaide in South Australia. She spent her twenties in Alice Springs, which became the setting for the Red Centre Series.

Emily enjoys the short story format, and has been published in local anthologies. The genres range from crime to romance, with some contemporary fiction for good measure.

She was a marriage celebrant for 24 years, and has married couples in many different locations, ranging from private gardens, to beaches, to caves or rural locations. Many of her clients remain friends to this day.

She usually writes with a black and white cat at her elbow, demanding an equal share of attention. Writing tends to be fuelled with regular coffee boosts, and occasional squares of very dark chocolate.

http://emilyhussey.com.au,
https://www.facebook.com/EmilyHusseyAuthor/
https://www.goodreads.com/Emily_Hussey
emily@emilyhussey.com.au

www.ingramcontent.com/pod-product-compliance
Lightning Source LLC
Chambersburg PA
CBHW071754110726
47908CB00006B/1806